In the Oakland of 1989, Mirai San Julian is a young woman with a fascinating life and a rich past. She restores historic carousels—her dream career—working from her own studio in a former roller skating rink. Though black herself, she spent her first years in a Basque immigrant community in Nevada, the adopted child of a single mother. And after the mother's death, she was raised by her Aunt Joy in a Catholic Worker house.

Mirai has a lot going for her—but then, why is everything suddenly falling apart? Her current, year-long carousel project is veering crazily out of control, in both schedule and budget. The guy who dumped her only months before has shown up married and—as far as Mirai is concerned—to the worst possible person. Her mother's death long ago is looking less and less like an accident. And Joy, the one person who has had her complete trust, may know more about that death than she has let Mirai believe.

Mirai knows how to restore a carousel, but can she restore relationships with those she loves? Can she strip the old paint of past wrongs to prepare her life for new, more vibrant colors? And will her eyes be clear enough to spot the brass ring when it finally comes within reach?

Author Online!

For more about Anne L. Watson and her work, plus a reading guide to this book, please visit her at

www.annelwatson.com

Also by Anne L. Watson

Skeeter: A Cat Tale
Pacific Avenue
Flight
Cassie's Castaways
Willow's Crystal
Benecia's Mirror
A Chambered Nautilus
Departure

ANNE L. WATSON

Joy

Shepard & Piper
Friday Harbor, Washington

Library of Congress subject headings:
Merry-go-round—Conservation and Restoration—Fiction
Catholic Workers—Fiction
Basque Americans—Fiction
Basques—United States—Fiction
Earthquakes—California—Loma Prieta, Oct. 17, 1989—Fiction
Loma Prieta Earthquake, Calif., 1989—Fiction
Oakland, CA—Fiction
Nevada—Fiction

Version 1.2

*For Aaron—
and Mimi too,
with thanks*

Joy

Part 1

1

THE USED BOOKSTORE ON FOURTEENTH STREET had been there as long as I could remember. It smelled of yellowed paper, old leather, and dust. Browsing the shelves, I always—faintly—heard rain, even in dry weather. The sound would stop like a broken cassette tape if I listened harder, or if I looked out the door to the dry street. As I turned back to the stacks, it would start again. Isolating, soothing, almost hypnotic.

Patrons often stayed for hours, standing in the aisles like mannequins—the owner tolerated readers, but he didn't bother to make them comfortable. Like the books, they tended to have torn jackets and heavy general wear. Also like the stock, some of the customers were rare collectibles—classic California eccentrics. It was a great place to strike up a conversation with someone interesting. It was where Aunt Joy found Charlene.

I'd guess most people who lived in Oakland in 1989 were wary of strangers. Not Joy.

She and I had lived there for twenty-five years, ever since I started school. Long enough for her to have learned city ways— the friendly smile and the quick retreat. But Joy had no use for such behavior. We were from Nevada, a little ranching place called Paradise Meadow. Instead of learning to act like a Californian, Joy turned Oakland into a small town so it would fit her. She talked to anybody, anywhere. She gave people her phone number, invited them to dinner, made strangers into friends. Sometimes it drove me nuts.

The spring day she told me about Charlene was one of those times. We were walking around Lake Merritt, as we often did in the afternoon—supposedly for exercise, but really for people-watching and talking.

"How did you meet her?" I asked.

"Oh, we got talking." Joy was offhand. That figured. When it came to answering questions, she was the world's worst.

"Wasn't it you who taught me not to talk to strangers?"

"Oh, for pity's sake, Mirai—that's for children. Children don't get to vote or drink wine, either. Or drive." Not that Joy did any of those things.

"One of these days," I told her sourly, "you are going to fall into a conversation with Jack the Ripper."

She ignored the small matter that Jack had been dead for over a century. "What would he be doing in a *bookstore*?" she asked.

"Is that where you met Charlene?"

"Oh, yes. I was shopping for cookbooks at Holmes. She was, too."

She seemed to expect that to reassure me. As if a bookstore were the only place she picked people up! She talked to the meter reader, to dog walkers, to people in line at the bank or the bus stop. After so many years as the director of a Catholic Worker house, Joy didn't think anyone was a stranger. Most of her "guests"—the house term for her nonpaying residents—were people she'd found that way. Her volunteers, too.

I'd argued about this with her before, and had no intention of doing it again at any length. In self-defense I shut up, and we walked on silently for a couple of minutes. Then she came to her real point.

"She has a big house a few blocks from St. Martha's," she said. "And she's looking for a roommate. I got her card in case you want to talk to her."

"Why in the world would I want to move in with someone you just met in a bookstore?"

"Maybe because you're tired of sleeping on the floor of your studio? You're not moving back in with Will, are you?"

Will—my lover. Nonlover. Unlover. Whatever the word would be. Ever since things had fallen apart, I'd been too down-hearted to look for a real home. But I couldn't go on like that forever, as Joy was patiently pointing out. With a sigh, I took the card and put it in my pocket.

Joggers, nannies, and dogs circled on the sidewalk, and waterfowl swam around and around the lake. It reminded me of a carousel, and that reminded me I needed to get to work arranging my trip to Idaho to restore a historic one. This carousel was a prize job for me and my restoration crew—it had come from the workshop of the legendary Charles Looff. But I had to order materials, pack for the trip, set up testing . . . . I had a long to-do list, all of it important. What a time to face moving. I sighed again.

"You know you can come back to St. Martha House any time," Joy said.

I didn't say, *Anything but that.* I thought it, though, and she probably knew I did. I shook my head and didn't meet her eyes.

We stood silently and watched the lake for a while. Sun pennies danced across the water like skipping stones. A rowing club passed in their board-thin boat. Their wake shattered the reflection of a Victorian mansion on the shore.

I glanced up to the mansion's ornate rear deck, half-expecting to see ladies in long bustled dresses, going to the lakeshore with picnic baskets. That was the problem with working in restoration: It was the thin end of a wedge. First the charming, imaginary past, children on a carousel in twenties dresses, Victorian picnics. Once the door was open, the real past sneaked in.

THE REAL PAST, WITH ALL its questions: Christmas shopping with Joy. Mid-sixties, it must have been—I was eight or nine. Joy in her soft wool coat, with gloves and hat for downtown San Francisco. A salesclerk wrapped a purchase for Joy and counted change.

"What a cute little girl," she said, beaming at me. "Is she your maid's daughter?"

At that age, I lived in a fantasy world where I was Joy's real niece. This was the first time it had occurred to me that any stranger could tell I wasn't.

Joy drew me close. She beamed at the woman like St. Francis on a good day.

"Please allow me to introduce my niece, Mirai San Julian," she said. "And what's *your* name?"

The clerk flapped her jaw silently and quickly found another customer to wait on. Joy knelt to study my face. I tried to swallow my tears, but I couldn't.

"Everyone knows I'm adopted," I said. "Everyone knows I don't belong."

"*Adopted* means *chosen*, Mirai," Joy said, pulling a Kleenex from her purse and giving it to me. Her hand was pale against my small brown hand. How could I have imagined anyone would think I was hers?

"*You* didn't choose me," I sobbed. "*Mama* did." Joy ignored the shoppers swirling around us.

"Mirai, listen to me." Her voice was low and private, but intense. "I *did* choose you. I loved Zuzene best of anyone, and she chose you. And now she's gone to heaven. And I'm choosing you again every single day, Mirai. I'm choosing you right now."

And she hugged me closely, kneeling in the crowd. "Peace on earth, goodwill to men," trumpeted the Muzak while a dozen people glared because we were in their way.

I drew a deep breath with a sob left in it and relaxed against her. I knew that whatever Joy said was true. She never lied, not about the smallest thing. Sometimes that even made me mad, but that day it was all I had to hang onto. Joy said she chose me, and Joy never lied.

"I choose you, too, Joy," I mumbled. I was almost certain she heard me.

THAT WAS MY EARLIEST clear memory. To me, the years in Nevada were as imaginary as a Victorian picnic. And I was starting to wonder why.

Lake Merritt's "Necklace of Lights" shone their answer to the dusk. It was time to go home.

2

AT LEAST THE MOVE turned out to be easy. In less than a week, I had a new address.

And a new friend—I had to admit, Joy's instincts about people weren't all bad. Charlene and I hit it off right away. She was older than me, younger than Joy. Maybe about forty-five, it was hard to say. Charlene was a big woman—tall and heavy. Her long, dark blonde hair was elegantly arranged in a "put-up" style I didn't know the name of. If she wore makeup, she used it so skillfully that it looked natural. She had an easy, casual way of talking, but there was authority behind it, a sense that this lady had been in charge for a long time and had managed well.

I loved her house. Apart from being too near St. Martha's, the place was wonderful. It was a big Victorian, perched on one of the hills that surrounded Lake Merritt. It had gables and towers, chimneys and bays, all trimmed with every goofy piece of wood gingerbread its builder could dream up.

Besides the usual rooms, it had a butler's pantry, a breakfast room, and a servants' stair. On the second floor were four bedrooms, the house's only bathroom, and a tiny "fainting room," where tight-corseted Victorian ladies had recovered from walking up the front stairs.

Charlene was a fund-raising consultant, so she worked at home. She had somehow squeezed an office into the fainting room, complete with a large Buddha statue in the corner. It startled me the first time I saw it—I thought Charlene had a visitor. And then I thought, well, in a way she does.

Like almost every other room in the house, the office could just as well have been called a library. It figured that Joy had met her in a bookstore. Charlene's collection included books that were beautiful and probably valuable, but she also had ordinary books that just happened to interest her. The books were all over the house but meticulously arranged, not heaped like the collections of all the other book lovers I knew. Charlene had even invented an improvement on the Dewey decimal system so she could keep track of all of them.

My bedroom had a view of the tiny backyard and a redwood fence covered with trumpet vines. I loved the room's openness, the tall windows and high ceilings. I should have felt right at home, but I had a hard time settling in. I kept imagining the other people who might have lived there. By now there must have been a crowd of them, and I wondered if there was room for me.

Also, I missed Will. Not the way he'd been at the end, critical and destructive. It was the early memories, the good times, that hurt.

Nearly a month after I moved in, I began my fourth effort to unpack. Or it might have been the fifth—I'd lost count. Boxes were stacked so high, the bottom ones were caving in. I felt caved in, too, whenever I looked at them.

I was getting nowhere until Charlene peeked through the doorway, carrying two steaming mugs. I smiled and waved toward a chair. She came in and handed a mug to me. Swirling her purple silk caftan, she sat in one smooth motion like a dancer.

She looked around. "Moving's grim," she said. "When I moved into this house, it was absolutely perfect chaos. It took me nearly a week to get settled."

Gee, nearly a week. Considering the size of the house and the number of books, she must have put in some manic days. Nodding wisely, I sipped coffee and set the cup down crooked. It overturned, and a coffee waterfall cascaded to the floor.

"Whoops," said Charlene, laughing. "Hang on a sec. I'll go get something to clean that up." She took my mug with her and brought it back full. In her other hand was a jumbo roll of paper towels.

"I'm such a klutz," I said. "It even bugs Aunt Joy, and she's headed for sainthood. Better fasten your seat belt. Here," I added, setting the mug down more carefully this time. "Let me do that."

"It's okay," said Charlene. "Why don't I help you unpack? That way, you'll be comfortable when you come home from your trip." And, she didn't add, she wouldn't have to live with the mess while I was gone.

"I could shut the door."

"No, no, let's get it done. Then you won't have to handle it later."

"If you're sure you don't mind," I said. "Do you have a box knife? Mine is in a box with my other tools—"

"And you need a box knife to open it," Charlene finished.

If there'd been anyone to bet with, I'd have bet she'd have one with a new sharp blade, and that she'd be able to lay her hands on it in less than fifteen seconds. I would have won. I sliced the tape on the nearest box.

"Don't you label them?"

"No, I like surprises." This one was full of towels.

Charlene glanced at the wadded mass of blue terrycloth. "I cleared off a shelf in the linen closet for you," she said, motioning toward the hallway.

When I opened the closet door, I saw her linens were sorted by color, folded and stacked perfectly. I folded my towels before I put them on the shelf, but the edges wouldn't line up. Compared to her designer-looking stacks, my towels looked like the kind that might be saved for washing a dog. I closed the door to hide them and returned to the chaos in my room.

I slit another box open. Books. I grabbed a stack of them, dropping a few. As I was loading the bookcase, Charlene picked up the knife and caught my eye questioningly, gesturing at the next box. I nodded.

She opened it and leafed through its odd lot of sketches and photos. "What are these?" she asked.

"The photos go on the bulletin board." At least I'd hung that. I fished in the bottom of the box and grabbed a bunch of push pins, sticking my hand in several places. "Ouch."

"Want me to help?"

"No, they have to go in a certain order."

Charlene's face telegraphed her thought precisely: *Mirai has something she keeps in order?* I stifled a laugh at her astonishment and sorted the pictures: Gandhi, Mother Theresa, Frida Kahlo, Joy, Abraham Lincoln, Lara Holtzer—my tenth-grade art teacher—Georgia O'Keeffe, Martin Luther King, an old photograph of Zuzene.

"Quite an assortment," Charlene said.

"It's my family," I said, without thinking. She looked at me curiously, waiting for me to go on.

"When I was a kid, I minded that I was adopted. It was obvious I didn't belong, to Joy or anyone else."

"You could easily be her niece," Charlene protested.

"Most people assumed I wasn't. So, Joy said I could have any relatives I wanted. She bought me the bulletin board, and she said I could make a family tree on it, anyone who was special for me. She said that's a person's family, more than blood relatives."

I tacked the pictures to the board, connecting them with thin ribbon to form a tree. Zuzene at the top for my mother, then Joy as aunt, and the others fanned out as cousins. I noticed how old the pictures all looked: The newspaper photo of Mother Theresa was yellowed, and Zuzene was curling at the edges. I used some extra push pins to make her stay flat.

Charlene studied them. "They're like Cao Dai saints," she said.

I was grateful she hadn't laughed at my make-believe family on the board. "What's Cao Dai?" I asked.

"It's a Vietnamese religion. I have some books about it. It's kind of like Baha'i. They have unusual saints—people they've decided were voices of God. Victor Hugo, for one. They have a cathedral in Vietnam with incredible statues."

"I never had Victor Hugo on my board."

"You mean they change?"

"Oh, sometimes. Karl Marx was a cousin for a while when I was in high school, then I took him down. Even if what he said was right, the results led somewhere I didn't want one of my cousins to go. I even had Malcolm X, but he didn't last long."

Charlene laughed. "So, you disinherited them."

"If you regard being on the board as an inheritance, I guess I did."

"Gandhi and Malcolm X—that's quite a scope."

"*C'est la vie.* My *vie,* anyway."

"Who's the woman at the top?"

"That's Zuzene—my stepmom. Joy's sister. She died when I was little."

"Oh, I'm sorry."

"Don't be. I hardly remember her."

I knew the bare facts: Zuzene was an artist in Reno; she had died when I was five. Sometimes I had quick flashes that might be memories. They always disappeared, like slides being shown too fast. The "mother" on my board was as much a stranger as Mahatma Gandhi.

I opened the next box, and we went on finding places for clothes, books, and tapes. When everything was done, Charlene helped me make the bed. As far as I was concerned, it was the last time it would ever be made unless the fairies came and did it.

Charlene turned and gave the board a last look as she left. "I wish I could pick *my* relatives," she said.

3

MY STUDIO WAS IN a former roller rink on Peralta Street, near the Oakland army base. The rink had been abandoned for years when I took it over, and I hadn't changed it much—in fact, not at all, outside. Not the peeling paint or even the broken light bulbs that used to spell "Rollerland." I hadn't even taken down the Closed sign on the ticket booth.

Graffiti artists had decorated the front with jagged writing. I didn't care—it made the building match the neighborhood. A liquor store down the street had a few steady customers—*un*steady customers, actually—who hung out on the sidewalk near its doorway. They spare-changed me occasionally—not that I encouraged their habits by giving them anything.

Dingy as it was, the studio was perfect—big and cheap. Too rundown to fix, in too bad a neighborhood for anyone to want to tear it down and build new. I figured it was mine until Urban Renewal caught up. Which was likely to be never, considering how redevelopment had screwed up San Francisco's Fillmore and Mission.

On the first of May, jiggling the key to open the front door, I heard the telephone ring. *Damn.* I reached it as it stopped, but in a few seconds it started again.

I grabbed it. "Mirai San Julian Restorations."

"Mirai?" *Damn again.* It was Will. Half a year after our breakup, it still hurt to talk to him.

"Yes?"

"Is the trip to Peregrine Falls still on?" He didn't sound like he cared much. Since the trip was set for May 7, it was a hell of a time for him to weasel out, if that's what he'd called to do.

"Yes, of course it is." I made an effort to sound civil. Will was not the person I most wanted to speak to, but I was stuck. He was my band organ restorer, the only one I'd ever used. I was counting on him for the job in Peregrine Falls. Stupid, stupid, to get involved with a colleague. But I had.

No point telling him I needed him on the project. My neediness, as he put it, was the reason things hadn't worked out.

"Just wondering," he said.

"I can't blame you for wondering." I was thinking fast. "You might take a look and back off. It's been so long since that band organ worked, it may not be fixable. But I'd like someone who knows what he's doing to be the one to say."

"What do you mean, not fixable?" he snapped. "I haven't found one of those yet."

"Oh, okay. I'm relieved you think you can do it. I'll be at the Clown Motel. Give me a call when you get in—team meeting is Monday morning. We'll have lunch with the restoration committee after we've had a chance to look at the machine. Meeting with the owners on Tuesday."

Making it clear he wouldn't be alone with me, that there wouldn't be any more scenes.

"Got it."

We hung up, and I sat and felt stupid for a while.

Will was talented, sexy, with a young Robert Redford movie-star look. In other words, he had everything that *would* attract me—or almost any woman, for that matter.

Except I knew better than to get involved with a consultant. Relationships were like carousels: The new ones were glittering delight. And they ended up covered with the emotional equivalent of what restorers call "park paint"—the thick, toxic glop that crusts every machine I get my hands on. Wooden animals I could fix, but getting the park paint off a relationship was another story.

Never again.

I giggled in the middle of my misery, picturing the people "again" could involve. My mechanic, Mr. Papadakis, at least seventy years old. Evangeline—"just Evangeline"—my jill-of-all-trades scene painter, mirror restorer, repairer of anything. Harvey Engstrom, my electrical engineer, very married and proud of his twin daughters. Not much temptation there.

The laugh did me good, but I knew I had to be careful. Consultants and close associates weren't the only ones I had to stay professional with. There were—God forbid—apprentices. And clients, and restoration committees, and other carousel artists. These last were competitors in a way, but really, we worked in a loose guild we'd dubbed "the Carousel Mafia." *Don't mess with the Mafia.*

But I never met anyone else.

On May 4, I stopped by the studio to get the kit of tools I'd need in Peregrine Falls. Barbara, my assistant, was there. I hadn't expected to see her, since we'd let our workload drop to almost nothing in anticipation of the Peregrine Falls job. She was on the office phone when I came in, but she joined me in the workroom before I'd even set my backpack down.

Even in her usual jeans and T-shirts, Barbara looked great. But today she had on heels and a silky-looking dress that matched the blue of her eyes. Her long blonde hair was arranged in an elaborate twist. She was gorgeous, dressed for an occasion. She definitely hadn't come here to work.

She laughed when she saw me sizing her up. "To tell you the truth, I stopped by to use the bathroom," she said. "Then the phone rang."

"Who was it?" I asked.

"No one." She saw my puzzled frown. "I mean, not *no* one. A crank call."

"You mean a breather?" Damn. I couldn't have nuisance calls tying up the studio phone.

"No, more like kids. Giggling." She shrugged. "Nothing important."

I rolled my eyes. Thursday afternoon seemed like a funny time for kids acting up. Maybe not, though. For all I knew, they taught crank phone calling as a subject in school now.

"Where're you going?" I asked, motioning at her getup.

"Opening at the Oakland Museum."

"You look stunning. You ready to leave?" I asked, giving the tool bag a last-minute check.

"Not yet. I didn't get to the bathroom."

I laughed. "The phone strikes again."

"Aren't those keys on the desk the ones for the carousel?"

"Oh, God." I grabbed the key ring. "Thanks. I can just see me jimmying the lock. Good start, huh?"

"Like that night you got locked out of St. Martha's."

"Jesus. How long ago was that?" I asked. Sometimes I thought Barbara remembered my life better than I did.

"Ten years? At least that. It was kind of memorable."

It had been, except I tried *not* to remember things like that. I'd occasionally crashed at the house during my dropout days. This had been one of those times, and I'd gotten locked out. I no longer remembered how, or why no one was there to let me in. Or why I decided to shinny in a window. Or which of the neighbors called the cops.

"Hmm. . . . I'd rather forget it, to be honest." I put the carousel keys on my key ring so I wouldn't forget them again.

"Have fun in Peregrine Falls," she said.

"I will. I wish it was in the budget for you to go." I left her to lock up.

The next stop was St. Martha House, to help Joy with dinner for the residents. There were never more than a few of these "guests"—St. Martha's was the smallest of Oakland's Catholic Worker houses. It was an important one, though, because Joy took in people who were too disturbed for larger shelters.

The building was a big old stucco house that stretched around three sides of a front patio. The tile paving in the patio was cracked and uneven because of the peppertree in the middle, but Joy loved the tree and wouldn't even discuss cutting it down. Typical Joy.

I noticed the yard was getting overgrown again, with sweet alyssum and California poppies running wild. Most of Joy's volunteer helpers were retired women—the heavy yard work was beyond them.

Joy sat on a bench beside the tree, wearing a denim cook's apron over her jeans and turtleneck. She played a lighthearted tune on a small wooden flute, her fingers dancing above the holes. She started to put it down when she saw me, but I motioned for her to finish. She came to the end with a flourish and set the instrument in her lap.

"Is that a Basque flute?" I'd often seen her play it but hadn't paid that much attention to the instrument.

"No, it's an ordinary recorder."

"And the melody?"

"That's Basque. It's a dance tune."

"Where'd you learn it?"

"Some of the people at Papa's hotel played the *txistu*. That's the Basque flute—like a recorder, but it's played with one hand. The other plays a drum."

"It's a pretty tune," I said, hoping she'd play another.

She only gazed at the tree. The late afternoon breeze from San Francisco Bay ruffled its branches and made me shiver. I'd hoped for spring too soon, as I did every year.

"I wish you'd tell me about your family," I said. "Why don't we ever visit?"

"Everyone's gone," she said slowly. "It's been years . . . . I don't know, Mirai. I've been in the city so long, I doubt I could go home again."

She still called it home. "You'd *know* people though, wouldn't you?"

"Only a few of the older ones. If they're even still alive. I haven't kept up with babies or things like that. It's a tiny town, nothing much to do. I'd be an outsider."

I couldn't believe Joy could be an outsider anywhere. "Stranger in Paradise," I kidded.

She smiled, but I thought she looked strained.

"Wouldn't they be glad to see you?"

Her eyes didn't meet mine.

"They're narrow. They don't mean any harm, but it's their way. It goes with all the good things in a small town—it's probably impossible to separate one from the other. When I chose the city, I stopped belonging in Paradise Meadow."

She stood and slipped the recorder into her apron pocket. "Anyway, we need to make dinner, or our guests will go hungry tonight. Let's get some herbs on the way to the kitchen."

We followed a brick path to the gate, gathering herbs as we went. Rosemary crowded the path, and Joy broke off a few

extra twigs to neaten it. I'd always loved the scent of rosemary—
something like ginger and pine—and I breathed deeply, enjoying it.

Through the gate was the sunny backyard, filled with Joy's
vegetable garden, freshly tilled now and planted with seedlings.

"Garden looks good," I commented.

Joy gave it a brief, exasperated look. "The snails are driving
me crazy this year."

"Put out some beer for them."

"That tends to cause more problems than it solves."

It took me a second to catch on, but then I got it. Typically,
at least one of her guests had an alcohol problem. It wouldn't
do to have beer sitting around.

Joy opened the door, and I followed her into the kitchen.

It was large, facing south, with light pouring through its
uncurtained windows. Today, it was cool and still. The quiet
ticking of an old schoolhouse clock only added to the feeling of
peace. Paper bags of donated food were lined up on the counters,
but the volunteers had left for the day.

We set down the herbs and washed our hands. Joy checked a
stew bubbling slowly on the stove. She smiled into the fragrant
steam, happy to be taking care of needy strangers. But *I* needed
something from her, too. I needed a family, not imaginary friends
fading on a bulletin board.

She opened the restaurant-size refrigerator and lifted out
a deep bowl of salad. I unwrapped dark rounds of bread from
one of the bags, and Joy took a snaggletoothed knife from her
rack and reached for the cutting board.

I noticed her hands—when had they started looking so
old? Ringless hands, ropy-veined and dry. *Joy isn't old, she's only
fifty-seven. That isn't old.*

"Joy," I said, and she looked up. "I want to know about your family. Why don't you come along on the trip to Idaho, and we'll go by Paradise Meadow on the way home?"

"It wouldn't be like it was when I lived there," she said. "The hotel's probably been torn down by now. Most likely, no one would even remember me."

With her expression set in a stubborn blank, her face suddenly seemed as elderly as her wrinkled hands. But I didn't believe, not that day with the sun slanting into her kitchen, that Joy could get old. Or that she was a person anyone could forget.

"Of course they'd remember!" I said. "The town is only a few hundred people, isn't it?"

"Yes," she said slowly. "But if you want to hear family stories, you won't find them in Paradise Meadow."

I drew in a deep, ragged breath. Joy was my favorite person in the world, but asking her to discuss the past was useless. I might as well ask a carved wooden horse. *Straight from the horse's mouth,* I thought, a flicker of amusement overriding my annoyance as I watched her go on with the dinner preparations.

Positioning the loaf on the board, she made the sign of the cross on its crust. The familiar gesture, the late-afternoon sunlight, the scent of herbs and bread, the peace of St. Martha's—my love for Joy came back in a rush. I wanted to put it in a crystal, like a mustard seed necklace. To hold on to it, preserve it, safe from harm, forever.

4

"CHECK IN?"

At least the woman behind the counter of the Clown Motel wasn't dressed in circus getup. I pushed some clown figurines aside so I could pass her my credit card without breaking anything. Behind her, Barnum and Bailey posters were layered on a wall decorated with clown wallpaper. A clown-face clock grimaced beside them. Polka dots covered the counter, like a color-blindness test. The effect was dizzying.

"Smoking or non?"

"Non." I wondered if the smokers had to smoke clown cigarettes while they were here. I imagined the rooms: pictures, bedspreads, lamps, even the carpets, everything covered with clowns. Maybe the towels. Maybe even the toilet paper?

"Checkout time is ten o'clock," she said. "We don't have a restaurant, but there's a coffee shop down the street—the Clearwater Cafe."

"Thanks."

"Enjoy your stay. Let me know if you need anything."

As I turned to leave, she was rearranging her china clowns on the counter.

I trudged to my room at the far end of the patio. I slung my suitcase onto the bed and glanced at the phone. I knew I ought to stay there so my team members could reach me when they got in.

But first I wanted to see the carousel alone. Having time in the beginning to look and think on my own would make the carousel mine in a way I couldn't explain. That sense of possession was necessary to get me through the year or more of hard work it would take to make it sparkle again. I grabbed the backpack I used for a purse and went to the lobby.

"How do I get to Northern Lights Park?" I asked the clerk.

Her smile was threadbare. "I can give you a brochure if you're interested, but it isn't open yet."

"I know. I'm here to restore the carousel."

"Oh!" she said, and *did* smile then, with the goofy look people got when I mentioned carousels. "It hasn't run for years! Can you fix it?"

"Oh, yes. It just takes work. It's not only me—there's a whole team. I don't know if they're staying here or not."

She glanced at her book. "A few people are coming in today," she said. "Are some of them on your team?"

"Maybe."

I got out quickly then. I wanted that carousel to myself.

I stopped a man on the street and asked for directions to Northern Lights Park. "It's not open," he said.

"Yes, I know. I need to meet someone."

He gave me directions, and when I half-turned at the corner, I saw him staring after me.

I hurried the few blocks to the park. Using the keys my client had sent me, I slipped in quickly through a side gate and locked it again behind me.

The carousel was at the edge of the park in a shabby barnlike building. When the carousel opened, the big doors on every side would roll up and disappear. The shadows inside would heighten the glitter of lights and whirling mirrors. But now the building was abandoned. I unlocked a small door and stepped into blind dark.

I'd studied everything I could find about this carousel. It had all its original animals. Like many carousels of the early twentieth century, it was a menagerie—it included everything from a goat to a sea monster. There were two chariots, designed for ladies' modesty. . . . In my mind, 1906 blossomed again. I could see the ladies in their Edwardian dresses, their hair piled high. Beside the band organ, Charles Looff, the carousel's maker, stood glowering at me, stocky and mustachioed. I could read his mind: *Who is this tramp woman in blue canvas trousers?*

"Times have changed," I told him. "It's okay. I'm here to fix it. Remember me? I worked on the one in Silver Spring. Tell your guys, would you? Tell them to give us a hand."

My voice rang hollow in the closed-up building. I turned on the lights and blinked at the mess. Far, far worse than I'd been led to believe. I'd expected park paint, but not in every color of the rainbow. Pink, purple, chartreuse . . . . Dear God, had the painters been drunk? Even the jewels in the harnesses were buried in paint. The horses, originally fitted with real hair tails, had nothing left on their rears but obscene-looking sockets. As I stepped onto the carousel, part of the floor felt shaky and rotten.

I walked among the animals, touching their faces, knowing how they'd look when I was finished. The horses would be dapple gray, palomino, bay, and roan, like real ones, with new horsehair tails. Looking through the dirt with a restorer's vision, I saw bright new paint, the trappings and harnesses gilded and shaded. I could make them special again, the pride of Peregrine Falls.

Whenever I'd coaxed a carousel back to life, the town would have a party to celebrate. Dignitaries would speak, usually at length. Everyone who'd helped the project along would be recognized and applauded. Finally, I'd be asked for a few words.

"A few words" was exactly what they got. I'd tell them I hoped they'd enjoy the carousel, and invite them to get in line behind me to buy a ticket for the first ride.

I'd mount one of the jumpers and the carousel would start. A moment of pure triumph, and it wasn't the newspapers and the speeches that made it that, it was the swooping animals and the gongs, the colors and lights. With a little luck, the band organ might even be tinkling my favorite carousel tune:

After the ball is over,
After the break of morn,
After the dancers' leaving,
After the stars are gone . . . .

I'd have one ride. After that, I'd slip away and go home, or to the studio. I always had another mess to start on, and another one after that.

For this carousel, the opening was scheduled already—Memorial Day next year, a little over a year away. A lot of work even for a team, a lot for my studio, almost too much for me and one assistant. I locked up and went back to the Clown.

Avoiding the lobby, I walked through the patio, toward my door at the end of the balcony. I was brought up short by the sound of "Nellie Gray," played on the banjo. The last thing I wanted to hear—it could only be Will, right here in my motel.

Once, his banjo had made me smile just as the band organs did. Once, *Will* could make me smile, too. No more. I considered how much trouble it would be to switch to a different motel and discarded the idea right away. Since I had to deal with him, I'd better get used to it.

On every trip for the past two years, Will and I had been together. Now I went to my room alone like a banished child. I wished I could call Joy, but Sunday was her busy day, distributing packaged food to street people in Richmond.

On an impulse, I called Barbara, thinking some girl talk might cheer me up. No one was home but the answering machine. I left a message for her to come to Peregrine Falls in the morning. Screw the budget. I needed a friend more than I needed the money her expenses would amount to.

Lying on the bed in the dimming late afternoon, I waited for the crew to call me, waited to give directions and make plans. Like the carousel itself, I waited for something to happen.

> *Many a heart is aching,*
> *If you could read them all—*
> *Many the hopes that have vanished*
> *After the ball.*

5

Next morning, I picked out Will's car parked on the street in front of the coffee shop. No room for doubt—Will had a real screamer of a car, an old red Mustang convertible.

Not that he described it that way. His version started off with "1964½" for the model year and "poppy red" for the color, then veered into details about the color of certain key engine parts—at which point I had always zoned out so far, I didn't hear the rest of the speech.

There it sat, parked at the curb in Peregrine Falls, Idaho, already collecting a few admirers. Not even counting the vanity plate—ORGAN4U—the car had so much of Will's personality attached to it, I felt mildly nauseated. As an alternative to kicking a fender, I slammed into the coffee shop.

"Whoa, Mirai! Remember us?"

The crew had gathered at the only big table in the Clearwater Cafe. I'd been so wrapped up in my own problems, I hadn't even seen them. They were all there—Evangeline, Harvey, Mr. Papadakis. And Will.

Neither fight nor flight was practical. I sat down at the table. The waitress hurried to me with a coffeepot and mug. I ordered the special and sipped my coffee. *Clearwater* was certainly the word for that coffee—they must have named the restaurant after it. I glanced around the table, skipping over Will.

Mr. Papadakis caught my eye. "What's the agenda?" he asked.

"We'll go to the park as soon as we're done here. Check out the carousel, then have lunch with the committee. We have to give the owners a preliminary report tomorrow morning."

Evangeline smiled. "How long are you staying?" she asked me. "All week. You?"

"I'll stay awhile. I may want to work on things in place." In Evangeline's case, "awhile" could mean several months. She had an answering service, but no permanent address. At the moment, I envied her.

Harvey shook his head. "I'm leaving tomorrow night. I'll come back later, when the work on the building starts. For now, a couple of days will do it."

It was Will's turn, so I *had* to look toward him then. He sat quietly, holding a coffee cup. Will had never worn jewelry, but now a ring glinted on his finger. A plain gold ring on the fourth finger of his left hand. A wedding ring.

I stifled my shock fast to keep the others from seeing it hit my face. "And you?" I asked carefully.

"Just long enough to get the organ dismantled and shipped. There's nothing I can do here, and I need to get home," he said.

Will and I had broken up six months ago. And he'd gotten married since then. Still on his honeymoon. Yes, he *would* need to get home—I could see that.

The waitress brought my order, and I made myself put a bite-sized piece of food into my mouth and chew it.

"Did you see it?" asked Evangeline.

Swallowing wasn't easy, but I managed.

"See what?" I asked. Did I see Will's wedding ring? Did I see this coming? I had no idea what she meant.

"The *carousel,* Mirai. Did you see the carousel yet?"

Oh, right. The carousel. "Yes, I did. It's a mess."

"Are the rounding boards painted over?"

Rounding boards, the outer crown of the carousel, originally had mirrors or painted scenes. When the murals began to look worn, the owners often slapped a coat of paint over them. I concentrated on what I'd seen the day before.

"Only the gilding, but it's a sloppy job."

Evangeline sighed. I didn't know if it was relief she wouldn't have to restore them completely, or anticipation of painstaking hours of picking off a lot of gold that had been splashed in the wrong place.

Gold in the wrong place. Yes, that could happen.

"Mirai?"

I jerked my mind back to the crew again. If I didn't focus, I was going to make a fool of myself. They knew Will and I had been living together, and they could see I didn't have a wedding ring on *my* finger. *Keep it professional,* I told myself.

"Sorry, woolgathering. This is terrible coffee. Is there anywhere I could get something decent?"

"I brought a coffeepot," said Harvey. "I'll make you a cup before we head out. Is Barbara coming on this trip?"

"She'll be here for lunch. After I saw the carousel, I told her to come on up." *After I saw the carousel and after I heard Will playing. I thought I was going to need a buffer, and boy, was I right.*

Harvey nodded. "Pretty bad, is it?" he asked casually.

"Disaster." I assumed he meant the carousel. "It looks like it was painted by a troop of monkeys."

"How's the electrical?" asked Mr. Papadakis.

"Didn't check it except for the house lights. They work, but I wouldn't bet on anything else," I said.

The others were finished with breakfast, and I couldn't eat mine. We crossed the street to the Clown. Harvey walked me to my room.

"I'll bring the coffee in a couple of minutes," he said. I nodded and unlocked the door.

Inside the room, I sat on the edge of the bed. *I'll bet anything she's white.* I pushed self-pity away and stifled my tears. I didn't know if I was sadder or angrier, but I knew I couldn't afford to let go now. I couldn't let the crew or anyone else see me red-eyed. No way was I going to give Will the satisfaction, either. I bit my lower lip, took a few deep breaths, and answered Harvey's tap at the door.

He came in, holding a plastic mug in one hand and a notepad in the other.

"You okay?" This was as close as Harvey was going to get to a personal question, I was sure. I nodded.

"See you at the carousel," he said. The door closed quietly as he left.

When I got to the carousel, I found the crew gathered at the door. I unlocked it, and they scattered to their tasks. They were quieter than I'd ever known them to be—usually we got in a lot of yakking and kidding while we worked. That day, the talk was low-voiced and brief.

I set myself to inspecting the carousel in as much detail as I could. Until I got the animals stripped, I was partially guessing how damaged they were. Clever finishing could cover a host of sins. But the animals didn't look too far gone, except for three at the side of the outer row where the floor was bad.

Those three were dire. I guessed there'd been a roof leak after the park had closed. The paint on all of them was peeling, and one, a goat, was coming apart. I'd have to send those to Portland Carousel Works to be rebuilt. The others looked like they could be restored in the studio.

I unwrapped my tools and began scraping away layers of paint and dirt from an inside-row jumper. When I got down to the lowest layer, it was orange. Not a factory color. I'd check a few more, but it looked like the original paint was gone. That was a shame, in a way. On the other hand, it did simplify restoring the carousel for park use.

The door opened, and a plump, white-haired woman bustled in. She paused, peering in the dim light as she sized us up. I stripped off the surgical gloves I wore when I worked on paint and walked to meet her.

"I'm Regina Meissner," she said. "You must be Mirai. We talked on the phone."

So we had, at length and more than once. She surveyed the team, scattered around the carousel. "What are you finding?" she asked.

"I've been scraping paint layers with a scalpel. It looks like the animals were stripped at some point."

"I'm not surprised. The park did a lot of stupid things. But how can you tell?"

"Here, I'll show you." I led her toward the horse I'd been working on and trained a flashlight on the patch I'd scraped. Around a dozen paint layers fanned out like a rainbow.

"This is what we call paint seriation," I said. "You get a view of every color, top to bottom. You can see the oldest coat of paint was orange."

"But there's a white layer under that," she objected.

"The white layer is primer."

"How can you tell?"

"There's no layer of dirt between the orange and the white." I handed her the lighted magnifier I used for checking tiny details. "See how fresh the white coat is, compared to the orange one? It was never exposed. That means it's a prime coat—which is exactly what I'd expect anyway."

Several people had arrived and gathered around while I was explaining.

"Does it matter that it's orange?" Regina asked.

"It matters a lot, because the original factory paint job wouldn't have been a color like that. The historic paint jobs were always natural colors. I wouldn't draw a conclusion from only one horse. If I check a few others and get similar results, we'll know the animals have been stripped."

I looked around my circle of listeners. They were nodding, following my reasoning attentively.

"Does that mean they're less valuable?" Regina asked.

"Yes and no. If you were going to sell them to individual collectors, it would. Since you plan to keep running the carousel, it makes our work simpler. At least we don't have to concern ourselves with restoring old paint. Or did you want us to try to reproduce the original colors?"

"Not particularly," said Regina. "We don't want to spend our money on research. What we need is a carousel that will look beautiful—something to attract people. Tourists and local patrons both. On the other hand, we don't want it to look modern."

"I'll work out a color proposal and send it to you," I said. "First, we have to strip the old paint and see what condition the animals are in."

"Some of them don't look good," said one of the men.

I gestured toward the three animals I'd decided to send to Portland. "Does the roof leak?"

He glanced toward that side of the machine. "Yes, and nobody told us. We could have lost it all. As it is, the city dithered and dickered until we did a temporary roof repair ourselves. I'm afraid those animals are ruined."

"They can be rebuilt. I assume you're restoring the building." I hoped they could find a decent contractor. It was obvious that restoration would involve a lot of work.

He nodded. "The city has asked architects for proposals. The council decided to develop the park to attract business downtown, so we finally have a little money. And they want the antique carousel to be the focus of the whole design."

"It may work," I said. "There aren't many of the old carousels left."

"I think everyone's here who's coming to lunch," Regina said. "This isn't the whole association, only the Committee for Restoration. I'm sorry—I should have introduced everyone—Tom, Stella, Lois, Angelo, and Helen. This is Mirai San Julian, our restoration consultant."

They half-raised their hands as she said their names. I hoped I could keep them straight. They all looked like they were over sixty, and I hoped that was because they had more time than younger people, not because they were the only ones who cared.

I introduced the crew. After some general chatting, Regina checked her watch. "Shall we go?"

"My assistant was supposed to join us," I said. "She should be here any minute."

"The restaurant is only a few blocks away. We can leave a note here on the door."

I gathered my tools, careful not to cut myself, and put them into my toolbox. Regina locked the carousel behind us and led the way to the restaurant.

When I got there, I washed my hands and checked the mirror. I felt tired and grubby, but I didn't look bad. My hair was cut in a short natural, so at least it didn't get messy. I moistened a paper towel with cold water and patted it on my face and neck. It would have to do.

In the dining room, I spotted my party at a table next to the window. The plate glass showed a view not of purple mountains' majesty but of an asphalt parking lot. As I took my seat, Will's chair scraped back.

"Barbara's out there looking lost," he said. "I'll go and get her."

After a couple of minutes, they came to the table and I introduced her to the committee. As she sat next to Will and reached for a menu, I noticed something on her hand.

A plain gold ring. On her fourth finger.

The twin of Will's.

Part 2

6

"YOU'RE JOKING," SAID CHARLENE. Her voice was flat, but the toaster popped in a kind of exclamation point.

"It's not funny," I snapped. I grabbed a slice of toast and slathered butter on it.

Charlene's chair creaked as she leaned back, seemingly unperturbed at my tone. She sipped coffee and closed her eyes for a second. "How did your crew take it?" she asked, reaching for the other slice of toast.

"No one could look at anyone. Will left Tuesday night, and I told Barbara she could go, too. Things lightened up once they were gone, but everyone was embarrassed. Polite. Professional. Awkward as hell."

"Did they know from the beginning?"

"You mean at the café? I don't know—maybe he told them. Or else they noticed his ring, too."

"What did you do?"

"Went poker-faced. Got through the trip as best I could. Did the stuff I was supposed to do. It wasn't easy."

She took a bite of scrambled eggs. "No, I'd guess not. What now?"

"Fix the carousel. I doubt I'll see Will again, until the opening party anyway. I haven't decided what to do about Barbara."

"You have several choices."

"I feel like firing her ass." Saying it made a flush of rage rise through my misery. It would feel so good to tell her to get the hell out of my studio.

Charlene nodded. "Uh-huh, of course you do. But is that best for you?"

"It would feel good."

"Yeah, I bet. So, is that what you want to do?"

"Well, I don't know. She *is* my oldest friend."

"Why'd you hire your best friend to begin with?"

"We met in high school art class. I went to Cal and she went to San Diego State, but we stayed in touch. She got interested in carousels when she saw what I was doing."

"Yeah, but working with your best friend is usually a mistake."

"Joy said the same thing when I hired her. But what was I supposed to do when Barb asked me for a job? We were doing fine till *this* happened. At this point, though, it looks like the 'friend' part is history. I might as well can her."

"Maybe, maybe not. What else do you have to lose if you do?"

"I need her, or someone. I have a tight schedule for fixing this machine. I could replace her, but I can't afford the time to train a new assistant. And if I can *her,* I'm out a band organ restorer too."

"Aren't there other people who could fix the band organ?"

"Sure. I haven't *used* anyone else, though."

I wished now I'd started the project with someone else. To tell the truth, I'd had an idea maybe Will and I would make up if we worked together—but I wasn't going to tell Charlene that. She was waiting for me to explain, so I faked a reason.

"I'd rather not lose anyone," I said. "And the rest of the crew would have to take sides—or they'd feel like they had to. It would be a mess."

"Your other alternative is to be above it all. What's wrong with that?"

I got up and stood at the long kitchen window, looking down the hill to a dizzying view of the lake. I toyed with the prisms

Charlene had hung to catch the morning sun, but the sun was past the window now. Too late for rainbows.

My anger flared up again like a chaparral fire. I turned to Charlene.

"Mainly that I'm *not* above it all," I said. "I've had my share of guys, and I seriously thought Will was the one. And Barbara and I were like sisters. Then, presto! Bye-bye, love, and bye-bye, sister. Whenever I saw either of them, I felt like crying."

"That was probably mostly shock. Suppose it wore off?"

"You mean, I should work with her like nothing happened?"

"Tough, huh?"

"Yes it is, but I'm stuck. The carousel reopening party is already scheduled—Memorial Day next year. I've got a contract—I have to get it done."

"It could be a lot worse."

"I can't think how."

"The guy's a jerk," she said. "Better you found out sooner than later."

"After a year of living with him, I'd hardly call it sooner."

"Could be worse. It could have been two years, or five. Could have been five years and two kids. Don't bet your butt that Miss Barbara is in an enviable position. Being married to a son of a bitch . . . . I don't believe I'd care for it, myself."

"At this rate," I said, "it looks like I'm not going to be married to *anyone.*"

"Better no one than a bastard. Frankly, I have no wish to pair off. I like my privacy, and I like having my own way. That's why I've never worried about being fat."

I started to protest, but she kept right on. "Don't do the reassurance number. I don't need it—you'd be surprised how many men are turned on by big women. All the same, I don't want a guy."

"I'm not sure I do, either. Not after this."

"Oh, you'll meet someone else, and it's likely to be someone a lot better. Most men *are* a lot better. Springing a new wife on you at a business meeting, staying at the same motel . . . . What kind of sadist *is* he, anyway?"

"Maybe he didn't mean it the way it came off," I said. A gray tiredness washed through me. Leaving the window, I plopped down in my chair. Charlene poured the last of the coffee into my empty cup.

"Uh-uh," she said. "Will had to know exactly what he was doing. Barbara might be dumb, or awkward, or innocent. But not him."

"He didn't expect me to ask her to go there."

"That could be. But he didn't have the courtesy to tell you he was married before he turned up with a wedding ring, and in front your crew, too. After that, the part with Barbara was a detail."

I nodded. "At least she made him change motels."

"How do you know it was her idea?"

"I saw them going to check out. He was arguing about it."

"*Hoo*, boy. Some husband *she's* got. Honey lamb, Will has a screw loose. Count your blessings." She scraped her fork across her plate to get the last of the eggs. It sounded like fingernails on a blackboard.

"You think I should pretend nothing happened?"

"Just keep thinking, *Better you than me, babes.* What did Joy say, if I may ask?"

"I haven't told her yet. I wasn't in the mood for charity and forgiveness."

Charlene stood and gathered the dishes. "She may surprise you," she said.

Joy did. When I called to tell her, she was quiet for so long, I wondered if I'd told the whole story to a broken connection.

"Joy? Hello?"

"I'm here. I'm a bit stunned. Mirai, can you tell me what exactly happened with Will?"

"I told you. He got married. To Barbara."

"I mean, why did the two of you break up to begin with? If you don't mind my asking."

"He said I was too needy."

Another long silence.

"What was that supposed to mean?" she finally asked.

"What he said was, 'You're too needy—don't expect me to be the family you never had.' I don't know what the problem is. I do great with work, but I strike out with men over and over."

"Do you think a therapist could help?"

"No way. I've seen women try that when their love affairs don't work out. They end up in love with the therapist, and that's even worse."

"The idea is you learn how to deal with the feelings."

"Nobody does. They have another bad experience, and this time, they've paid a ton of money for the privilege."

"So, what are you going to do?"

"Fix the carousel, fix another carousel. Tell the next guy to buy a ticket on the carousel, 'cause he ain't going round with me."

Silence. "I'm sorry," she finally said. "I'm sorry, Mirai. I blame myself."

I was astonished. Joy, for all her devoutness, wasn't given to guilt. "How on earth could it be your fault?" I asked.

"I wasn't much of a family for you," she said, and I could hear misery in her voice. "I thought I could do it, but it didn't work. Maybe it's the way I live, here at St. Martha's. Maybe that was no way to raise a child. I see now that I left you wanting more of a sense of belonging than you got."

"St. Martha's is great. I look at other people's families and I think I was lucky," I said.

"Thank you. I'm glad you do—but when you were young, I know you felt very different, very isolated."

"I was a brat," I said. It was true. By the time I was in high school, my yearning to be Joy's real niece had vanished. I wanted to be like other people. I thought of those others as "nice people," and they included everyone except us and our houseful of crazies. And I wasn't exactly the type to suffer in silence, either. My Mission District dropout days had come right after that. Joy's saintliness had gotten a good workout for a few years, there.

"You weren't a brat," Joy said. "You wanted what everyone wants, a family of your own. Nothing could be a more normal wish, and I didn't let you have it. I thought it was best, but I was wrong. And I'm sorry."

"Joy, you could hardly help it that anyone could tell I was adopted. You can't possibly regret who you are or what you've done for me."

"No. . . . But now I understand why you were asking about family again before you left. I've always put off telling you. I had good intentions, but wrong is wrong. I don't know. . . . I have letters my father sent me and a box of his papers. . . . "

"Can I see them?" I interrupted. I imagined going through an old journal, finally knowing how the past was like while it was happening.

"They're in Basque."

"I can read Spanish. Even a little French."

"It's not like Spanish, or French either. It's not like any other language, sort of a mystery. I can translate, I suppose."

"What kind of papers are they—photos, or journals, or what?"

"Papa didn't keep a journal. There's records from the hotel, letters . . . . Things like that."

"We can go through them together," I said. I imagined evenings sitting in front of the fireplace in Charlene's living room. Imagined Joy reading mystery-language letters from the past. Joy, reading a story to me, the way she did before I could read.

This time, it would be *my* story.

7

ON THE SATURDAY AFTER I got home from Peregrine Falls, two people were waiting for me in the littered entryway outside my studio door. One was a young guy in scruffy jeans and a T-shirt. The other was Barbara. They were standing a couple of yards apart, and Barbara was half-turned away from him.

They watched me park the van, get out, and walk toward the door, neither saying anything. They watched me drop and retrieve my keys and papers. The guy chased down a few of my papers that were skittering along the sidewalk in the breeze.

"Hi," I said, as he handed them to me. "What's up?"

"Hi," he said. "My name's Louie. Louie Martin."

"Hi, Louie. I'm Mirai San Julian and this is Barbara . . . Tremayne." I managed to say Will's last name without my voice wobbling.

Barbara cut in. "Mirai—"

"Be with you in a minute," I told her. She scuttled into the studio, looking over her shoulder like she was scared he might be following. When she was gone, I turned to him.

"This your place?" he asked.

"Yes." I didn't know what he was getting at. "Why?"

"My brothers and I used to skate here."

"Uh-huh."

"I was wondering what you do."

"Restore carousel animals."

"Oh." He paused for a moment. Then he asked, "Do you need any help?"

In this neighborhood, that question might be more complicated than it seemed. It could be a come-on, a gang shakedown,
the first step in a burglary plan. It could be a real request for a
job. I looked him over.

Louie was a medium-sized man, Hispanic, I guessed. He
looked like he might be in his early twenties. His jeans and T-shirt
were shabby, but not fashionably shabby. Apparently sober. No
tattoos or tracks, as far as I could see. No gang colors. Just a guy.

"What did you have in mind?" I asked. "You need training
for most of what we do."

He didn't seem discouraged. "I could clean and paint. Whatever you need."

I looked at the dismal front of the building, paying attention to it for a change. He had a point that the building needed
cleaning and painting, and he'd taken the trouble to make it
tactfully. Also, I remembered that someone was going to have
to unload thirty-nine carousel animals that were coming from
Peregrine Falls.

"I can't use anyone full-time," I warned. "And it would only
be minimum wage. And a lot of what I'd have is heavy work."

"That's okay. I'm a student at Merritt College. The quarter's
over in a couple of weeks. So, I could use a job. You got paint?"

"Not for the building, but I can buy it. Give me a few days.
Can you work part-time till school is out?"

"Sure."

"I could use some other guys next Tuesday, too, if you know
two or three who could help unload a truck."

"Yeah, I know some guys," Louie said. "Hey, thanks." He
shook my hand and walked off.

Inside, Barbara sat at a table in the old concession area, hands
in her lap. I wondered if she was wearing her ring.

"What did *he* want?" she asked.

"Work."

"Oh. You didn't *hire* him."

A statement, not a question. It irked the hell out of me.

"Actually, I did." I got a spiteful joy out of her surprise.

"What's he going to do?"

"I'll have to find out what he *can* do," I said.

"You're not going to *train* him."

Until that minute, it hadn't occurred to me I might. Then it seemed like a wonderful idea.

"Depends if he has talent." I kept my voice neutral, but I was enjoying her dismay.

"Hell, he's probably an illegal. I don't know why you want to mess with some guy off the street, anyway. There's plenty of art students in the Bay Area."

"Because he's interested. And he had enough initiative to come here and ask. Art students tend to feel a bit too . . . entitled. A lot of them don't make particularly good employees." Let her make whatever she wanted of *that*.

Barbara's hands came together on the tabletop. I noticed she *was* wearing her ring. She picked at her manicure, a fancy job complete with acrylic nails. She was ruining it fast—not that it was going to last ten minutes with work on carousel animals. Supposing she still planned to do that.

She saw me looking at her hands and hid them in her lap again. "Mirai . . . I'm sorry about Peregrine Falls. I didn't mean it to happen like that."

"It was awkward," I said, keeping my voice calm—the only alternative to yelling at her.

She looked up from shredding her cuticles. "It was my fault," she said. "I hadn't worn my ring to work because I was afraid to tell you. But Will didn't know that. He thought you knew." Her voice was shaky—she was close to tears.

I remembered what I'd overheard as she was dragging him to check out of the motel.

"*—nothing to do with her, Barbara. Screw Mirai. What do you care what she thinks, anyway?*"

"*Will, please—*"

I didn't want to imagine that scene with me as the wife. Begging, placating—that wasn't who I wanted to be. *That's women for you,* I thought. *Anything to get a husband.*

Charlene's commonsense advice and Joy's lessons in charity battled with my anger and jealousy as I stared at Barbara's flushed face. Everything I wanted to say and do would be ruinous to the carousel, my contract, my business.

Barbara broke into my thoughts. "Mirai . . . I want you to know. I wasn't dating Will when the two of you were together."

I didn't believe her. But I didn't want to take the consequences of saying that.

"Don't sweat it," I finally said. "It worked out pretty weird, but I understand how it happened."

It sounded forced and insincere. Hell, it *was* forced and insincere. At the moment, that was the best I could do.

BARBARA CALLED IN SICK on Monday, her voice theatrically hoarse.

"I've got a terrible flu," she said. "I probably won't be in till next week."

"Oh, what a shame. Hope you feel better soon. Take care of yourself."

The flu story was transparent but I didn't mind. I needed a break from her.

I managed fine alone. I called the freight company to pick up a horse I'd finished for a collector in Chicago. It was a beauty, an Illions stander with rose garlands and a gilded mane. I'd loved working on that horse.

"Bye," I said, as I finished crating it. "Take care of yourself."
This time I meant it.

That wrapped up the studio work. I kept busy for a couple
of hours in the office, clearing the desk and filing a towering,
lopsided stack of papers. I sent a bill to the Chicago client and
a reminder to another one. I inventoried supplies and made a
shopping list. And then all that was left to do was wait for the
freight guys.

I wandered out into the rink. I'd partitioned off workrooms
for sanding and painting, and a secured storage area. The skating
floor was huge, triple the size I'd ever need, even for a full carousel.
When all the lights were on, it was bright, but I didn't use more
light than I needed, and today that wasn't much. The far end of
the rink was dark, and the high roof was deep in shadow. The
building's usual noises were soothing, even the screech of the
ventilators in the gusts of afternoon wind from the bay. Cavern-
ous and dingy as it was, the studio felt cozy, familiar, and mine.

When the shrill of the doorbell broke into my reverie, I
was sorry to answer it. I was reluctant to let go of the horse in
its crate, sad in the sudden quiet when the truck was gone, the
floor empty.

The Peregrine Falls carousel would fill it again—fill the space
with animals, and the day with the busy decision-making I loved.
I turned my mind toward that, like a kid looking forward to
Christmas. Will and Barbara were a raw spot in my mind, but
I dismissed them for the moment. May they roast in hell. *Not
nice,* I admonished myself. *Don't say that in front of Joy.*

Thinking of Joy reminded me: I had to get home. Joy was
coming after dinner, and the story of Paradise Meadow would
begin.

8

"I'VE ALWAYS WISHED I'D KEPT some of Zuzene's paintings," said Joy. "Never more than now. Her work would explain so much." She leafed through the small stack of papers she'd brought.

"Why didn't you?" I asked.

"She kept saying she'd do a painting for me, but she didn't get around to it. Of course, no one expects to die at thirty-six. As far as the ones she had on hand, well, I inherited them. But I sold them, and her house, to get the money for the down payment on St. Martha's."

"What were they like?"

"Oh . . . like layers. What you saw depended on where you stood, but they weren't abstract. In fact, they were real as photos. There were pictures and subpictures. A leafless tree would turn into a plowed field as you stepped away from the canvas. There were tiny miniatures in the shadows, and hugely magnified parts of things. She had one painting that looked like an ordinary flower at first, then you saw the blossom was dwarfed by a shadow of its own seed."

"They must have been wonderful."

"They were, and I can't even describe them properly. For a while, she painted on blocks of wood—I saw a show like that once at the Lowie Museum. She might have gotten the idea from Indian art. I don't know."

"She didn't say?"

"Zuzene didn't discuss ideas. In fact, she was quiet about everything. She mostly 'talked' by painting."

"What papers did you bring?" I asked, gesturing toward the pile in her hands.

"Letters from Papa. I still haven't dug all his papers out of the attic. These are letters he sent me when I was at college in Missoula. He wouldn't write in English, even though he knew I rarely used Basque. He wouldn't *read* letters in English, either. He returned one to me with a note clipped to it: 'This appears to be for someone else.' He wrote that in Basque, of course."

"He sounds stubborn."

"He was. No one more so. Anyway, I translated a few for you. Here goes."

She started to read.

April 10, 1953

Dear Nekane,

"Wait," I broke in. "Who's Nekane?"

"Me—it's my Basque name. Joy was the name I picked to replace it. Of course Papa kept calling me Nekane."

"Oh." It was confusing that Joy had a name I didn't know. "Does Nekane mean 'Joy' in Basque?"

"No, the English equivalent would be Dolores."

"That's the opposite! That means sorrows!"

"I like to make the best of things."

I was bewildered for a second. Then I laughed. Typical Joy. She began again.

Dear Nekane,

The hotel is all right, although that "Bonehead Billy" is here again, drunker than ever. I don't know why a Paiute would want to stay at a hotel where everyone speaks Basque. I wouldn't even have let him check in, but I can't afford to turn anyone away these days. Seems like there's fewer shepherds every year. The Sheepherder Bills were supposed to fix that. I can't say I've seen much difference here.

It's just as well. Since you've been gone, I've had no luck getting help, and I'm too old to run this place alone, even with business as bad as it is. God only knows, Zuzene will never come back, and she couldn't manage the hotel if she did.

That damn Billy has been singing most of the day. He's enough to make me think the Volstead Act was a good idea, even though I didn't exactly go along with it at the time.

I have to go. Someone has to fix dinner for ten people and the cook I got now is useless. I don't know why you think you need to go to college. High school was plenty good enough for your mother.

Aita

"Was Aita his name?" I asked.

"Oh, no. His name was Estebe. Of course, I wouldn't have dared call him that. No, *Aita* is 'Papa.'"

"He sounds pretty old-country."

She smoothed the letter and folded it with the translation inside. Her hands moved gently over the old paper.

"He was," she said. "That's hardly surprising—he was born in 1873."

"In the Basque country?"

"Legally, the town where he lived is part of Spain. He came to America when he was fifteen. He went back to Spain after Zuzene died."

I noticed she was tugging the sleeves of her sweater farther down her wrists. I passed her a knitted afghan, and she spread it over her knees.

"What did he mean about the Volstead Act?" I asked.

"That was prohibition, you know. Like most Basque *hoteleros,* he didn't pay any attention when wine was outlawed."

It took a second for that to sink in. "You mean your father was a *bootlegger?*"

"Not exactly. He wasn't like Al Capone. But the Basques didn't 'get' Prohibition. Wine was part of their culture, and they served it, law or no law."

Joy sounded apologetic, but I thought it was funny as hell.

"He certainly guilt-tripped you for going to college," I said.

"He didn't 'get' education for women, either."

"What did he mean, Zuzene couldn't run the hotel?"

"They didn't get along. You'll hear a lot about that. Ready for the next one?

"Sure." Actually, I *wasn't* sure.

She cleared her throat and picked up a paper.

July 8, 1953

Dear Nekane,

> *I drove into Reno to visit Zuzene, and she dragged me to a show she's got at a gallery downtown. I couldn't*

believe what she did. She had three pictures, sort of hooked together. They showed your mother—in the first one she was arriving, getting off a bus, the second, she was surrounded by pots and pans, and babies, and clothes on a clothesline, and the third showed her as she got on the bus again. That's not right, to show your shame that way, show it to everyone. I was so mad, I went home without speaking to her.

And what's more, she had called that picture "Madonna Ostatu," and I could tell she was making fun of me as a hotel keeper and laughing at Our Lady too.

When I got home, I had to throw Billy out of the hotel. He was counting on me being gone all day, and he had a bad woman in his room. I'm not naming names, but you know who I mean.

The town had a big to-do here for the Fourth, I don't know why they do that every year. Most of them plan to go home someday. Wherever home is—Italy, the Pyrenees, somewhere else. Very few of them ever do.

Aita

"What was all that about your mother?" I asked. I knew she had left him, but I'd never heard the details.

"She was from out of town," said Joy. "I don't know why she came to Paradise Meadow. She didn't know anyone there—the priest at the Catholic Church was the one who sent her to the hotel.

"Papa was nearly fifty and she was eighteen. I have no idea why they married. She didn't like Paradise at all—didn't make friends, other than the priest's housekeeper.

"She lasted a few years at the hotel, working like a slave, and she had Zuzene and me. And then she left. We never heard from her again."

"Jesus," I said, shocked. Joy threw me a slightly reproving glance.

"Sorry," I added. "Why did he take the title of the picture personally?"

"*Madonna Ostatu* would translate as 'Our Lady of the Basque Hotel,' more or less. He thought Zuzene was making fun of him and Ama and the Virgin Mary too. He never forgave her for that. Among many things. If she'd been a boy, they'd have thrown punches at each other."

"Ama—is that your mother?"

"Not her name—it means 'Mama.' Her name was Rosa. He never said it again after she left." Joy's eyes were slick with tears, and her voice broke.

"I'm sorry, Joy. I didn't know you still minded about all this."

She wiped her eyes and tried to smile. "It's all right. If nothing else, you might find out that families aren't all good."

"When Charlene saw my board, she said she wished she could pick *her* relatives."

"By the way, where *is* Charlene tonight?" Joy asked.

"I told her you were coming over to read family papers, and she said she was going to work in her office. She's very considerate."

"All the same, let's get together at St. Martha's, next time. I don't want to keep driving her out of her own living room."

"Maybe she could sit with us sometimes? Or is it too private?"

Joy looked surprised, then wary. "Some of it's personal. It's up to you. Ready for another?"

"Not tonight. I have to get up early."

In fact, I felt overwhelmed by what she had already told me. Zuzene was a serious artist, Joy had a name that meant "sorrows," Estebe—I was determined to think of him by name, none of that "wouldn't-have-dared" stuff for me—was a bootlegger, whether Joy was willing to give him that name or not. And Joy's mother had deserted her. All along I'd been thinking *I* was the black sheep of the family.

She folded the afghan and gathered her papers. "I won't have trouble translating if we go at this pace. I was afraid you'd want them all at once."

That night, I went to bed with my head full of buses and bad women, skeleton-tree paintings and Billy the Paiute. If I dreamed about any of it, I didn't remember it in the morning.

9

THE TRUCK IDLED IN THE STREET, belching a diesel stink that made me slightly high. Louie and three of his friends unloaded it quickly—we didn't have a permit to block traffic.

When they finished, I paid them cash, and they called their thanks as they left. I was too excited about the carousel to pay much attention—I barely remembered to call "Thank *you*" as they left. Then I drew a deep breath and walked across the skate floor. I opened the storeroom door for one more look.

It was filled with wooden animals wrapped in moving blankets and plastic—the workroom was ready to go. I felt a rush of bone-deep happiness. I could have spent the rest of the day looking and planning. I fell into a near-dream, could almost feel the tools in my hands.

A sudden sound of water in pipes startled me. Louie emerged from the men's room.

"I thought you'd taken off with your friends," I said. "You can go, if you want. I won't be doing any more today."

"Could I see one of the horses?" Louie asked.

I laughed. "On this machine they're not all horses."

"They're not? What else is there?"

"A menagerie can have all kinds of animals. This machine has a greyhound, and a giraffe, and a whole bunch more. There's a goat, but I sent him and two horses to Portland for major repairs. They were falling apart. Anyway, you'll see them before long."

He was taking in my description with so much interest that I decided to go ahead and unwrap the first animal.

"Let's get some tools," I said. I led the way to the storage racks in the former skate rental area and selected some box knives. We took them to the storeroom, and I selected the mummy labeled "R1-1."

"What does that mean?" asked Louie.

"First row, first animal. What's called the lead animal. On a menagerie carousel, that's usually a lion or a tiger. This one's a lion."

"Which is the first row?"

"It's the row right behind the chariot, or the main chariot. Careful with the knife. They're damaged enough."

When we'd unwrapped the plastic sheet and the mover's quilt, Louie stared blankly at the lion.

"He's *purple*?"

I laughed. "No, they're supposed to be natural colors. Some-one went crazy with the paint."

"Oh. What do we do now?"

"Take a lot of photos of the animal the way it is now. Make notes. Then send them to be stripped. Then we do photos and notes again. You see a lot more when the paint's gone. I'll bring my camera in tomorrow and get started. Right this minute, though, I have to go. You ready?"

Louie nodded, and with a glance or two at the purple lion, got his jacket and mine from the coat hooks in the concession area. As I locked up, he surveyed the front of the building.

"Want me to start cleaning tomorrow?" he asked.

I shook my head. "Tomorrow I need someone to take animals to El Cerrito. Can you drive my van?"

"Sure. What's in El Cerrito?"

"The paint stripping place."

"Oh, okay. First thing, right?"

"No, I have to take pictures first. But you could help me with that too—move the animals around, work with the lights, that kind of thing. Okay?

"Sure."

"I should be through with at least a few of them by late afternoon, and you can take them then. We'll clean next week."

"Okay, see you tomorrow."

I watched him walk down the street, bouncing with each stride. Memories of my dropout days between high school and college made me smile—the street kids with their hippie gait, hands stuffed in pockets, feet dancing. Louie was a little like that—still some kid in him, and maybe there always would be. He was having fun working on the carousel. He made me remember that I was supposed to be having fun myself, in case I'd forgotten.

I checked my watch and headed for my van. I needed a shower before going to help with dinner at St. Martha's.

"I HAD A JOB AT THE MALL," the woman said. "It was that big mall up to Richmond. I didn't make it on time too much because of the bus. So, they fired me."

Of the three guests at the table, I knew the two men, Frank and Pete, but not her. She was new, and I hadn't caught her name. I'd heard that kind of story at St. Martha's, though, over and over. It didn't need a name anymore.

"That's a shame," I said. I didn't ask for details—at St. Martha's, the details were likely to be a well-aged jumble of memories, delusions, and wishes. The woman handed me her bowl, and I refilled it with soup.

"I was a carpenter foreman," Pete said. "I got fired, too." He shrugged.

"I had a job," Frank chimed in. "I forget what I did. It was a while ago."

Joy caught my eye and smiled. No matter how odd her guests were, she never wavered in her affection for them.

"Were you thinking of getting another job, Ginny?" she asked the woman. *Ginny,* I reminded myself. *That's her name.*

"My little boy doesn't like me to go out to work anymore," Ginny said.

Joy handed her the bread platter. Ginny put a chunk of the homemade bread on the side of her plate. Then she crammed another in her pocket. Joy tactfully studied her own plate. I pictured Ginny filling all her pockets with bread, then stuffing her cheeks like a chipmunk. Any minute now, she'd dash away to her room and bury her loot for the winter. I looked firmly down at my own plate—there was no way I was going to be able to keep a straight face for the next few minutes.

"Rich guys have cars," said Frank.

Pete looked up from his dinner. "They can afford to live anywhere, but they also got the transportation to go where they want." Scrawny with a bedraggled beard, he looked like a speed freak—and for all I knew, he *was* one. Or a junkie—I'd seen enough of those too.

"How's the work going?" Joy asked me. She looked around the big oak dining table, smiling at each of the guests, checking bowls to see if anyone needed more. "Mirai restores old carousels," she told them.

"It's fine. We're starting on the first few pieces tomorrow."

"I took my little boy to the merry-go-round at the zoo," said Ginny. She stopped talking abruptly, seemingly lost in her memories of her child and music and the dancing animals.

"What's your son's name?" I asked.

"Bobbie. Well, Robert."

"How old is he?"

"Thirty." Ginny fiddled with her spoon. "Maybe twenty or twenty-five. Or twenty-eight. I forget. He used to be younger."

Yes, I could see he might well have been. I tried to keep up a sane conversation with her. "Where does he live?" I asked.

"I don't know. His father stole him. They don't talk to me."

"Rich guys," said Frank. "They take your kids and everything."

"HOW'D IT GO?" asked Charlene, looking up from her desk in the fainting room as I dragged myself to the top of the stairs.

"Typical dinner at the asylum."

"Could I volunteer sometime?"

I sat down in a chair that occupied most of the floor space in her office. "You short of crazies in your life?" I asked.

"*Short* of them? I *collect* them."

"Uh, Charlene. You're supposed to collect things that are *rare*."

She laughed. "Not me. My book collection isn't only rare ones. I'm interested in all sorts of things. I even collect words."

"Words? Like what?" I asked.

"Let's see," she said, miming the removal of a lid from a box. "Here's a *complete* collection of every word that means 'iridescent.' Every single one. Very rare and valuable."

I fell in with her skit, if that's what it was. "Let me see," I said.

She pretended to pull them out and hand them to me. "Here's *opalescent*. And a first edition *nacreous*. *Prismatic*. *Shot*. *Shimmering*."

"Uh, oh. I dropped *shimmering*." I bent to retrieve the word from the carpet and held it up for inspection. "Hmmm. . . . It's not smushed." I handed *shimmering* back to her.

She packed it carefully into her imaginary box. "So, why are Joy's boarders nuttier than we are?"

"They don't know where fantasy stops. And they're miserable. And their lives don't work—they can't get by."

She thought for a minute. "Guess that's as good a definition as any for the line between goofiness and insanity. How does Joy handle all of it?"

"She's a saint. Also, she took psych courses at Cal after she got this job."

"An informed saint. I'm intrigued. Would you ask her if I could volunteer?"

"I'll give you her number, and you can call and get on the schedule." I stood and did a few shoulder rolls against the day's tiredness. "See you in the morning. I'm beat."

"G'night."

I turned back after a few steps and peeked through her door. "Charlene?"

"Umhmm?"

"*Chatoyant.*"

Charlene grabbed a dictionary, and I spelled the word for her.

"Damn!" she said when she'd found it. "Where did you learn a ten-dollar word like that?"

"Art class at Cal."

"Figures. *Merci beaucoup.* My collection is complete."

"No collection is ever complete," I said, and skipped down the hall.

10

Joy's NEXT VISIT WITH the letters got off to a rocky start, because I dropped a tray loaded with teacups and then cut my foot on the shards while I cleaned it up. Charlene made more tea, Joy helped me bandage my foot, and we sat down to hear tales of Nevada.

"What was Zuzene like?" asked Charlene, handing a cup to Joy.

Joy opened her folder of papers. "You've seen photos of her, haven't you?"

"Mirai has one on her tack board. But a black-and-white still photo doesn't say much."

"It's hard to describe her in words, either." Joy thought for a moment, then continued slowly, as if choosing her words one by one. "She was small, maybe five-two, and skinny—she often forgot to eat. Dark hair, dark eyes. That doesn't add up to what she was like—neither do her photos, really."

"Mirai's picture of her has an odd quality," said Charlene. "She seems to be looking *through* the camera, not at it."

"She didn't really look at people, either," said Joy. "I think she mostly looked inside her head, at pictures she hadn't painted yet."

"Intense," said Charlene.

"Really," I said. "I can see where she wouldn't have gotten along with your father."

Joy nodded. "He was a European *paterfamilias*," she explained to Charlene. "An extreme one. Blunt and uneducated, but intelligent in his own way. I'm having to translate his letters for Mirai because he insisted on writing to me in Basque.

"Read one," I said. "He comes through so clearly when you do."

Joy unfolded a paper and cleared her throat.

November 5, 1953

"How old would he have been then?" asked Charlene.

Joy thought. "Seventy-four or -five," she said. "But that's misleading. Aita never got old."

"Why was he writing you letters?" Charlene asked. "I thought you lived at the hotel."

"I went to college in Missoula and got a job there after I graduated. I didn't go back to Nevada until Zuzene died."

She resumed.

Dear Nekane,

At All Souls' Day Mass, this new priest we got was reading the names of this year's dead, every one of them. He's from California—maybe that's what they do out there. It was hard to listen to, even the names of people I didn't like.

I got a big surprise when he said Danel's name. I doubt if you remember him—he and I weren't friends anymore. We used to run sheep before you were born. After we fell out, I wished he'd go away. Now he has, and it didn't feel as good as I thought it would. May God have mercy on his soul.

I don't know if you knew about Larry Trivigno—he died last summer in Korea. He was the only young one on the list. Either you or Zuzene might have gone to school with him.

A couple of the others I guess you already heard about—your friend Carolyn's grandmother. And Tony Delgado's father. Lots of people. There were a few Indians too.

I went to Reno to see Zuzene last week. Waste of time. She's painting on blocks. Blocks is perfect for Zuzene. She's still around two years old, if you ask me. They look awful. You can't tell what anything is.

Aita

"Who was Danel?" I asked.

Joy shrugged. "One of the few people Aita really hated. I never knew why. Aita would cross the street to avoid talking to him or even looking at him."

"What was that crack about the blocks?"

"Aita thought Zuzene was crazy or retarded," said Joy.

Charlene seemed startled. "Why?" she asked.

"Zuzene was distant—she seemed to be one step from vanishing. And she wasn't a good student, except in art classes. None of that made sense to him, and her being as strong-willed as *he* was only made him madder."

"Were the blocks the ones you described last time?" I asked.

"Yes, it was a blending of sculpture and painting. Possibly inspired by Northwest Indian art. Papa thought they were stupid, but they were beautiful. And they brought good prices. One of those blocks is in a museum in St. Louis."

"Your dad was evidently not much of an art critic," Charlene said.

"More a horse expert. Zuzene was, too, but they didn't even agree about that. He didn't like the *way* she judged horses. He knew the rules, she was intuitive. Aita hated Zuzene's horse. In the end, he swore it was the horse that killed her."

"I thought she got lost in the desert," I said.

"Wait, wait!" Charlene waved her hands. "I want to hear the whole story. From the beginning."

"There isn't a whole story," Joy said. "Only a bunch of pieces like a jigsaw puzzle that won't go together. Zuzene rode out into the desert one summer night. Her horse came back to the stable the next morning with the saddle on, but no Zuzene. She was found two days later nearly ten miles from Pyramid Lake. She had a head injury. She died before they got her to the hospital."

"She rode alone into the desert?" asked Charlene.

"Zuzene did ride into the desert alone sometimes. She knew better, but she loved to ride Taba and she loved to be alone."

"Taba?"

"I think it means *sun* or *sunlight* in Paiute. He was a big palomino mustang, a stallion. Aita didn't trust him. But Taba was incredibly gentle with Zuzene."

"All the same, a stallion," I said.

"Zuzene was careful," Joy said. "She didn't go riding at night or into the desert at all in the summer. That time, she did both. Also—when she did go riding alone, she would at least tell someone where she was going. Usually her neighbor Andrea. But again—only that one time—she didn't."

"I think I remember Andrea," I said.

"That's who she left you with, that night. You were five. You *might* remember."

Only a flash, a back turned towards me, a shrill voice talking into a yellow telephone on a kitchen wall.

"If she left me at Andrea's, why didn't she tell Andrea where she was going?" I asked.

"Who knows? Andrea had an idea it had something to do with a boyfriend. No boyfriend ever turned up." Joy folded the letter carefully. "I doubt we'll ever know what happened."

Charlene looked at her sharply. "What about the head injury?" she asked.

"Aita said Taba must have kicked her. They didn't find evidence of anything else."

Joy glanced at me, then at Charlene. I had an idea she knew more than she was willing to say in front of Charlene. Maybe more than she was willing to say at all.

"I'm afraid that's the only letter tonight," said Joy. "I haven't had time to work on the rest."

I didn't mind—I'd heard enough for one evening. We sipped our tea for a few minutes. When we'd emptied our cups, Joy gathered her stuff, and I stood and hobbled to the door on my bandaged foot to let her out. Charlene took the cups and the teapot to the kitchen to wash by herself. Most likely, she figured enough had been broken for one night.

11

"Damn it to crimson *hell*," I yelled.

Louie ran to look at the lion he'd brought back from El Cerrito.

"What's wrong?" he asked.

Barbara looked up from photographing a giraffe. "Another one for Portland?" she asked.

"*Shit*," I raged. "Yes. Another one for Portland. Who in *hell* invented wiggle nails?"

Louie blinked. "What's that?"

"Look here," I said, pointing to the corrugated fastener at the joining of the lion's front leg. It was rusty, surrounded by a patch of rot. That had been smoothed with a filler that looked like Bondo. And the whole mess had been hidden with paint.

"Can't we just paint it?" asked Louie. "It didn't show before."

"No, it's rotting. It has to be rebuilt. We'll have to send it to Portland. Can you build a crate?"

"Sure."

"There's a couple of crates in the storeroom, but neither of them is big enough. Take them apart and make a big one. Get lumber if you need it, though. Damn. Why did it have to be the lion?"

"That was the side of the carousel with the leak," Barbara said.

She was right—I shouldn't have been surprised the lion needed repairs. But I felt superstitiously disturbed that the lead animal was in worse shape than I'd thought.

"Let's go over the standers carefully before we ship the lion," I said.

"Why the standers?" asked Louie.

"They get more wear. They're the prettiest animals, so they get ridden more. They're also on the outside, nearest the weather."

Barbara nodded toward the giraffe. "This one's okay. The giraffes were on the other side."

"Carousels turn," I reminded her. "We don't know that the roof only leaked over one part of it."

"The floor was only damaged in one area," she said. Her voice was tight, irritated.

"We can hope," I said. "Roof leaks aren't the only thing that can happen, and now we know the park had a cover-up artist on staff. Bondo, for God's sake."

"What's wrong with Bondo?" asked Louie.

Barbara rolled her eyes. "It's for cars, Louie."

She hadn't been happy that I hired him. Now that we were finding out how much work would be involved in restoring the carousel by the deadline, it was obvious that a helper was a good idea. But she didn't seem to have let go of her annoyance. Everything she said to him had an edge to it.

So did almost everything she said to *me*.

Ignoring her tone, I turned to Louie. "Most products that work on metal don't work on wood," I said, keeping my tone bland and teacher-ish.

"Makes sense," Louie said. "You wouldn't glue a piece of steel with wood glue."

"That's right, it wouldn't hold. When you use metal filler on wood, though, it may seem fine in the beginning. It takes a while for the damage to show."

Barbara's back was turned. She seemed immersed in her photography. That and maybe suddenly stone deaf as well. I watched her carefully for a minute. Whatever she was thinking, she kept it to herself.

I sighed. I doubted we'd ever be friends again, but I didn't want us to be enemies. I'd controlled my anger over Will. I hadn't canned her—I hadn't even said any of the nasty cracks I was thinking. It wasn't working, and I didn't know why. Maybe at this point, nothing I could do would make a difference.

I turned to Louie. "Can you get him crated by tomorrow afternoon? We need to ship him to Portland as soon as we can."

"Sure thing."

Louie sorted through the stored wood, whistling a tune I didn't recognize. The shutter of Barbara's camera clicked again and again, always out of tempo with Louie's tune. It sounded like an animal's teeth snapping. I decided I didn't *want* to know what was on her mind.

When Louie started building the crate, Barbara put her camera away.

"I can't work with that pounding," she said. "Anyway, I have to get home."

Home to Will. I pictured them kissing hello.

When she was gone, Louie turned to me. "What's with Barbara? She doesn't like me?"

"It's complicated, Louie. It doesn't have much to do with you."

He didn't look reassured, and I didn't know what else to say. I could hardly explain the whole Will-and-Barbara mess to him.

"She mad at *you*?"

"Not exactly that, either. Don't sweat it—it's personal stuff."

He hesitated. Then he said, "Uh, I was wondering—"

"It doesn't have *anything* to do with you." I tried to keep the testy tone out of my voice, but I wished he'd drop the subject.

"No, I didn't mean that," he said quickly. "I was wondering .... You have a lot of space here."

"Yes?" I wondered what he had in mind. This wasn't sounding good.

"Well, I'm an assistant coach for a basketball team. Could they practice here at night?"

"Basketball?" I couldn't believe I'd heard him right. "What for?"

"We need a place to play."

"But it isn't a basketball court."

"We'd bring in portable nets."

"Don't they have parks or YMCAs or anything around here?"

"They're so crowded, it's hard to get a turn."

"Louie, I can't open the studio for a bunch of guys I don't even know."

"You said you and Barbara would be here in the evenings."

"All we need is for a ball to smash into one of the animals."

"I don't see how it could. Would you at least talk to the coach? He'll tell you we're okay."

I rubbed my eyelids. *Wish I had earlids to rub. Or to close— that would be even better. Everyone around me seems to be three- quarters crazy.*

"He can give me a call. But honestly, Louie, I don't think so."

His disappointed-puppy look wasn't lost on me. The carousel had to get finished, and I had to have employees to finish it. Why couldn't people just work for money? Everyone had to have the most bizarre extras. Barbara's price included the whole Will tangle, and it was beginning to look like Louie's involved turning part of my studio into a rec center.

"I have to call Portland Carousel Works and let them know we're sending the lion," I said. It was as good an excuse as any to go hide in the office.

12

DOWN THE HALL, THE PHONE rang and rang. Crank call, I thought, turning over in bed and waiting for it to stop. It did, and I pulled the comforter to my neck, hoping to drift back to sleep. It was blind dark, not nearly time to get up.

The phone started again, and rang on and on. I threw the covers back, exasperated. I lurched down the hall to the fainting room, ready to tell off the caller.

"Mirai?" Joy's voice.

"Uh . . . what time is it?" I asked.

"Mirai, are you awake?"

"Almost. What's going on?"

"I need to go to the airport."

"What for?" A hard pit of fear was spreading outward from my stomach. Joy had never called me like this. I grasped at a stupid hope. "Do you need me to pick someone up for you?"

"No, I need to go to Paradise."

"Paradise?" I was stunned. "What for?"

"Come get me and I'll explain it in the car. I'm sorry to call at this hour—it's an emergency. I got a seat on a puddle-jumper flight to Reno at five."

"Okay. Coming."

I threw on yesterday's clothes and grabbed my pack. Down in the kitchen, I checked the clock—three in the morning. I chugged half a cup of leftover coffee, grabbed a bagel from the breadbox, and got on the road.

Joy was waiting at the curb in front of St. Martha House. I loaded her suitcase into the back seat of the van.

"What's going on?" I asked, as she fastened her seat belt. "Why are you going to Paradise Meadow in the middle of the night? You told me you didn't know anyone there anymore." My voice echoed in the predawn quiet of the street.

"I didn't," Joy said. "I have an old friend, Jakinda—we grew up together. She married and moved to Cedar City shortly after I left for college. Now she's gone back to Paradise. She's dying of cancer. Her daughter-in-law called me."

"Why?" I sounded like a broken record. Or a talking doll. Pull the string and she says "Why?"

I tried again. "I mean, why does your friend urgently need to see you at three in the morning?"

"I don't know why Jakinda wants to see me. Her daughter-in-law didn't say. People get quirky ideas at the end, sometimes. I don't even know exactly why Jakinda went back to Paradise. Maybe it had to do with her son's death. Her husband's been gone for several years. I think her daughter-in-law was the only person left."

"How in the world did she find you?"

"4-1-1, I'd imagine. Jakinda knows I live in Oakland."

Joy was quiet for a few minutes, as if she had something on her mind. I watched the road closely, as if I were driving in heavy traffic, not on the empty freeway long before dawn.

I heard rustling from Joy's direction. She was pulling papers out of her purse.

"It's kind of a coincidence—I worked on more of Aita's letters the other day. He was worried about the atomic bomb tests at the Nevada Test Site. I didn't know exactly why he went to Spain, but that may have been part of it. He'd lost his parents at Guernica, and his views on the military weren't exactly typical for northern Nevada. Anyway, I brought the letters along in case you want to read them while I'm gone."

"What's a coincidence? Guernica?" I knew it was a painting by Picasso, knew it showed a bombing. But it didn't seem real. *Guernica* had no more meaning for me than *Agincourt* would have. I couldn't see any connection with Joy's father.

"Aita came to America in 1888," she said. "His family lived in Guernica, and it was bombed on a market day in 1937. All of them were killed."

"But he didn't go to Spain until much later. What does Guernica have to do with it?" I asked, glancing away from the road long enough to eye the folded papers.

"Aita didn't like the military. And Nevada in the early fifties was very military. The Cold War was at its height. He couldn't even discuss his worries with his neighbors, because they would have thought he was a communist. He shut up. And then he left. Zuzene had died, and I think he felt free to go because he didn't have her anymore."

"I thought they didn't get along," I said, bewildered.

"They didn't. But he thought she was crazy, and that meant he had to be there to help. Basque families. You don't walk away from the odd ones."

"But she didn't need his help."

"He didn't see it like that. Oh, speaking of help . . . ."

"What do you need?"

"I need you to get the volunteers organized to take care of St. Martha's while I'm away. The guests are all in halfway decent shape. Frank's drinking has been under control for months—I don't think he'll start again, at least not for a while. If anything goes missing, look in Ginny's room. I have a list of phone numbers in here, too"—she waved her clutch of papers—"and the things I was going to do this week. I'll call when I get there and give you that phone number in case you need to reach me."

"Oh, okay." I needed coffee. My head felt like it was filled with cotton. I figured I'd sort out my confusion later.

At the airport, I pulled into a loading zone and heaved the suitcase out of the van. Joy inched her way out of the passenger seat like an old lady. I looked away.

A skycap bustled to the curb and I passed the suitcase to him, along with a tip. Joy kissed me and followed him into the terminal. She didn't look back.

Belting myself into the driver's seat again, I glimpsed the papers on the passenger seat. Unwanted as a summons. Anxiety stiffened my neck muscles, so I breathed deeply for a few minutes before I started the van. All I needed now was a traffic accident.

When I got home, I sat on the living room couch without turning on the light. I knew I'd toss and turn if I went to bed. I had a headful of why's like a two-year-old, and no one to ask. Charlene's mantel clock ticked into the dark, in case anyone wanted to count the seconds till dawn.

Part 3

13

I HAD A STIFF NECK when I woke. I dragged myself off the couch and into the kitchen, where Charlene was pouring herself a mug of coffee. After one look at me, she passed me the mug, instead.

"Thanks," I mumbled, slumping against the Hoosier cabinet. She found another mug in the dish drainer and filled it for herself.

"Let's sit in the dining room and you can tell me," she said.

I followed her into the cool, dim room, concentrating on hanging on to the mug. Mirai clumsiness wasn't what was needed right now.

"Joy called," I said. "Early."

"I heard the phone ring. Is something wrong?"

"She needed a ride to the airport. One of her Paradise Valley friends is dying."

"I'm sorry. I didn't realize she had friends there."

"This lady used to live in Cedar City, but she moved back to die."

"Cedar City." Charlene looked thoughtful. "What's wrong with her, if you don't mind my asking?"

"Cancer."

"Oh, I see."

"I don't. What do you mean?"

"Cancer clusters. Utah, Central Nevada . . . . There was a lawsuit about it."

"I didn't know. Is it some environmental problem?"

"Kind of. It was the nuclear testing in the fifties. At least, that's what I read."

"Joy gave me more of her father's letters this morning, and she mentioned something about that. She said it was a 'coincidence.' . . . Where did I leave those papers?"

"In the living room, maybe? Where you were sacked out?"

I checked the living room, but I didn't see them. "They must be in the van," I called, and went out to get them.

Back in the kitchen, I shuffled through the papers and arranged Estebe's letters in chronological order. I started to read the first.

May 19, 1957

"Wasn't the last letter a while before this?" Charlene asked.

"She might have lost some. Or maybe he didn't write that often. Or else she's translating them out of order."

I started again.

May 19, 1957

Dear Nekane,

> *I got something to tell you that worries me a lot. A man stayed at the hotel, he was from Utah someplace. He was a sheepherder, but his whole flock got wiped out by those A-bomb tests. He said most of them died with burns on their mouths from the grass they ate. Some of them had burns all over.*

> *He and some other men sued the government, but the trial was rigged somehow and they lost. The government men said nothing happened, and the judge believed them.*

He got out of there. The government says the bomb tests are safe, but he don't trust them. He's moving on, might as well, since he lost everything. Looking for a safe home for him and his family. He's wondering how far the dust or whatever it is from the bombs could travel.

I remember after Guernica, Franco said nothing happened, too. I got neighbors who say we have to do this to beat the Russians. I don't get it. Our own government is A-bombing us. What could the Russians do that's any worse?

For the first time since I got here, I'm thinking of going back to Spain. Your sister says no way is she going—she's an American. You are too, I guess. If I go there, I'll never see either of you again, most likely.

I don't know. Maybe it's too late. I'm an old man, Nekane. Probably everyone I knew in Spain is long gone. And I have so much to do in the next few months at the hotel. Maybe next year. Next year I'll go.

Aita

There was a note in Joy's hand at the bottom of the letter.

This letter was in English—the only one that was—but I typed it anyway, because Aita's writing was nearly illegible. I guess he didn't know Basque words for what he had to say.

Seeing Joy's neat, round writing made tears sting behind my nose—I missed her already.

We sat for a while without saying anything. Finally I asked, "Want to hear another?"

"Not right now. What about St. Martha's? Who's taking care of that?"

"Me, supposedly. At least till I get the volunteers organized to take over. I have to go there this morning. Joy left me a list of things to do."

"I'll help," said Charlene.

I gave her a quick look. I didn't want her to get swept up in my problems and neglect her work.

"I said I was going to volunteer, didn't I?" she asked.

"Uh-huh. Do you have any idea what you're getting into?"

"No, but that's true every morning when I get out of bed."

"And you still get out."

"It's a bad habit."

When we got to St. Martha's, I parked at the curb and we surveyed the building for a minute. Through the French doors in the walls around the patio, we could see that all the lights were on. Except for that, it seemed the same as ever. Still, I was hesitant to go in.

"We won't ever finish if we don't ever start," said Charlene, opening her door.

I unhooked my seat belt and climbed out. I felt silly—what was I expecting, dragons?

The front yard was as ragged as usual, but geraniums and Nile lilies at least made it bright. We crossed the patio, but the front door was locked.

"Let's go through the kitchen," I suggested.

We skirted the building, past Joy's well-tended herb bed. Now in midsummer, the vegetable garden was starting to pay back for all the spring work. It would need a lot more tending if the vegetables weren't going to go to ruin. I'd have to find someone to do that while Joy was gone.

The back door was locked, too, but the residents were in the kitchen. I knocked and Pete let me in.

"Where's Joy?" he asked before I was even through the door.

"She got called away on an emergency," I said. "Didn't she leave you a note?"

"We didn't look," said Pete.

Frank, behind him, nodded.

"We made our own breakfast," he said.

I could see that they had. The counters were covered with left-out food, crusted pans, kitchen towels, and dirty dishes. On the floor was an assortment of food wrappings, eggshells, potato peels, and crumpled paper that hadn't made it into the garbage can. Yellow and brown gunk dripped off the stovetop. The kitchen looked like it would take hours to clean. I reminded myself that the residents weren't all that functional, and I swallowed my annoyance.

"That's nice," I said, trying to smile. Charlene looked at me like I was nuts, but she didn't comment.

"We made French toast," said Ginny. "I used to make French toast for my little boy."

That explained the gunk on the stove. Egg and cinnamon.

"I made hash browns," Pete added.

Ah. The potato peels.

"Why don't you guys watch TV for a while, and we'll straighten up?" I asked.

They trooped obediently into the living room, and the racket of morning cartoons filled the air.

"Could you turn it down, please?" I called.

"I don't hear good," said Pete. He didn't turn it down.

I caught Charlene's eye and shrugged.

"The volunteers usually say a prayer before they start," I said.

"Good idea."

We both bowed our heads. I'd meant to say the St. Francis prayer, which was what we usually did, but Charlene spoke first.

"Jesus Christ, help us clean up this mess," she said. "Amen."

I suppressed a snort. "Amen," I echoed.

She surveyed the kitchen, arms folded. "Shoulda brought my paint scraper," she grumbled. "How's the dining room?"

The havoc in the kitchen had led me to assume all the mess must be in there. How much more could they have done? When I checked the dining room, I found out. Half-full serving dishes were piled high on the mantel, spoons still in them. Wadded paper napkins soaked up leftovers in the abandoned plates on the table. The string of a tea bag dragged from a mug like the tail of a drowned mouse.

"Was this breakfast for three?" Charlene asked. "Or did they give a party?"

"I think it was only them."

"Wow. Does Joy have some laundry baskets?"

"What for? We're not going to start doing laundry, are we?"

"No, baskets make it easier to handle a big mess. Get as many as she has."

I didn't know how laundry baskets were going to help, but I got four of them from the service porch. When I gave them to Charlene, she handed one back to me and picked up one herself.

"Put trash in yours," she said, "and I'll put dirty dishes in mine."

"What are the other baskets for?"

"The third is for food, and the fourth is for whatever needs to be put away elsewhere in the house. One basket at a time, both rooms."

Holding a basket, I circled the dining room table, picking out items to throw away. Charlene followed me, gathering dishes. We did a second circuit in the kitchen.

"Next round," Charlene muttered, setting the basket of dishes on the counter.

When we'd filled the third and fourth baskets, Charlene loaded the dishwasher. I carried the trash to the dumpster. Then we turned to the other full baskets.

"I'll find places for the food," she said. "You'd know where the other stuff goes better than I would."

It was like a treasure hunt in reverse, finding the right place to put the odd things the guests had hauled out when there was nobody to stop them. While I was at it, I picked up a few things, too, including the bottle of cinnamon and six forks from Ginny's room. Finished, I returned to a surprisingly orderly kitchen, with Charlene scraping the last of the crust off the stove. She polished it with a dishcloth.

"Where's the mop?" she asked.

"Back porch. I'll get it."

With the floor mopped, the kitchen and dining room looked like a picture in a home magazine. I checked my watch. The cleaning had taken no more than twenty minutes.

"How'd you learn to clean so fast?" I asked.

"I used to be a nanny-housekeeper."

Before I could absorb that, the phone rang. It was Joy.

"I'm here," she said. "I called your house but no one was home. I figured you were at St. Martha's. How's it going?"

"Charlene and I are doing fine," I said. "No problem at all."

14

I GOT TO WORK LATER than usual. Barbara and Louie were eyeing each other like a pair of cats. Or rats. Or whatever animal doesn't like other animals of its own kind. Like a pair of humans.

Hearing my footsteps, they turned toward me.

"One of the zebras has to go to Portland," Barbara said.

"Mirai, did you call my coach?" Louie cut in.

"The fire inspector said we needed to get the extinguisher recharged." This from Barbara.

"He'll only be in until two." Louie again.

I considered screaming. However, that didn't seem likely to solve anything.

"Louie, hang on a second. Barbara, what's wrong with the zebra?"

"Wood split. It's been fixed with fiberglass cloth."

My profits on this job were going to go to Portland Carousel Works. I sighed.

"Louie, make us a crate, would you? I haven't called your coach yet, but I will." I kept my voice down. It wasn't easy.

The phone rang. When I answered it, Will asked to speak to Barbara. Without comment, I passed it to her. I turned away politely, but I eavesdropped on her end of the conversation.

"Hi, Honey. . . . We don't? There was chili in the refrigerator last night. . . . I was going to go after work. . . . Could you go out for a sandwich? Uh-huh. Oh, okay. No, I'm not busy. . . .

No, not at all. Mirai just got here. . . . I'll be there in an hour. . . .
Love you." She hung up. "I have to go," she said.

"Are you coming in this afternoon?" I asked.

"I doubt it."

I looked at her in astonishment. I couldn't think of a thing
to say. I couldn't believe she was leaving, apparently to go to
the market and fix lunch for an able-bodied male. I didn't see
any trace of my friend Barbara in this man-pleasing automaton.

The silence stretched beyond discomfort. *Say something,* I
told myself. *She can't do this. I'm the boss. What does she think
she's doing?*

"If Louie's going to be hammering, I can't do anything anyway," Barbara said.

I finally found my voice. "Barbara, we have a tight schedule
here. We'll miss it if you leave as soon as anyone makes noise."

"Sorry. I have a headache. I'll do it later." She got her purse
and left.

I sighed. I had an idea who would work double to make up
for her taking off, and it wasn't Barbara.

If the only reason I wasn't firing her over Will was that I
needed to get the carousel done by Memorial Day, and she
wasn't helping me get the carousel done . . . . I sighed again.
There was still one reason. If I canned her, it would look like it
was over Will, and then *he'd* quit the project. There were other
band organ restorers, but it would be tough to get anyone else
to come in with the job half-finished. I kicked myself for not
easing him out before the project started. What had made me
think I could work with him?

Louie was staring at the closed door like he had a lot on his
mind. "Hey, Louie," I said quietly, "the crate."

"Oh, right. What was that about?"

I shrugged. I didn't want to discuss the scene with Louie, so I went into the painting room and checked the stripped and sanded animals waiting there. I'd be painting them a few at a time, switching among them to give each coat time to dry. The first group included three horses and a giraffe.

When we had animals stripped, they came back with a fair job of sanding, too—good enough for most furniture, but *not* good enough for the glassy finish of a carousel figure. Hours of tedious sanding awaited us.

In the past, Barbara and I had worked together, chatting. We'd discuss the project and the customers, of course, but sanding was a long, dull job. Our talks would veer into our personal lives—plans and dreams, weekends and boyfriends.

Maybe I'd talked too much about Will.

The words of an old song came to me.

> *When you get good lovin',*
> *Never go and spread the news,*
> *Or your girlfriends will double-cross you,*
> *Leave you with the empty bed blues.*

Not that my conversation had been *that* graphic. All the same, I felt a twist of embarrassment at the memory of those confidences. A picture rushed into my mind, strong and clear— Barbara and Will, lying in bed after making love. Her blonde hair trailed over his bare arm as she gazed into his eyes. She told him something I'd said about him. The circle of arms was complete, and I was outside it. They laughed at my foolishness.

Don't be paranoid, I told myself. *Why would she remember, why would they discuss me? They have far more interesting topics of conversation.*

The glass eyes on carousel figures always seemed more human than animal—it could be disconcerting. The prospect of solitary sanding under their gaze was less than inviting. But having Barbara there with nothing to say—that would be even worse.

Then again—the idea came to me with the sound of Louie's hammer on the crate—I could train *him* to do at least some of it.

I thought it over. Sanding was critical, and I'd have to supervise him to make sure it was done right. And Barbara was unhappy at the idea that I might train Louie—probably afraid for her job. Too bad. She could hardly complain I'd taken her work away—she was the one who walked out. She wasn't nervous *enough* about her job, in my opinion. Too busy being Mrs. Tremayne.

By the time the hammer stopped, I'd decided to try Louie at the sanding.

AFTER DINNER, I TOLD Charlene about Barbara and the phone call.

"Too bad I didn't make you bet with me," she chortled.

"What bet are you talking about?"

"That Barbara was going to find out that being married to an SOB is no fun. I missed out. I might've won your shop—lock, stock, and carousel horse."

"You might not have wanted the shop," I said.

"Why? I thought you had a lot of work."

"I do. But when the animals are stripped, new problems can show up. Sometimes, bad repairs have been buried in paint and putty to make them invisible."

"Until you strip the paint, huh?"

"Right. Then they have to go to a place in Portland for major work. If many more of them turn out to be damaged, I won't make much profit on this job."

"What are bad repairs?"

"The kind that make the problem worse in the long run."

"Such as?"

"Metal fasteners will, because moisture condenses on them, and then they rust . . . . You get the idea. In the end, the piece is in far worse shape than it was to begin with."

"Don't you allow for that when you bid?"

"I allow for some of it. But if I figure in everything that might show up, I'll never win a bid. So, on some jobs, I lose money."

"Can't you charge the client for it?"

"I could. I hate to do it, though. The misjudgment may have been my fault—I was upset when I evaluated the animals, and I may not have checked them for damage as thoroughly as usual. And as far as money goes—they don't have it."

"Neither do you, babes."

She was right. I hoped it wouldn't come to that, though. Asking for extra money made me feel like a beggar. With any luck, I wouldn't find any more damage. I'd be okay if there wasn't much more of it. Maybe I could dicker with the guys in Portland for a better price, too. I'd sent them a lot of business over the years. They might give me a break for a higher number of animals.

Charlene was studying my face. "Honestly, that phone call . . . . Did you imagine, that could be you? How would you feel if your husband acted like that?"

"Yeah, I did think of that."

"Did he ever pull stunts like that when you were living together?"

"He wasn't the most liberated guy in the world. But he didn't take it that far."

"Count your blessings it's her, not you."

I nodded. I did feel that. I also felt homesick for the good times. I remembered a picnic Will and I had gone on once. I'd felt so beautiful and so replete that I'd lain in the grass and mentally given heaven an I.O.U. for all the happiness that had come my way. Now I wondered if heaven had come to collect.

Charlene was watching me. I changed the subject.

"Louie wants me to let him and his friends play basketball in the empty end of the studio."

She frowned. "Wouldn't there be risk to the animals?"

"No, the ones we're working on are in the paint room or the sanding room. And the others are stored on special racks in a locked storeroom. Noise could be a problem."

"Would your insurance let you do it?"

"I don't know. Louie wants me to call his coach."

"And you're going to?"

"I guess so, if only to shut him up. I doubt it will work out. Might as well get it over with."

Charlene didn't answer, but she gave me a look that asked if I'd lost my mind. I called Louie's coach from the living room phone, but he wasn't in. I left a message for him to call me, hoping he wouldn't.

15

WHEN I GOT BACK TO THE KITCHEN, I found Charlene cleaning up our meal.

"Oh, I'm sorry," I said. "I didn't mean to leave that for you."

"It's okay. I don't mind doing for you once in a while." Charlene had set the dishes in the dishwasher as precisely as a flower arrangement. She closed the dishwasher and turned the dial.

Raising her voice over the roar of the machine, she said, "Those new letters Joy left you—want to read another?"

"Sure."

I dug in my pack and pulled out a crumpled mass of paper. I leafed through sheets of phone numbers and instructions for St. Martha's and found the letters.

"Let's go to the living room where it's quieter," I suggested.

We settled down in our places. I wished Joy was in hers. The room seemed incomplete without her to read to us.

June 15, 1958

Dear Nekane,

I guess Zuzene has told you the news. Has she? Now she's decided to adopt a child. At first I was sure she'd really gone crazy, but when I thought it over, I could see some good in it. Not that your sister has it in her to be a decent mother. But she says Andrea is going to be a babysitter.

Anyway, I don't think it's such a bad idea. She wouldn't be able to get a Basque baby, of course, because no Basque would give up their baby. She might get some cute little guy anyway, and I'm not that narrow minded, as long as it's not an Indian or a Mexican. It would be fun to have a grandson. I could take him hunting someday.

It is getting hot already. I'd like to air condition the hotel someday. Not this year. Or maybe I'll go back to Spain before long. Not if Zuzene means it about the grandson, though.

Aita

I held my breath when I'd finished reading. I hadn't expected the letter to be quite so personal.

"Oh, shit," said Charlene. "Joy's father was expecting he'd get a grandson."

"A *white* grandson," I added.

"Son of a bitch," said Charlene. I didn't know if she was referring to Estebe, or if her comment was only an expletive. "You might have guessed it, though."

"I hadn't." I couldn't understand why I felt so crushed. Why should I care what some dumb old guy thought about me? His loss, not mine. He'd never known his only grandchild.

"When did Estebe die?" asked Charlene.

I pulled myself together to answer her. "Mid-sixties. But he was in Spain by then. He left America shortly after Mama died."

"Why did he keep saying your mother was crazy? I mean, if you don't mind my asking. She doesn't sound crazy to me. Maybe he didn't have much experience with artists."

"I don't know. We'll have to ask Joy. I don't remember her."

"If she *had* been psychotic," said Charlene, "she wouldn't have been allowed to adopt a child."

I winced. "Even a black child?" I asked.

"I don't think so. For that matter, did it ever occur to you that there's not an awfully large black population in northern Nevada to begin with? Where did she find you?"

"It did occur to me. Will said once that I shouldn't be asking *Joy* about my past, I should be looking for some Vegas hooker about sixteen years older than me."

"Ouch," said Charlene. "That crack has it all—sexist, racist, ageist. Did he miss anything?"

"Not that I can think of. He wanted me to quit talking about it, and I did. Joy got the same result by being evasive. At least until now."

"Yes, but are her father's letters really telling you anything?"

LOUIE'S COACH RETURNED MY CALL the next morning.

"I'm glad I finally caught up with you," he said. "This is Barry Donovan, Louie Martin's coach. He told me you might let the team use some of your studio space for basketball practice. That's so generous—I wish more people in the community were aware of the need."

"Need?" I asked, blankly. I'd been ready to tell him there was no way they could use the studio.

"The need for recreation for teens. Since Prop. 13, the cities haven't been able to do much."

"I see," I managed.

"Yes, the kids have to hang out on the streets—in the long run, drugs and gangs cost the city far more than a few basketball courts. It's a false economy, but very few people understand that."

We were getting further and further from my intention to tell him they couldn't use the space.

"I have to check my insurance," I said. "I have quite a few valuable carousel animals here. . . . "

"Don't worry about that," he said. "The Boys and Girls Club is fully insured. Also, we'll work with you to make sure your things are safe."

That did make a difference. I still didn't think I'd like having them around, but now I couldn't think of an excuse to say no.

"Anyway," he said. "I'd like to see what we need to do to get your extra space ready. Let me know when it would be convenient."

It was too late to say, "One week after Hell freezes over." I told him Saturday afternoon would be fine.

16

I STARTED ON THE STACKED-UP filing, rationalizing that I wasn't "cleaning up for company." Except I knew I was. Before I'd gotten far, the phone rang again.

"Mirai, this is Linda Gonzales. From St. Martha House."

"Oh, hi, Linda."

"I'm sorry to bother you. I've left messages for Joy, and she hasn't returned my calls."

"How's it going, there?" I hooked my desk chair with my ankle and rolled it closer so I could sit down. Might as well make myself comfortable.

"Not good, I'm afraid. The guests can be hard to control."

Linda sounded almost desperate. I wondered where Joy had met her—at the market, at church, on a street corner? The volunteers meant well, but some of them soon found themselves in over their heads.

I chose my words carefully. "They *are* more or less mentally disturbed."

"I know that, Mirai, but we're not qualified to run a hospital."

"What's the problem exactly?"

"Today it's Ginny. She's gotten a doll from somewhere. . . . Honestly, Mirai, I think you'd better come and see for yourself. She's behaving quite oddly."

"I'll drop by after work."

"Good. I'll stay till you get here so we can talk. When's Joy coming back?"

"I don't know. I thought she would've called the house and told you."

There was a silence at the other end of the line.

"Linda?"

"Yes, I'm here. I'll see you this evening, honey. Bye."

"Bye, Linda."

I looked at the papers in the "File" basket and realized I didn't have time for them. I needed to finish color plans for the animals so I could start finish coats as soon as they were primed.

I pulled out my sketch pad and Prismacolor pencils. Looff typically coordinated harness colors for all the animals on a carousel, but with individual detailing. Most of the harnesses would have had touches of gold or silver. I rubbed the edge of my pencil on the edge of the pad, sharpening it to a finer point. Carousels whirled in my mind. *Dapple gray*, I thought, *with the breastplate golden and the saddle a Prussian blue. . . . A new, white horsehair tail. . . .*

The phone rang once again.

"Mirai?" Barbara's voice.

"Yes?"

"Something's come up. . . . I'm going to be late."

I could imagine what might have "come up." I clenched my teeth in fury.

"Mirai? . . . Mirai?" She hesitated, then hung up. I listened to the dial tone for a few seconds, fuming, then set my receiver down as gently as a crystal wineglass. My hand was shaking.

Turning to my sketch, I tried to recapture the image. *New, white horsehair tail. . . .* I drew a galloping horse, with its tail streaming behind it, tendrils wind-braided. . . .

Barbara's blonde hair, splayed across a rumpled pillowcase.

I threw the pencil against the wall.

BARBARA CAME IN SHORTLY before lunch. I could think of half a dozen things I'd like to say to her, but I knew I'd be sorry if I did. There was no way Louie and I could finish that carousel on schedule without her. I pretended there wasn't a problem.

"Hey, lady," I said, giving her a fakey smile. "What we need is to get the stripped ones sanded more, and I need you to show Louie how to do it. Help him, would you? I'm tied up with color sketches."

She nodded and left the office. I checked the sanding room a couple of times, but they were working peaceably, and Louie seemed to be doing everything right.

But when I looked in a few minutes after three, Barbara was gone. Louie glanced up from the giraffe's saddle and gave me a half wave, still holding his sandpaper.

"Where's Barbara?" I asked. *Jesus, do I have to sound like a cop? Whatever she's up to, it's not his fault.*

"She went home. She said to tell you she'd be in tomorrow morning, but she might have to go at lunchtime."

It was clear that what I had was a part-time assistant, when I needed full time and then some. Barbara and Will had me over a barrel. It was infuriating. Here I was, putting up with the risks and expense and overwork of running my own business, choosing to do that so I wouldn't have to deal with a boss—and I was being intimidated by an employee. It was a classic case of "Heads they win, tails I lose," and I wondered how I had ever let it get started.

I saw Louie studying my face, so I cut off that train of thought. I felt a little guilty about him. I'd been reacting to his request to use the studio after hours with a lot of the anger I hadn't been able to turn on Barbara for the mess she'd made. *Not that I plan to turn the place into a basketball arena, but I don't have to be so snotty about it.*

"Well, let's see how you're doing," I said, checking the smoothness of the three animals with my fingertips. "Good work. These are ready to prime. Let's take them along to the paint room."

Louie walked behind me, wheeling a horse on its stand. "Why do you have separate rooms?" he asked.

"To keep the sawdust out of the paint."

I poured primer into a smaller can and selected a clean brush. "Make a thin coat," I told him, showing him how. "The first coat is called the 'finder coat' because it 'finds' the rough spots in the sanding."

I handed him the brush and watched him as he tried to do it the way I'd demonstrated.

"It's watery paint," he said. "Mirai—can someone be allergic to sawdust?"

"There are toxic sawdusts—rosewood is one—but I haven't heard of anyone reacting to the woods that were used for carousel animals. Why?"

"Barbara kept sniffling and blowing her nose while we were sanding."

I put my hand over Louie's and corrected the angle of the brush. When I let go, he rearranged his grip, trying hard to get it right.

"Barbara's not allergic to sawdust, or she'd have died by now," I said. "She must be coming down with a cold."

"She said she wasn't. I guess she was upset."

He was starting to glop primer all over the place. "Look out," I said. "Don't let the paint collect in the detail—brush it on lightly."

"Why don't you spray it?"

"Some artists do. I don't like the noise of a spray rig. And the cleanup's a bitch. Anyway, the old guys didn't use sprayers."

"Do we do everything like they did?"

"No, if a new material is better, we use it. But not unless. Or if there's a reason why we can't do it the old way."

"Like what?"

"We use three thin coats of primer where they used one coat of white lead paint. White lead is good paint, but it's not legal anymore. They used primer to fill in carving imperfections, but today's primers aren't thick enough."

"Three coats!"

"Yes, and they have to dry thoroughly. And you sand in between. It's slow."

I watched him for a while, only half my mind on him and the horse. The other half was wondering whether Barbara had been crying in the sanding room and why she, of all people, might be unhappy.

For the rest of the afternoon, I kept having flashes of a picture of Barbara crying over her work. I finished the priming with Louie and showed him how to clean the brushes. He left at quarter after five.

At five thirty, I locked the studio and dragged myself out to the van. Navigating Friday evening traffic, I drove more or less on automatic pilot: stop, start, stop again. All the way to Saint Martha's, I saw Barbara sanding a giraffe and crying. I sort of wished she'd leave me alone. At the moment, she wasn't a person I wanted to feel sympathy for.

17

At St. Martha's, I paused in the door of the living room. The three guests were sitting on the couch, so engrossed in the television that they didn't even glance my way. Ginny had her doll cradled on her lap, stroking it as she watched the show. It was spooky to see a grown woman do that.

I went into Joy's tiny office, where Linda was waiting, and shut the door behind me.

"You see," she began, "Ginny got hold of that doll. She seems to think it's a baby."

"Yes, I did see," I answered, trying not to sound impatient. "She wouldn't be here if she weren't pretty odd. She isn't hurting anything."

"Well, she may be. I think she took the doll. You know she does . . . take things."

"You mean, she's shoplifting?"

"No, it looks used. Not much, but she didn't get it from a store."

"I couldn't see it very well. What kind of doll is it?"

"That's the bad part. It's one of those Cabbage Patch Kids. It's probably worth something. Also, those dolls have adoption certificates and everything. It isn't one that's likely to be overlooked."

"Damn it to hell. Why couldn't she have swiped a Betsy Wetsy or some other doll no one would miss?"

Apparently I wasn't reassuring Linda—she looked more and more rattled. "I don't think they make Betsy Wetsys anymore, Mirai."

"Did you ask her what she was doing with it?"

"Yes, of course."

"What did she say?"

"All I could get out of her is that its name is Robert."

"Oh, shit." Her son's name. I tried to rub away the headache that was starting at my temples. "Do you think she swiped it from a kid?"

"I think it's likely."

"Look on the bright side—she might have stolen the kid instead."

Linda's eyes got round. "Oh, golly, I didn't think of *that*. What should we do?"

I tried to imagine how Joy would handle it. Nothing came to mind.

"I don't know how we'd find the owner," I said. "Even if we could get the damn doll away from her, which I don't know how we could."

"I don't, either. Maybe she'll get tired of it in a few days."

"Then what?" I asked. "Put a picture of it on milk cartons?"

Linda gave me a funny look. "Ginny must have gotten it in the neighborhood," she said. "Could we tack signs to the telephone poles?"

"Like when someone loses their cat?"

"Can you think of anything else, Mirai?"

"No." My headache was getting worse. I needed to get home and take some aspirin, maybe have a hot, steamy bath.

"I hope Joy calls soon," said Linda.

"Me, too."

As I left, I walked through the yard's too-high grass without really paying attention. All I wanted was to get home.

I WISHED I COULD TALK to Charlene, but she was out for the evening, supervising the caterer at a fund-raiser for a city councilwoman. Grabbing a carton of yogurt and a bagel from the refrigerator, I went upstairs to my room.

I was sure I'd seen one more letter in that pile of papers I'd gotten from Joy. I dug through the stuff on my desk and finally found it. Found the original, anyway—there was no translation. I searched through everything again, but no luck.

Joy had been so flustered when she left, she must have picked up the wrong sheet. Or maybe she'd meant to translate it but forgot. Or maybe I'd just misplaced it. I studied the page, trying to make out a few words. Nothing. All I could read was the date, four months after I was born.

· Frustrated, I put it aside, meaning to remind Joy when she called. If she ever called. I was starting to worry—it wasn't like Joy to be inconsiderate, but I hadn't heard from her for days. Not since that first morning when Charlene and I had cleaned up the crazy breakfast at St. Martha's.

Crazy. Crazy Ginny and her baby doll. Crazy Zuzene and her baby. Was Zuzene crazy? Estebe thought so, but was she?

Sitting on the bed, I looked at my bulletin board. Zuzene's picture stared past my head, as it always did. Isolated—she'd been isolated all her life at her own wish, and then suddenly decided she wanted a child when she was in her thirties.

How, as Charlene had asked, had Zuzene ever adopted a black child? *Maybe* today, but in northern Nevada in 1959? She might have known my mother—an artist might have had all sorts of friends, even if she lived in a narrow-minded community. But as far as I knew, Zuzene was a loner, with few or no friends of any description. Why would a loner have adopted another woman's baby?

I regarded the photos of my "family" on the board. None of them looked like people who would know a thing like that. Maybe Karl Marx or Malcolm X could have told me, but they were long gone.

ON SATURDAY MORNING, I WOKE feeling like I did on dentist days. *It's not going to be a fun day.* It took me a minute to remember why: Louie's coach would be visiting the studio in the afternoon. I fished in my memory for his name. Barry Donovan, that was it.

I could picture him already—Oakland Irish, one of the hangers-round in the Bay Area's shamrock pubs. Green beer on Saint Paddy's Day, and too much beer every day. Potbellied guy with a comb-over, maybe sixty years old, cheering on his scruffy team of street kids.

My stereotyping made me feel ashamed, but I blamed it on the way he'd made me feel guilty. At this point, I'd have to at least *try* letting them practice. I didn't have much doubt how it would end. Barbara would have a cow, and I'd have to side with her. God knows, I'd gone through enough to keep her and Will on the job—I could hardly let them walk out over *this.*

That made me feel better. I dressed and got my pack. Then I went downstairs, quietly so I wouldn't wake Charlene. I didn't know when she'd come home from the fund-raiser, but it must have been late.

After a quick breakfast at a coffee shop, I drove to the studio. The streets hadn't filled with traffic yet, and the breeze from the bay was fresh and cool.

The studio neighborhood was quiet in the early morning, sleeping off its Friday-night drunk. As I parked, I noticed the building's crummy facade and felt slightly embarrassed to have Louie's coach see it. I'd pulled Louie into carousel work so fast, he hadn't had a chance to do the cleaning and painting I'd hired him for. I shrugged. Let Barry Donovan find somewhere else to play ball if he didn't like it.

When I got to the front door, it was unlocked.

Nearly panicked, I yanked it open and dashed in, expecting the studio to be a shambles. I calmed down at the sound of a radio playing classical music. Out on the skate floor, Barbara faced a blue sea monster, a camera to her eye. She lowered it as she heard me come in.

"Hi," she said. "I wasn't expecting you."

"I wasn't expecting you, either."

"I *said* I was going to make up some time."

"I forgot, I guess." *Forgot* seemed a lot more polite than *didn't believe you.*

"I need to document a few so Louie can take them for stripping on Monday."

"It might be a good idea to lock the door when you're here alone."

"That's true." Barbara caught my eye and smiled. "It might be a good idea to come in cautiously if you find it unlocked and don't know why," she added.

"That's true, too."

Remnants of caring about each other, death throes of the friendship. Kind of a shame it couldn't be finished quick and neat, like putting a sick old dog to sleep. Maybe I'd always regret that things had worked out this way. Like Estebe, listening to the list of the dead on All Soul's Day. *"He and I were friends then. Later I wished he'd go away. Now he has, and it didn't feel as good as I thought it would."*

Barbara looked like she was going to say something. Before she did, the phone rang.

It was Joy. "Charlene said you were probably here," she began.

"Oh, dear. She was out half the night at a fund-raiser."

"She said I didn't wake her, but she sounded like I did. I told her I was sorry."

"Are you still in Nevada? Your crew at St. Martha House seems to be having problems."

"The guests don't handle separations well. We'll sort everything out when I get home. How's the carousel going?"

"Big problems. Every time I turn around, I'm sending another animal to Portland for major repairs. How's your friend?"

"Slipping away fast. She told me she was talking with her husband yesterday, and her husband died very young, years ago."

"Joy, I'm so sorry."

"It's not that hard for me, except I feel terrible for Jakinda. Fifty-something may not seem that young to someone your age, but it's terribly young to die. And she lost a child to leukemia, and a grown son last year."

"Was it because of the testing?"

"Oh, yes. I mean, no one can prove that it was, not in a particular case. But there certainly has been an epidemic of cancer in that area. The people who lived there in the fifties are still in court—or their families are. I think a lot of the ones who were exposed are dead."

"Jesus."

"I doubt He had anything to do with it, Mirai."

"Sorry." I paused. Change the subject. "Do you know when you're coming home?"

"I'll stay here as long as Jakinda wants me, or until she dies. It won't be much longer."

"I miss you. Take care of yourself."

I sat in the office for a while, feeling bleak. Barbara left with a wave in my direction, but I didn't say good-bye.

18

I pulled out the Prismacolors again and started on the sketches. Certain color combinations were traditional—the most popular colors for the horses were dapple gray, bay, roan, and palomino. The trappings would be painted to bring out the colors of the animals, brightened with gilding and glass jewels.

I sketched a palomino with creamy mane and tail, and added red and green trappings picked out with thin black lines. As I held it at arm's length, squinting to get the overall effect, the door opened and Louie came in.

"What are you doing here on a Saturday?" I asked.

"Sanding animals."

I laughed. "That should impress your friends," I said. *"How was your weekend?' 'Oh, it was great. I sanded animals.'"*

He grinned. "Oh, my friends think I have a cool job."

"Keep 'em thinking that. We may need help."

"Doing what?"

"Sanding. Or varnishing."

Louie looked surprised, almost indignant. *"I* can do that."

"Louie, those animals need *seven coats* of varnish. You won't finish unless we get some help."

"Seven coats! Why?"

"Did you ever notice a kid on a carousel horse?"

"Oh, you mean they kick it or something?"

"They do everything. And the adults—they don't wreck the animals deliberately, but most of them are too out of shape to

get on without scraping the saddle with their foot. At least the
kids usually wear tennis shoes."

"So, you need more helpers?"

"Let's not worry about that today. You know Barry's coming
by this afternoon?"

"Yeah, I know."

"Think he might want to sand?" I joked.

"I doubt it," he said, taking me seriously.

I doubted it, too. Sanding was so boring that nobody wanted
to do it—but it had to be done perfectly. Maybe some of Louie's
friends would be interested, at least for a while. Whatever it took
to get the project finished.

"Let's get going, then." We each chose a primed animal from
the painting room and rolled them back to be sanded. Louie
watched me closely as I stroked the wood with my fingertips,
reading imperfections.

"Mine feels fuzzy all over," he complained.

"It's only had one coat. That's what the first coat is supposed
to do—it raises the grain so you can sand off all the loose fibers.
Keep on feeling for rough spots as you sand. When you find
one, circle it with pencil so you'll know to use filler on it before
the next prime coat."

We worked a while longer. The only sound was the swish-
swish of the sandpaper. Finally, Louie said, "Mirai . . . you said
I'd need a lot of training to do this."

"Not to sand, but to do the whole restoration, you would."

"Where do you study?"

"Barbara and I went to art school."

"Did the old guys go to art school? The ones who made the
carousels?"

"No."

"How did they learn it?"

"Family trade, most of them. Some just apprenticed to someone."

"Could I learn it from you?"

My piece of sandpaper was nearly used up, so I chose another. "You can learn a lot here if you want to. But I don't know everything—nobody does. It's better to work at several places or go to art school."

"I can't afford art school."

"Could you get a scholarship?"

"I'm not really that great a student."

"Aren't there recreation programs where you could take some art classes?"

"Uh-uh. Not anymore."

There it was again, the problem Barry had brought up. None of the cities or school districts had money anymore, not since the property taxes had been slashed by Proposition 13.

It was the kids who paid—for the past ten years, there'd been no funds for schools or libraries or rec centers. None for parks, either, and California's carousels wouldn't last forever without maintenance. To top it off, there was no money to train anyone to do it.

I remembered an old sight gag with soldiers standing in a row and the sergeant calling for a volunteer. The "volunteer" was the soldier left when all the others stepped backward. When it came to who would teach Louie, it looked like that was me.

"Why do you want to restore carousel animals?" I needed to know why he was asking, whether he really understood what they meant.

Louie took a minute to answer me. He trailed his finger over the area he'd been sanding, the swirled mane of a jumping horse.

"They're so beautiful," he said. "When I'm working on them, I wonder about the old guys, the carvers. I can't believe someone really made this. I can't believe anyone would let it get lost."

Good reasons—more or less the reasons all restorers did what they did. "Okay, Louie, I'll do what I can to train you, since you're interested. But you'll have to do homework."

His face lit up. "Do you really mean it?"

"That I'm giving you homework? Damn straight I do."

"No, I mean, you'll really train me?"

"That too."

It was probably my musings on the property tax revolt that made me such an easy sell when Barry came in that afternoon. Otherwise, I might still have found a way to wriggle out of the basketball idea.

Louie introduced us. He was completely different from the way I'd pictured him. The only thing I'd gotten right was the "Irish-American" part, and that had been obvious from his name. So much for stereotyping.

Barry Donovan looked around thirty-five. He was tall and lanky—I couldn't remember why I'd thought a basketball coach was likely to be anything else. His curly black hair and deep blue eyes told me he was "black Irish," a term I'd found confusing when I first heard it. It didn't mean he was black and Irish, only that he was—supposedly—descended from the luckier sailors of the wrecked Spanish Armada, who—again supposedly—washed up on the shores of Ireland and joined the gene pool there.

Pushing aside inappropriate thoughts about the man's looks and the merging of gene pools, I said I was pleased to meet him.

"Louie's told me a lot about your work," he said. He touched Louie's horse lightly, as if he were afraid it might break. "It's beautiful. How old is it?"

"This one was built in 1906," I said. "It's what they call the Coney Island Style."

He looked surprised. "I didn't know there were different styles of carousels."

"Oh, yes. You wouldn't find anything this elaborate in the merry-go-round of a traveling county fair. And there's one style with saddles and trappings that's *much* more plain and realistic. Different makers had their own twists, too."

"Who made this one?" Barry asked.

"A man named Charles Looff. I don't know if you ever saw the one that was at Playland at the Beach, but he made that one too."

"Is it gone?"

I nodded. "It's still intact, but it got moved to Long Beach."

"What fascinating work," he said, looking more closely at the swirls of the horse's mane.

"It's *hard* work," I said. "Louie's been a big help."

"Mirai says I can start being a real apprentice now," Louie said all in a rush, like a little kid telling about his birthday.

"What does that mean?" Barry asked. "Isn't that what you've been doing?"

"Not really," I said. "I hired Louie to clean and paint the studio, a couple of months ago. It didn't work out that way, though, because I have a big contract and my assistant hasn't been well."

"So, then he started doing the carousel stuff?"

"At first it was scut work, like sanding. Now he says he'd like to learn the whole business. That means reading, and art projects at night—exactly like school."

Barry smiled at Louie. "You lucked out, buddy. But you may not have much of a chance to play basketball."

"Well, that's how it goes." Louie's words belied his expression. If his smile got any broader, he was in danger of having the two ends meet at the back of his head.

"The team can still use the place." I listened to myself saying that and wondered if I had lost my mind. "That is, if it works for you. You want to see the extra space?"

"If you point me in the right direction, I could check things out without interrupting your work. Maybe you'd be free some evening to have dinner with me and talk about schedule?"

"I think I could do that," I said.

19

SUNDAY, I MADE MYSELF get up and go to early Mass. I tried to pay attention, but I couldn't concentrate the way I liked to. The problems at St. Martha's, and Joy's friend, and my own tangle with Will and Barbara, what Barry was up to, the lousy condition of the carousel animals . . . . My mind kept wandering to first one and then the other. I hoped God would realize I was sending an S.O.S. and not just goofing off.

I dawdled around Lake Merritt Park after Mass, idle and discontented with myself. It was a few minutes after eight, still cool, even on an August morning. Oakland got very few hot days, but today would be one of them. The families would be converging on the Children's Fairyland soon, enjoying the lakeshore. There would be giggling and tears, the wonder of the petting zoo, and the disaster of dropped ice cream cones.

I stooped and picked up an object from the grass. It was flesh-colored, sort of—what the crayon boxes used to call "flesh" until political correctness caught up. But even white people weren't really this color. It was a plastic doll's arm, left over from someone's Saturday at the park, I supposed.

I put it carefully on a bench and sat down on the cropped grass. In the sun, the ground was warming up fast, but the shady patches under the trees still held a shivery dew. I inched farther into the sun and lay back, throwing one arm over my eyes to block the glare.

I only napped a minute, but I dreamed that a doll walked up and politely asked for her arm. I helped her fit it onto her shoulder.

"Thank you," she said. "It was my *right* arm, you see."

In my dream, that made perfect sense. But when she walked away, I woke confused.

I stood and dusted myself off. The day stretched in front of me. I could go into the studio and work. In fact, I probably should, but I decided to skip it. I needed a day off.

As I headed home through the still-empty park, I saw a hopscotch chalked on the pavement. I couldn't resist. I hopped back and forth on it, remembering the balance of it: one, two, three, four-five, six, seven-eight, nine, and turn on ten. I didn't even care if anyone noticed I was way too old for such a thing.

ON MONDAY, I BROUGHT a bottle of sparkling apple juice and a carrot cake to work with me. I laid out a party on one of the concession area tables, complete with a paper tablecloth and plastic champagne glasses. I cut slices of cake and set them on paper plates.

Barbara raised her eyebrows. "What's the occasion?" she asked.

"Louie's becoming an official apprentice," I said. "He's decided he wants to learn to be a carousel restorer." I braced myself for her reaction.

"Congratulations," Barbara told him. That was all, and she sounded perfectly pleasant. Maybe she'd decided she liked Louie, once she'd gotten to know him.

I poured three glasses of juice, and we toasted Louie. As I began to eat a slice of cake, the phone rang. I ran to the office to get it.

"Mirai San Julian Restorations."

"Mirai? This is Linda Gonzales."

"Hi, Linda. What's up?"

"Ginny left the doll in the laundry room yesterday and hasn't paid any attention to it since. Do you want me to go ahead with the poster?"

"Go ahead and make the notices, and hide the doll. Wait a couple more days, and if she's really forgotten it, put them up."

"Okay, sounds like as good a way to do it as any. Thanks."

I started to get up to go back to the table, but Barbara appeared in the doorway.

"Mirai, could I talk to you?"

I was afraid it was about Louie, and I didn't want to discuss it. But I had to hear her out at least once. I motioned toward the office's guest chair.

She shut the door behind her before taking her seat. "I really have to apologize," she said.

That was the last thing I'd expected.

"What for?" I asked. Not that she hadn't done plenty. But I wasn't sure which part of the "plenty" she meant.

"I think Will is having an affair." Her voice cracked, and she pulled a tissue out of her pocket and blew her nose.

"Why would you apologize to me about that?"

"I suspected it was with you. And I've been pretty nasty."

"With *me*?" I'd heard some weird stuff lately, but this one was beyond any of it. "Why with *me*? I'm the *last* person who'd have an affair with Will."

"He still talks about you—how cool you are, how gorgeous you are, how talented you are. And I'm sure he's got *someone*."

"Jesus, Mary, and Joseph, Barbara! He never fucking told *me* he thought I was cool and talented and gorgeous!"

Barbara blinked. "He didn't?"

"Hell, no. He had a magic eye for my *faults*, though. Every damn one of them."

"Mine too. He told me I'm too needy."

"At least the man's consistent." I blurted this out before I remembered that Barbara and I weren't supposed to be friends anymore. But it didn't matter. I caught Barbara's eye and we started to giggle, even though she was crying too. It seemed the friendship was tougher than I'd thought.

"So, *that's* why you did things like pop in here unexpectedly 'to use the bathroom,' for Pete's sake. As if I'd be getting it on with Will on the concrete floor. And leaving at funny hours, and coming in late, and acting pissed off . . . ."

"Well, that's what I'm apologizing for," she said. "I kept going home at odd times, thinking I'd catch him in the act. It didn't work."

"What makes you so sure he's running around at all?"

Barbara twisted a hank of her shiny blonde hair into a pretzel. "At first I *wasn't* sure. It was things like a faint scent on his skin, inconsistencies between what he said and what he did. There's also been a bunch of hang-up calls on the phone."

"Those might have been nothing. I've gotten a *lot* of those lately. I got one this weekend."

She looked shamefaced. "That was me. I figured if you were with Will, the two of you would be at a motel or something, on account of your roommate. When you answered the phone, I realized it wasn't you he was with. I'm sorry."

"Well, it's good to know the calls will be stopping, anyway."

We started to giggle again. If Louie could hear any of this through the office wall, he must have been thinking we'd both gone nuts.

"So," I finally managed, "do tell. Why are you sure he's got another woman now?"

"He went to a bluegrass concert Saturday night. I didn't go—
I don't like bluegrass."

"And?"

"There wasn't a bluegrass concert Saturday night. I mean,
there *was* one, but it got canceled at the last minute."

"Did you mention that to him?"

"Yes, and he said he went to his studio to work on the Peregrine Falls band organ. But he didn't."

"How do you know?"

"I called the studio, and no one answered."

"Maybe he was in the men's room."

"All six times?"

"Did you ask him about that?"

"It's no use. He always comes up with an excuse that's barely
plausible. He makes me look like a jealous fool. Every time, it
gets twisted."

She gave an extra strong yank to the knot she'd made in her
hair, and seemed to realize what she was doing. She untangled
her hand and smoothed the hair down again. "Will says I'm
paranoid. I'm beginning to wonder if I am."

I had to admit, it didn't look good. Either Will was catting
around less than a year after the marriage, or Barbara was imagining things. And I'd never known her as the suspicious type.

In all honesty, I wasn't surprised. I'd had a hunch about the
same thing while Will and I were together. And once he'd married Barbara, I'd thought *she'd* been the third side of the triangle.

"What are you going to do?" I asked.

"I don't know. I don't want to leave him. I feel like I'm los-
ing my mind."

People in Victorian novels are forever wringing their hands,
but I hadn't seen anyone actually do it before. Now Barbara
was—squeezing first one hand and then the other as if they

were waterlogged. Her right hand twisted her left so hard that she flinched as her ring dug in. She noticed what she was doing and laid her hands in her lap.

"What makes it impossible is that I can't think of any way to make him admit it. He's always got a story, and he always says I'm imagining things. I wish, just once, I could catch him in the act."

I didn't have any suggestions—Will was beyond me. So I said, "Good luck," and got up from my chair.

She followed me to the table, but Louie had eaten his cake and gone back to work. He was doing the touch-up on a prime coat on the last horse in the group.

He mock-saluted me with the paintbrush. "I need to go pick up more animals at the stripper."

"Let's hope these are in better shape," I said.

Barbara and I finished our cake and she started sanding, scrubbing the sandpaper viciously against her greyhound. Good thing the people who rode that dog could never guess what emotion had gone into restoring it. I didn't try to talk with her as we worked.

Louie came back from El Cerrito shaking his head. Even he, inexperienced as he was, could see that two of the animals had to go to Portland. After that, I did some vicious sanding myself.

When I'd calmed down, I decided to call Portland and see if I could cut a deal with them. I'd gone to school with Matt, one of the company's three owners. I thought I'd lucked out when he answered the phone, but he was hesitant.

"Mirai, I don't know. I'll have to talk it over with Ben and Susan. I'd give you a break in a minute, but the lousy condition of these animals you've been sending us means we're doing a lot more work on them than we bid for. And Ben's been complaining we're getting behind on our *other* work, picking up all these extras for you."

"Well, would you talk it over and let me know?" I asked. "I think you would have given me a better unit price on ten animals than on three. All I'm asking for is the quantity price you would have given me if I'd known there was so much damage in the beginning."

"I'll see what they say." Matt sounded doubtful. "You're a good customer, and I'll remind them of that. Maybe we can work something out."

I got off the phone feeling depressed. If I had to pay the same unit price for all the animals that I'd been quoted for the initial three, I could go into the red. I hoped Matt could get Ben and Susan to see that.

In the afternoon, Joy called.

"Jakinda died this morning," she said. "I'm staying for the funeral. I'll be at the rectory of St. Ignatius Church—I'm staying with an old friend of Ama's."

"I thought you said you didn't know anyone in Paradise anymore," I said.

"I had no idea she was still here. I ran into her at the hospital. Anyway, I'll come home Thursday."

"Okay, I'll pick you up. Joy, I'm sorry about Jakinda."

"Don't be. She was in so much pain. And with her husband and her son both gone, she wasn't sorry to go. I was glad I could be with her at the last—she and Melanie weren't particularly close. And I enjoyed reminiscing with her and Garaze, the lady I'm staying with. Especially since you've been interested in my old letters and things like that."

"The last of those letters you left me—I couldn't find any translation."

"I thought I did them all."

"All but one, unless I lost it."

"Oh, well. I'll see to it when I get home. How are things at St. Martha's?"

"Better, I think. Ginny's lost interest in the doll, anyway. We're going to put up signs on the telephone poles and try to find the owner."

"That sounds like a good idea."

"Let me know when to pick you up at the airport."

"I will. Thanks, dear."

I primed carousel animals with Barbara and Louie for the rest of the day. I did it by touch, without giving much of my mind to it. I'd thought my problems with Will were over when I choked down the fact that he had married Barbara. But he didn't seem to be happy unless he was treating some woman like shit.

Still steaming about it when I got home, I banged the door behind me.

"Mirai?"

Charlene was stretched out on the couch, reading the paper. She folded it in exact quarters as I came into the room and laid it on the coffee table.

"C'est moi."

"Well, 'moi,' could you please not break the glass in the door? It's the original glass, and it would cost a centipede's worth of arms and legs to replace."

"Centipedes don't have arms."

"That would probably put the price even higher. Law of supply and demand, you know."

"Sorry about the door. I'll be more careful."

"Thanks. . . . What's bugging you, anyway—no pun intended?"

"As if Will hadn't given *me* enough hassle, now he's cheating on Barbara."

"What did she expect? She knew he was a cheater, didn't she? Besides, what do *you* care?"

"She's messing up at work. And besides, even if I *was* pissed at her, she's one of my oldest friends."

"Who's he messing around with?"

"Anyone who's interested, I imagine. Barbara says he always weasels out of it when she gets any evidence. Then he turns it on her, and tells her she's paranoid."

Charlene thought for a moment. "I have an idea. Are you up for something kinky?"

WEDNESDAY AFTERNOON, I CALLED Linda to make sure she knew Joy would be back on Thursday. She did, but St. Martha's problems were more immediate than that.

"I put up the signs," she told me. "And it wasn't any time at all before someone called."

"And?"

"I don't think this is going to be as easy as we thought."

"So, what's the problem? We return the doll, we apologize . . . . What more could they want? Are we supposed to say a hundred Hail Marys and fifty Our Fathers, or what?"

"No, not exactly. But when I answered the phone, a woman said, 'Oh, my God, it's the crazy house. How did you get my daughter's doll?'"

"So, what did you tell her?"

"I said that someone had evidently picked it up by mistake, and we'd been anxious to return it. She slammed down the phone and hotfooted it over here so fast, I barely had time to get to the door."

"And?"

"She was a little upset."

"A little?"

Linda sighed. "A lot upset."

"Why such a ruckus over a doll? It wasn't damaged or anything, was it?"

"The doll wasn't even half of it. The yard's pretty overgrown. She said she was going to complain to the city. I guess we can get fined or something. She went on and on."

I kicked myself for forgetting the yard. I'd meant to find someone to go over and at least cut the grass. Maybe one of Louie's friends. Or given that the neighbors were pitching a snit, I'd do it once myself and then hire a gardener.

"I'll see what I can do, Linda. Sit tight."

20

On Thursday morning, I had a complicated to-do list: pick Joy up at the airport, play gardener at St. Martha's, and try to pull off Charlene's scheme. I called the studio and told Barbara I was taking a day off.

Charlene came into my room to kibitz. "Don't overdo it," she said as I pulled a pair of shorts and a camisole from a drawer. "He'll catch on if you're not more subtle. You usually wear jeans—got any really tight ones?"

I fished in another drawer and found a pair that had shrunk badly the first time I washed them. They were so tight, I had to lie on the floor to zip them. When I struggled to my feet, they fit me closer than the paint on a carousel horse.

I rummaged in my T-shirt drawer and came up with one I'd bought in the boys' department at Macy's—much snugger than any woman's shirt. I was too skinny to have much of anything on top to flaunt, but that shirt, worn without a bra, would get Will's attention for sure.

"Got any makeup?" Charlene asked.

"Yeah, some." I bent toward the mirror to work on my face. Since I was trained in painting and shading, applying the stuff wasn't a problem.

"Careful," Charlene reminded me as I slathered it on. "Don't lay it on so thick that he figures it out."

I fluffed my hair up with an Afro comb and put on my usual tennis shoes. I pivoted for inspection, and Charlene whistled.

"Have fun," she said.

"I fully expect to."

When I got to Will's studio in the Berkeley Flats, I parked around the corner, out of sight. After I'd cut the ignition, I sat in the van for a long while. My hand kept going back to the key—*Get the hell out of here, Mirai, what are you doing?*

I'd have given anything to chicken out. On the other hand, Will was a royal son of a bitch. I made myself remember how he'd pushed me away and persuaded me it was my own fault for being "too needy." Now he was cheating on Barbara and telling her she was paranoid for suspecting him. He deserved whatever I could dish out.

I got out of the van and took a few deep breaths. It wouldn't do to go in there scared like a kid going to the principal's office.

My throat felt tight, so I said out loud, "The quick brown fox jumps over the lazy dog." My voice started out in a nervous squeak, but it was behaving by the time I finished the sentence. I looked around, embarrassed. All I needed now was an audience. But the sidewalk was empty.

I walked around the corner to Will's door and breezed in without knocking.

He was bending over a metal assembly on a table, but he looked up when he heard me come in.

"Hi," I said. "Sorry to bust in without an appointment, but I was in the neighborhood, and I thought I should take a minute to see how it's going."

"Could be worse." He sounded wary, so I hung out a smile for bait.

"Is it as bad as it looked?"

"The pneumatics are in bad shape, but the pipework is better than I expected. We'll make it." He gave the mechanism on the table a couple of strokes, but he wasn't looking at that—he was looking at my boobs.

I felt a glow of hope. Will always was a round-heels. I gestured toward the contraption. "Is it all as rusty as that?" I slithered toward the table and bent over for a good look. And to give him a good look, too. Actually, I had no idea what the rusty metal was—for all I knew, it was the works to the studio toilet—but it gave me a chance to get a lot closer without making him suspicious.

"There was that roof leak," he said. "And a lot of these parts are . . . uh . . . ferrous metal—so, yes, there's some oxidation. . . ." Typical Will, explaining to me that steel rusts. But he wasn't concentrating well. He was having a hard time, so to speak.

He brushed up against me, and I didn't pull away. I touched the metal object, as if to check its corrosion, and he reached out, too, first putting his hand alongside mine, then moving it closer. A casual touch turned into an exploratory caress.

"I've missed you," he said.

"I've missed you, too." I licked my lower lip quickly with the tip of my tongue, keeping my eyes on his. A bit whorish, but so what?

His hand crept up to my shoulder, then down to my breast. His fingers verified what his eyes had told him about my bra-lessness.

He pulled me close and kissed my neck. I shivered with readiness as his lips met mine.

The door opened, and the mailman came in, put the mail on the front desk, and left without comment. I pulled away from Will. My heart was pounding and it occurred to me that it wasn't only nervousness. Memories of Will and me, how good we were together, his familiar scent—I was getting turned on.

Shit—what *was* I doing this for? For Barbara? For revenge on both of them? To get Will back?

I stood there awkwardly. "This is no good," I blurted.

"Want to go to your place?" he asked. He didn't seem to be absorbing the idea that I might not want to ball him, only that I might not want to ball him in front of the mailman. I pulled myself together. Even if my motives were mixed, Barbara deserved to get the upper hand with this he-slut.

"My roommate's home."

"My house is no good. Barbara's always forgetting stuff and coming back. Let's get a room somewhere."

"The Hacienda Inn's down the street."

"Let's go now, babe. I want you."

"Go get a room and I'll be there in an hour. I have something to pick up before the place closes. But it won't take long." I gave the crotch of his jeans a light massage.

"Come on with me now."

"Just one little errand, and I'm yours for the rest of the day." I gave him a cat-eyed glance. "I'll call you from the lobby, okay?" I rubbed the magic location again, and his eyes glazed over like Orphan Annie's. I figured his reasoning power was shutting down, which was all to the good.

"Okay, but hurry."

"I'll be right back."

I drove to my studio and double-parked with the flashers on. I ran in like there was fire behind me.

"Barbara," I called.

"What?"

"We have to go somewhere *now*. Sorry, I need you right away. I'm double-parked."

"What's happening?" she asked, grabbing her purse.

"I'll tell you in the van."

When we got to the Hacienda Inn, I used the phone by the restrooms, with Barbara standing in confusion beside me. Will answered on the first ring.

"Hi," I said, laying on a sultry tone. "What room are you in?"

"Seven ninety-two."

"Are you . . . ready for me?"

"More than ready."

"Really, really ready?" I teased.

"I couldn't be readier."

"I'll be right there."

I hung up the phone and turned to Barbara. "He's in seven ninety-two," I said. "If he has a stitch on, my name is Mary Todd Lincoln. Go on up and ask him his definition of paranoia."

Leaving her gaping, I headed home. I was running late—but with any luck, so was Joy's plane.

21

CHARLENE MET ME ON the front steps. "Joy called from the airport," she said.

"Oh, my God. She's here already? When did she call?"

"A few minutes ago. I was going to pick her up."

"Thanks. I'll do it."

"I told her I'd help over there this afternoon," Charlene said. "Can I ride with you?"

"Sure. I was going to stay and do yard work at the house anyway."

We trotted to the van, and I headed for the airport. We were halfway there before I realized I was still wearing my seduction outfit. I decided it didn't matter much—Joy was anything but judgmental, and I probably could manage yard work in my tight jeans as long as I didn't get too ambitious. If not, I could run home and change into something more practical.

Joy was waiting alone by the curb. I pulled up, and Charlene got out and took her suitcase. Joy climbed into the front seat while Charlene stowed the bag in the back. My aunt leaned over and kissed my cheek, then fastened her seat belt. We headed to St. Martha's.

As we approached, I noticed that the sidewalk seemed unusually populated. Ordinarily, in California, the sidewalk is a good place to feel completely alone—no one seems to walk anywhere. But something had drawn a crowd today. Ten or twelve people were clustered in front of St. Martha's.

I parked, and the three of us approached the noisy group. I noticed that one person seemed to be trying to talk over all of them. Linda. She caught sight of us and began to wave.

"Joy!" she called.

Heads turned and people stepped aside to let us get past. Then one woman stepped forward.

"Mrs. St. Julian—"

Joy didn't correct her, she only nodded. The woman drew a deep breath and went on.

"This neighborhood is getting tired of having a halfway house on the block. As if it weren't enough that your people don't even behave responsibly, you keep your yard looking like a jungle. Your house has needed painting for over a year—it needs all kinds of work, and you're letting it go downhill. Our property values are crashing, and we're going to complain to the city council. Your residents are crazy—they ought to be in an asylum."

Joy's mild expression didn't change. "I've been away on an emergency," she said. "Has something happened?"

Joy's politeness seemed to rev up the woman even more. "Damn straight it has!" she said. "I went shopping with my daughter, and one of the loonies who live here stole her doll right out of her stroller!"

"How do you know your daughter didn't drop it?"

The woman took a deep breath. "We went into a store that doesn't allow strollers. She was playing mama. She tucked the doll in the stroller and told it not to cry—we'd be right out. Which we were, but the doll was gone."

"I see," said Joy.

"It could have been my *daughter* that got taken, not just the doll! We've had bicycles stolen, and someone broke into my husband's car. . . . We're afraid to live here anymore."

Joy didn't waver. "We have no bicycles," she said. "I'll accept responsibility for the doll, and I'm sorry it happened. I'll talk to my guest about it. But I don't think everything that happens here can be traced to our people. Crime happens in every neighborhood. And I'm sure you'd never leave your child in a stroller while you went into a store."

The woman ignored all Joy's points. She drew a deep, shaky breath and went on in a shrill voice. "And your house looks terrible. Look at that bougainvillea! Look at the lawn! Lawn? You can't even *call* it a lawn—it's a *pasture* or something! The place is disgraceful!"

Joy took in the disheveled appearance of the house. "I'm sorry it's been a problem for you," she said. "St. Martha House relies on volunteers, and sometimes there aren't enough to get all our work done. We're going to do yard work this afternoon."

The woman glanced at Charlene and me, waiting behind Joy. "I suppose this . . . *black hooker* from *Emeryville* or someplace, and this . . . *hippo* are the new groundskeepers?" she asked.

Joy's kind expression didn't change. She didn't speak, only met the woman's eyes. There was a murmuring from the rest of the group.

"Wait a minute, Nancy, there's no need to get personal," one man said.

The knot of people drew away, and the woman stood isolated, her hand over her mouth. Tears started in her eyes, and she turned and fled up the sidewalk and into a house a few doors away. A man followed her for a few steps, then returned to the now-silent group.

"My wife tends to be nervous about our daughter," he said. "I'm sorry she flew off the handle." He turned to Charlene and me. "I'm sorry she said what she did. She didn't mean it."

That seemed debatable, but we weren't inclined to get into it. He turned and followed his wife back to their house.

The group shuffled nervously. Couples glanced at each other, probably for cues what to do next. One man stepped forward and put out his hand to Joy. "I'm Jonathan Rose," he said. "We didn't know you needed help here. I'll be glad to pitch in with your yard work." Several of the others nodded.

"I appreciate that very much," Joy said. "Why don't you think over what you might be able to do, and give me a call in the next day or so? St. Martha House is in the phone book. I'm sure we can work together to keep the block looking the way you'd like. And I do apologize about the doll."

"No harm done," said Jonathan. The group dispersed quickly, with a few more murmured apologies and some fake-sounding laughter. We got Joy's suitcase out of the van and went into the house. Joy sank into a chair and closed her eyes.

She sat up again in a few seconds and focused on me. "That really is different from your usual outfit, dear," was all she said.

Part 4

22

On Friday, I went into the office prepared for the worst. Will had had it coming to him—I'd gotten him back fair and square. But there was no way around it: He must be furious. I figured he wouldn't break his contract, but I might have to find another mechanical music expert for the next job. Well, there were others.

I worked on color sketches for a while. I did need to get them done so we could start painting as soon as the priming was done. But my real reason for dawdling in the office was so Barbara could say anything she had to say in private when she came in.

She got to work more or less on time and came to the office. She sat down in the guest chair, but she didn't say a word. The suspense was killing me.

"Okay, tell me," I said. "He's madder than hell."

"You got *that* right." She sounded like *she* was, too.

"You did say you wished you could catch him in the act."

"I'm glad I didn't say I wished someone would wring his neck."

"Oh."

No use mentioning it was Charlene's idea. I was the one who'd done it. I sat there feeling stupid—how was I to know Barbara didn't mean what she said? "I could wring his neck" was different—everyone knew that was a figure of speech.

She was still sitting there looking at me. I wondered if she was going to quit.

"Sorry," I said. "I thought I was helping." I wasn't sorry. I felt pissed. All that trouble for nothing.

"It turned out all right," Barbara said. "I really did have him cold. When he answered the door, I pushed my way in, and we had a rip-roaring fight. Then it calmed down into a discussion about the marriage."

"Is he still doing Peregrine Falls?"

"He was ready to chuck it for a while there. Then he remembered it wouldn't be too good for his career if he broke a contract."

"Think he'll ever work for me again?"

"I don't know. By the time this job is finished, he may have gotten over it. He wouldn't turn down a good project. At least I don't *think* he would."

"What about the woman he was seeing?" I asked. "Or is it *women?*"

"I don't know."

I felt drained, and more than a bit guilty. And also, I felt a petty triumph: *I could have had him again if I'd wanted. He doesn't prefer you to me, does he?*

In the workroom, Louie was pounding together another crate for the animals we were sending to Portland Carousel Works. From what Matt had said when I asked, it didn't sound like they'd give me much of a break on the price, if any. I was barely in the black on this job, but I wouldn't lose money if no more animals had to go.

On Saturday morning, Barry and the team were waiting on the sidewalk when I arrived to open the studio. We'd hardly said hello when one of the local street guys shuffled up and asked us for spare change. I just shook my head, and to my surprise, so did Barry. Most people would have coughed up some change just to get rid of the guy.

Barry must have seen my look, because when the guy had left, he said, "I'll give anyone food, but not money. It's usually just fuel for some addiction. I don't want to help in their self-destruction."

"Amen to that," I said, "though I can't say I've had any of them over for dinner recently." At least Barry didn't think I was some cold-hearted bitch for turning the guy down.

I unlocked the door and let us in. The boys were carrying two portable goals, obviously homemade. I felt embarrassed to ask Barry if he'd built them himself.

"I made these in my garage," he said, reading my thoughts. "The guys helped. Then we made a few for other teams."

"You made equipment for your opponents?" I asked.

"Sure. If they don't get to practice, the games are no fun."

I thought this might be taking sportsmanship too far, but then, I wasn't into sports. For some reason, he reminded me of Joy—not that Joy cared two cents about ball games. Or agreed with us about panhandling—or did she? I couldn't remember Joy ever giving money to street beggars, either.

"You'd like my aunt," I said without thinking.

"Why?" he asked. Then he looked flustered. "I didn't mean that exactly like it sounded—I meant, why in particular? Does she work with young people?"

"No, she runs a Catholic Worker house."

"Oh, that really *is* something. That's a lot more important than what *I* do. I'm sure I'd like her very much." He hesitated. "If I didn't find her too intimidating."

"Joy isn't intimidating," I said, surprised. "Why would you think that?"

"I don't know. . . . People like that seem, oh, above it all or something. Saintly, maybe."

"She's not intimidating. Wait till you meet her."

"I'm sure I'll like her. And what about you? How did you get into such an interesting line of work?"

"Joy used to take me to the old carousels at Tilden Park and the San Francisco Zoo. Then the Save the Carousel campaign for Tilden in the seventies made me realize what it takes to keep carousels like that going—and that some people actually make a career of it. After that, I went to art school and . . . ."

I figured Barry was listening, but his eyes were on the boys as they ran back and forth, dribbling the ball and shouting. I caught his eye, and he smiled and shrugged apologetically. "I'm enjoying talking with you, but I'd better get in there and coach."

He trotted out among the boys, calling instructions and encouragement. I watched for a minute before I went into the office to catch up with paperwork. Too bad he hadn't said anything more about getting together.

23

Joy came to dinner on Sunday. It was a welcome-home meal, and I'd tried to cook something special. As a result, the food was worse than usual. I hoped she'd appreciate my intentions, anyway.

I'd been sorry that Charlene couldn't join us, but it turned out to be just as well. For one thing, Joy disapproved of our stunt with Barbara and Will.

"I can't imagine why you'd *do* such a thing," she said, squashing a mashed potato lump with her fork.

"She *said* she wished she could catch him in the act."

"Honestly, Mirai, did it occur to you that she shouldn't have asked you to do that?"

"She didn't," I said. "Not in so many words. But she was telling me all about how Will's been shafting her, and it's exactly the way he treated me."

"But you're not the person she should have confided in, dear. It could have been very painful for you to hear about her and Will."

"Actually, I think I'm cured of all interest in Will."

"I'm glad of *that*, at least. I doubt she wanted you to do anything—it sounds as if she might have just been letting off steam. Did you really take it as a serious request?"

"Not exactly, but I do think she was asking for help. The way Will treats women is wrong and mean, and I like Barb a lot."

"It worries me that you seem to have trouble saying no to people. Or," she put a hand up to deflect my protest, "you may go to extreme lengths to please people. I'm not 'aunt-ing' you here, Mirai, I'm talking from experience. One or two of the worst mistakes of my life were done in precisely that way, and I think you should know that."

"But aren't we supposed to help other people? Isn't that what you do at St. Martha's?"

"Helping isn't always the same as pleasing. Sometimes, the greatest service you can do is to refuse to help a person in a course of action that's not their best choice."

I remembered how annoyed I'd been about turning out to be the bad guy, and how dingy my triumph over Barbara had felt.

"There's a Basque saying," Joy went on, "that a married couple is like a pair of scissors—even when they're moving apart, it's not wise to come between them."

"I'll keep it in mind," I said. "You have a point when you say I give in to everyone. I even let Louie's coach talk me into letting their basketball team practice in the studio."

Joy laughed. "How in the world did *that* happen?"

"Wait till you meet him," I said. "I suspect that man could talk anyone into anything." Of course, it was pretty unlikely they'd ever meet.

After dinner, we sat in the living room for a while. Suddenly remembering the letter with no translation, I fetched it from my room.

Joy gave it an odd look. "This is one I'd decided to summarize rather than translate," she said. "I can't think how it got into the papers I gave you. I suppose I swept it up with the others because I was so flustered that morning we went to the airport."

"I noticed it was dated shortly after I was born," I said. "Since you don't want to translate it, I assume your father was objecting to his daughter's adopting a black baby."

"That was the gist of it."

"I thought Spaniards were more enlightened than that."

"In Madrid, they probably are. Country people tend to be narrower in their outlook, especially if they're immigrants. Not that I could say whether Papa was even typical for Nevada Basques in the 1950s."

"You might as well translate it."

"I don't see the point."

"I don't see why not."

Joy thought for a minute, then she said, "Remember the mocking rhyme the children used to sing? 'Sticks and stones can break my bones, but words can never hurt me'?"

"Yes."

"I think words can hurt more than anything else. Aita sent me that letter, and he sent a similar one to your mother. Zuzene was furious, and they had a falling-out. Not the first, and not the last. Shortly before she died, Zuzene told me she hadn't spoken to him for a long time. I don't really know, though. I broke with him completely. I only saw him once after that, at Zuzene's funeral."

"Joy . . . I'm sorry. But what else could you do?"

"Disagree strongly but not withhold my love. I think he would have changed his mind. In fact, I'm sure he would have."

I thought she was being idealistic, but that was Joy. It was interesting to know she hadn't forgiven him.

"So, there's no more letters," I said.

"No, that was the end. He sent me a few more, but I never read them. And then he stopped. I'll regret all my life that I acted that way."

I didn't know why that made me feel so bleak. What should I care about the letters of an old racist?

"There are other papers, though," Joy said. "You remember I told you I had a box of Aita's papers I hadn't really looked at?"

"Where did you get them?"

"Shortly after Zuzene died, Aita went back to Spain. A year or so later, he died. I sold the hotel. The box of papers turned up in the attic when I was clearing the place out. I wasn't feeling so self-righteous by then, so I took it home with me."

"You didn't look at it?"

"At first I didn't want to think about Papa. And then I forgot I had it."

"Where is it now?"

"At St. Martha's. In the attic, I think. I'll start looking for it."

I decided to ask Joy the question I'd been mulling over. "Joy . . . where in the world did Zuzene find me?"

"What do you mean?"

"Reno isn't Oakland. How did Mama find a black child in Reno?"

"I don't know that she *did* find you in Reno. Zuzene traveled a lot, the year before you were born. But besides that, don't think the West is an all-white venture. There have been African-Americans here since the Gold Rush or before. The notion that whites settled the West came from cowboy movies."

"Didn't you ask her where I came from?" My voice sounded sulky with disappointment, but if my tone bothered Joy, she didn't show it.

"I visited shortly after she got you, and possibly I did ask her then. It had been a long time since I'd seen Zuzene, and we had a lot of catching up to do. Mostly what I remember is you."

"Why did Mama travel that year? I thought she was a stay-at-home, a recluse."

"She was. But she wanted to be a good mother, and to her that meant doing some things she wanted to do first. She went to France for a while. Mostly she visited museums in different cities and looked at pictures. Zuzene wanted to be wholehearted as a mother, not regretting things she hadn't done. She had an idea that was why Mama had left, that she hadn't finished being footloose before she tried to settle down."

I mulled over our conversation after Joy went home. I remembered, as I had that long-ago day in the Christmas crowd, that Joy never lied.

Except that I wasn't eight years old anymore. I had put away childish things, including blind trust. And I started to wonder.

24

Summer was nearly over, and the carousel had to be done in May. We could still make the deadline, but it was going to be tight. The animals had all been stripped—now the chariots were at the stripper. And I was worried—problems with one or both chariots could break the budget.

I had to think about final painting too. The priming and sanding were going well, and I was ready to transfer my color studies to the animals themselves.

So, the studio was frantic, and I didn't have time to fret about Joy and Mama and Paradise Meadow. I fretted anyway.

With half my mind on the job, I painted the body color for three dapple grays, stippling shading at the muzzle, fetlocks, and knees. Louie watched carefully while I masked the teeth and put a first layer of pink on the insides of the mouths.

Straight from the horse's mouth. I always thought that what Joy told me was straight from the horse's mouth. Now I'm not so sure.

My hand slipped, and I got some pink paint on the horse's muzzle. I wiped it off carefully and stippled more of the dark color to conceal my mistake.

"Paint can always be changed," I told Louie. "Don't sweat the screwups, fix them."

It was good advice, but it would have been better to leave it at telling him rather than giving a demonstration.

I painted the base color for the saddles. Noticing the less-than-exact lines between the saddles and the bodies, Louie looked at me questioningly.

"Don't knock yourself out to make lines perfect on the under-coats," I told him. "It's a waste of effort. It all gets covered—*but*"—here I demonstrated with a cloth, wiping away a buildup at the edge of the saddle color—"don't leave any ridges, because those *will* show through."

"How will you paint the trappings?" he asked.

"On an animal with a lot going on in the body color, like a dapple gray, the trappings should be simple colors. It's the solid body colors that give you a chance to really go somewhere with the decorations."

"How many coats does it take on the body?"

"Over the three coats of primer? Usually another two. Sometimes three. On a marked horse like these dapples, count on at least one extra for the markings."

The basketball team trotted noisily past the open door of the paint room, with Barry trailing behind them.

He paused in the doorway. "Hey, Louie, you coming?" he asked.

I smiled at Louie. "You can go if you want," I said. We really didn't have time for it, but he wasn't a medieval apprentice.

Louie shook his head. "Let's keep going," he said.

"You sure?" I asked.

"Yeah. . . . I mean, when the ball game's over, it's done. These guys will be around for a while." His gesture took in the rows of animals in various stages of restoration.

Barry caught my eye and smiled, and I thought, *He's happy that Louie's finding what he wants to do. He likes them when they're kids, and he still likes them when they're grownups.* I smiled, too. For just that second, we were parents with a promising son.

Everyone's adopted, I reasoned. *Barry and I have adopted Louie, and Barry's got the team kids too. I have a dozen parents, people who've fostered me one way or another. So, why do I care so much about people I don't even remember?*

I waited for a wave of relief to flood through me. It didn't.

"You want this closed?" Barry gestured toward the door.

"Please," I said.

Even with the door closed, we could hear the ball ringing against the wood floor. I was sure I'd get used to it, and maybe Barbara would, too. She hadn't been nearly as temperamental lately. Anyway, it was the last week of summer. With school coming up, the kids wouldn't be here as often.

While the first coat on the dapple grays dried, we got started on three palominos. I loved palominos—the caramel of the body color and the manes like whipped cream. They almost made my mouth water. But as I worked on the body color, I remembered Joy's description of Taba: *A big palomino mustang, a stallion. Aita didn't trust him.*

I pulled myself back to the present. If Louie was foregoing his game for me, I had to give him my full attention.

"Don't let brushstrokes show," I cautioned him. "It's harder on a light color like this—every flaw shows up." I pounced the brush around to even out my texture. Louie watched carefully and did a creditable job when I passed him the brush.

When the body color was done, I painted the first coat of the saddle in a solid brown that made a strong line against the tawny body. *A big palomino mustang. . . . He came back to the stable the next morning with his saddle still on.*

"You have paint on the end of your nose," Louie said. I fast-forwarded to the present and rubbed my nose with the back of my wrist, still holding the brush.

We took a break and surveyed the general effect. Louie checked my color sketch, comparing it to the horse.

"How do you pick the colors?" he asked.

"If I don't know the original ones, I design something that's consistent with what that maker would have been using when the piece was made. I also look at the style of the animal and the style of the machine."

"What do you mean?"

"Well, for example, you might do buckskin horses instead of palominos if the carousel is Western-looking."

"Western? What would that look like?"

"It might have muskets, or bows and arrows. A buckskin horse would be darker and more yellow, and the mane and tail would be black instead of cream."

I corrected the angle of his brush. "With the old carousels, there were all kinds of phases and fashions. Sometimes there'll be armored horses, supposedly like the ones ridden by medieval knights."

"Supposedly?"

"Real knights rode big stocky animals, like beer wagon horses. No ordinary horse could have carried them. The knights' armor was heavy."

Louie grinned. "They should have had Harleys."

The idea of Sir Lancelot jousting on a chopper made me snort with laughter.

It was the last laugh I'd have in a long while.

25

LATE FOR A WALK WITH JOY, I hurried along the streets between home and St. Martha's. It wasn't so much the time that made me feel knotted up inside—it was a new distrust, a feeling that Joy wasn't really on my side. On my side in what, I couldn't have said.

I saw her waiting up ahead in front of St. Martha's. She didn't look impatient, but I jogged uphill the last half-block.

"Too much work lately to get any exercise?" Joy asked, watching me pant.

"What color did you say that kettle is?" I teased her. Joy had no room to talk about *me* working too much.

She laughed. "I've been playing catch-up since I got back from Paradise," she said.

We hiked toward the lake, keeping up a good pace. At least it was downhill. I got my breath after a couple of minutes.

"You didn't say much about your trip," I said.

"There wasn't much to say. Mostly I stayed in Jakinda's room and talked with her."

"Did she really get sick because of the nuclear tests?"

"Probably. No one can say in an individual case, but it's likely. Her husband and son died of cancer, too."

"Why didn't they know it was dangerous?"

"The government told them it wasn't. And by the time they found out, it was too late. Jakinda lost another son to leukemia years ago—he was one of several children in their neighborhood who died of that. He was six."

We walked on to the next corner in silence. "The children thought the radioactive clouds were pretty," Joy said. "They were pink—different from any clouds they'd ever seen. Well, of course they were different." Her voice had a bitter tone I'd never heard from her before.

"You said she talked about the past. . . . Was that what she was telling you?"

"Some of it. . . . She had a lot of regrets that she and Bill hadn't seen through the lies, taken their kids elsewhere. But there were some happy memories too. And some odd ones. . . . She told me something I'm astonished I didn't know—that shortly before she died, Zuzene was talking about getting married."

"Mama was getting *married*?"

The lake sparkled in front of us. Once again, it was studded with ducks and boats, and the Camron-Stanford House cast its spell on the far shore. Once again, the past seemed to be hiding inside, sliding past the windows like a ghost, ready to fling the door open and confront me. It wasn't pretty and nostalgic anymore. Victorian lady revenants, pink killer clouds . . . . I turned my head away and walked on, counting cracks in the sidewalk.

We slowed as we approached Children's Fairyland. Joy misstepped, cried out, and hobbled over to a bench. She sat down hard, grimacing.

"What's wrong?"

"Turned my ankle. Let's sit a minute."

We watched the kids lining up to turn the magic key that would activate each of the "talking storybooks." Years ago, I had loved Children's Fairyland. Now I felt like I was looking through a telescope at the moon.

"Who was Mama marrying?" I asked. "Did Jakinda say?"

Joy looked out across the lake, not at me. "She was marrying your father," she said.

"My *father*! How did she know my father?"

Joy spoke hesitantly. "Zuzene was your mother, Mirai—not your stepmother." She glanced at me, then studied the water again.

"*What?*" I was sure I hadn't heard what I'd heard.

She kept her eyes on the lake. "Zuzene was your mother. I'm sorry I told you she wasn't."

I couldn't think of anything to say. Everything that wasn't too mild was too much. Finally, one thought floated to the top.

"I wish you'd at least look at me. You're expecting the Loch Ness monster to surface over there by the Camron-Stanford House?"

"Sorry." Joy didn't pick up on my nasty tone. Her gaze flicked to my face for a second, then down to her lap.

I was filling with fury. "You've lied to me all my life, Joy. . . . Why?"

"I didn't want to. . . . But when you were five, when Zuzene had just died, I thought it would be wrong to upset your world any more than it was already. Later, there never was a good time to tell you. And what difference did it make? Zuzene was gone—I knew I had to tell you someday, but there were other reasons. . . ."

"You mean, you didn't want anyone to know that a black child was your niece, don't you?"

She looked straight into my eyes and said, "Mirai, have I ever introduced you to anyone as my stepniece?"

She had me there. Yes, she'd always said "niece." But I couldn't see any reason why she hadn't told me, unless it was some kind of racist shame. *The apple doesn't fall far from the tree,* I thought, thinking of the words from Estebe's letter: ". . . As long as it isn't an Indian or a Mexican."

"Why did the story ever get started in the first place?" My voice was tight and shrill.

"Your father's name was Alex Bowman. He taught at the University of Nevada at Reno. He was in the right place at the right time—an outstanding black man in a culture of tokenism. He was smart, sociable, and ambitious. And married. He wanted to climb the ladder at UNR. He even had political ambitions. All of that would have gone up in smoke if his affair with Zuzene had come out."

"You mean his illegitimate child with Zuzene, don't you? So, it was *his* idea that I should be 'adopted'?"

"His and mine. Zuzene was very much against it."

"Yours! Why would you help him persuade Mama to lie to me?"

"I thought Aita might accept you as an adopted child, where he never would if he knew the truth. Especially since Zuzene wasn't married—and your father was. Between the two of us, Alex and I persuaded her. It wasn't easy. She hated lying more than anything."

"I thought it was *you* who hated lying. I see I was mistaken."

Joy didn't answer. We sat in cold silence in the August sun.

"Where is he now?" I asked.

"Alex? I have no idea."

"Sounds like a great father."

"He was crazy about you, Mirai. He may have made some selfish choices—I think we all did. Alex loved you, but he wanted his career too much to risk a scandal. Zuzene wanted another woman's husband, and she wanted a child. Aita wanted a respectable Basque family. I wanted to avoid a family rift. I told you I'd made some terrible mistakes through trying to please people, and this is the worst of them. In our separate ways, we were all selfish."

"What happened to Alex's wife? He must have gotten a divorce, if Mama was going to marry him."

"Unless the marriage was a fantasy of Zuzene's. She wasn't always all that realistic."

"What is all this about Mama?" I asked. "You keep coming out with these hints and innuendos. Suggestions that she wasn't all there or something. Say it right out, why don't you? What was wrong with her?"

"I'm not qualified to diagnose people. I'd guess something in the area of high-functioning autism. But I simply don't know. That's another reason I didn't tell you all this earlier. I didn't want to start some kind of self-fulfilling prophecy that you'd be affected, too."

"You mean it's hereditary?"

"Not always. I've worried about your clumsiness, because Zuzene had that, too, and it's one of the symptoms of autism. But you're definitely not autistic, only a klutz."

Joy had, unbelievably, kept her voice quiet throughout this entire conversation. She always did this in an argument, as she had in the episode of the Cabbage Patch Doll. It was supposed to pull the discussion towards reason, and it usually worked, especially if her opponent didn't know what she was doing. But I did.

She gave me a loving smile that was gasoline on a fire. I jumped to my feet.

"I don't know how you can sit there so damn calm and smug and tell me you've lied to me," I said. "Lied about who I am, about my mother, my father . . . . You didn't even give me your own name—Nekane." I spat the name out bitterly, and saw Joy flinch.

I turned and strode away, along the Children's Fairyland fence. "Better not use the magic key," I said in the general direction of the children. "The story may turn out to be something you'll wish you hadn't heard."

26

AT CHARLENE'S, I RAN UP the front stairs two at a time, making as much racket as a herd of buffalo. In my room, I paused only a second before going to the bulletin board and tearing Joy's picture off it. I lobbed it at the trash can as Charlene came in.

"What's going on?" she asked.

"Joy told me she lied to me—I'm her real niece, Zuzene was my mother, I'm not adopted, they just said I was." I got it out in one breath, feeling like a two-year-old having a tantrum.

"Whoa." Charlene sat on the edge of the bed. "I've heard this one the other way around—that people are shocked to find out they *are* adopted. Never heard it *this* way. You serious—you're not?"

"No. Yes. I mean no, I'm not adopted."

"Well, except by Joy. I mean, she stepped in as mother when your mom died."

"Good for her. Joy the saint. Would have been nice if she'd admitted she was my real aunt."

"Would it?" She leaned against the headboard. "You must see how hard it would have been to tell you at that point."

"Well, maybe not right away. . . . I don't know. But I'm thirty, Charlene! When was she going to tell me? On her deathbed?"

Charlene snorted. "Probably. Lies can be very hard to wiggle out of. Why did they concoct this story in the first place? Last I checked, it wasn't the usual way to do things."

I smiled at her ironic tone. "I guess there were two reasons. One was that Joy hoped Estebe might accept an *adopted* bastard black granddaughter—she was sure he wouldn't go for a blood relation. And the other was that my father was some big noise at a university, and he was married. I mean, to someone else, not Mama. So, Joy and my father sort of pushed Mama into claiming I was adopted."

"There are usually a few signs to the contrary, like pregnancy," Charlene said.

"Mama went on some kind of world tour—I guess that was why," I said slowly, putting it all together as I spoke.

"Ah. I believe that kind of genteel flight was a custom even in Victorian days. Well, it does answer the question as to where they found you." She glanced at Joy's photo, lying facedown on the floor. "I take it you're pretty pissed."

"Wouldn't you be?"

"I guess. I mean, it's hard to imagine. So, what now?"

"I have a carousel to finish by Memorial Day. *That's* what now."

"What about Joy?"

"She's a big girl. She can take her walks around Lake Merritt by herself." I sounded like a spiteful kid and knew it. I was so angry—I didn't care if I ever saw Joy again.

Charlene only raised her eyebrows. She didn't try to change my mind.

I *DID* HAVE A CAROUSEL to finish. Summer was ending, and we were working long hours, always with an eye on the calendar. May of next year was bearing down on us like a runaway train.

When the first of the chariots was stripped, Barbara and I went over it carefully, looking for problems or major repairs.

For once, we got a pleasant surprise. Thanking heaven for small favors, I set Louie to priming and sanding it.

"Let's do some planning, Barbara," I said, and led the way into the office.

She perched on the guest chair, looking apprehensive in spite of my mild approach.

"You do nice work. I'd like you to take six of the animals and one chariot and do your own designs for them. I'll look them over, and if they're consistent with what I've got for the rest of the machine, we'll do them in your colors."

I hadn't offered a raise, because I couldn't yet, but to an artist, this was at least as good. I was considering offering her a partnership, supposing that her marital problems didn't mess things up again. This was a way of starting her on a partner's artistic autonomy, and she knew it.

"Which animals?" she asked.

"Any ones you want except the lead. And you might as well take the chariot that came back today."

"I'll start on designs tonight," she said. Her face filled with open delight—it made me think of the second a breeze hits a wind chime.

I didn't ask how homework would sit with Will. That was *her* problem.

As Labor Day weekend approached, more and more of the city traffic was campers and boat trailers. That was the only way I knew a holiday was coming—we weren't planning to take the day off. Louie was still priming and sanding. Barbara was working on designs for the chariot. I was everywhere, doing everything. I fretted about the schedule, day after day.

"We're not doing so bad," Louie said. "Why're we getting so frantic?"

"Memorial Day is the *opening*, Louie," I said. "We still have six animals in Portland, and we're on square one with them. Don't forget the seven coats of varnish and the drying time. And everything has to be finished here at least a month before the opening. All the animals have to be sent up there, and the carousel has to be put together. . . . Trust me, we're pushed."

He did some stretches and went back to sanding. He didn't even look up when Barry and the team came through the front door. I closed the sanding room door softly and started working on a camel.

The swishing sandpaper was like the whisper of secrets. *Shhh . . . shhh . . . shhh . . . she doesn't know. . . .* Through the walls came a muted drumming of the ball. Its hollow ring made a perfect accompaniment for my thoughts about Joy: *Hypocrite, liar, racist.*

Shhh . . . shhh . . . , said the sandpaper. *Shhh . . . she doesn't know. . . . Shhh . . . she's . . . she's—*

Almost like one of the family, the basketball finished. *Almost . . . like . . . one . . . of . . . the . . . FAMILY.*

A loud thump, followed by cheers. Someone had scored.

27

WE'D BEEN WORKING FOR the better part of an hour when there was a tap at the door. Louie got up and opened it, and Barry came in.

"The guys go back to school next week, so you'll be getting less noise," he said.

"They haven't bothered me." I said it more or less automatically, then realized it was true. Of all my problems, the team came somewhere near the end of the list. In fact, they weren't even on it. The studio would seem empty without them.

"We never did have that dinner."

"That's okay. The schedule sort of worked itself out."

That was true enough. With the hours we'd all been working, the team could drop by nearly any time and find someone there.

"I'd still like to take you to dinner."

"Sure," I said.

"Tomorrow?"

"Tomorrow's fine. Is eight too late for you? I usually work until seven, at least." It occurred to me that I hadn't even asked Barry where he worked or what he did. For all I knew, he was on a night shift somewhere.

"Eight's fine," he said. "Give me your address, and I'll pick you up."

AFTER THE GUYS LEFT, I got on with sanding my camel. Bitter and miserable as I felt, it was a relief to have someone want to spend an evening with me. *Grownups have their own friends,* I told myself. *No one else hangs out with their elderly aunt.*

Aunt. Joy was my aunt. Except she'd never gotten around to letting me know. Well, that was her problem. I needed to get on with my life. Right now, my life consisted of sanding a camel. By the time I was ready to leave, that may have been the smoothest carousel camel in the world.

When I got home, the house was full of wonderful smells. I went to the kitchen to investigate, and found a pan of lasagna on top of the stove, with one piece removed.

"Help yourself to the lasagna," Charlene called from the living room. "I got on a cooking binge this afternoon, so I'm counting on you to eat."

I didn't need to be told twice. I dished a good-sized helping onto a plate and carried it into the dining room. Charlene joined me, carrying a glass of red wine.

"Have some of this too," she said, raising the wineglass. "It's on the sideboard."

I'd skipped lunch and—come to think of it—hadn't eaten much breakfast, either. The first bite of lasagna was so delicious, it made my mouth sting with hunger and fulfillment, rolled into one. I poured a glass of wine to go with it.

The first sip went right to my head. *Careful. Don't get loaded.*

"So," Charlene asked, "How was your day, dear?" Her voice was a perfect send-up of a situation comedy, but I could tell she was serious behind the spoof.

"You should have been an actor," I said.

She didn't even hesitate. "Everyone's an actor. Some people choose roles better than others do. Closest I ever got to real acting was when I was a waitress in a wench bar."

"What's a wench bar?"

"Oh, you know. One of those places where you have to wear a costume that looks sort of old-fashioned and shows a lot of cleavage."

"Oh." I could easily imagine Charlene dressed like that, and having fun with it, too. "You've had some offbeat jobs. Nanny, waitress . . . . How'd you get where you are now?"

"Someone made it a point to teach me, same as you're doing with Louie."

I took another bite of lasagna. It didn't explode in my mouth like the first few bites had, but it was delicious. I drank more wine, feeling relaxed for the first time in days. My hands and feet felt warm and tingly.

"Anyway," she said. "How'd it go?"

"Oh, pretty well. Barry asked me out to dinner tomorrow."

"Ah-*hah*."

"No 'ah-*hah*' about it. He'll probably bring a couple of high-school ball players with him."

"Sounds kinky."

I flapped my hand at her—she was irrepressible. I finished my wine, thinking about Charlene. She'd done a lot of jobs I would have been outraged to do—nanny, serving wench, and lord only knows what. Far from being resentful, she had fun remembering them. She reminded me of a toy a pet parakeet of mine once had—no matter how the bird attacked it, it always righted itself. A *kelly,* that's what it was called. I poured another glass of wine, finished it quickly, and filled the glass again.

"You ought to be called Kelly," I said.

"Why Kelly? I'm not even Irish."

"Too complicated to explain." I was slurring a little.

"You getting soused? I mean, go ahead if you *want* to. But it's a bitch, getting soused accidentally—like being on a carousel that won't stop."

"None of them *ever* stop," I said. It sounded pretty profound at that moment.

"Hoo, baby. Good thing I don't have to eighty-six you, since you're at home." Charlene laughed and took the dishes to the kitchen. I noticed she took the wine bottle too.

I finished what was in my glass. I wondered what she'd say if I went and retrieved the wine—after all, she'd said to go ahead. But I didn't want to enough to get up. I sat and stared at the table. Charlene told me good night and went upstairs. I looked around the table and raised my empty glass to each of the chairs in turn.

A toast: Here's to you, Joy. And you, Alex—Dad. And you, Zuzene. And you, Estebe. Mom, Grandpa. May those of you who are not dead have a long life and a happy one.

Empty chairs, empty wineglass. Empty tears. I got up slowly and washed the glass in the kitchen. *Don't drop the glass, Mirai. You're just a klutz. It's one of the symptoms of autism. Get the glass clean for Clean Charlene. No pink in the bottom, no water drops. No smudges.*

I polished that glass as if I were covering up a crime. No fingerprints. Nothing left of me at all.

I went upstairs and lay down. I didn't sleep much.

Fix the carousel, fix Will. I fixed Will—I sure fixed Will. Joy, Zuzene, can't fix Estebe.

Fix the carousel, fix another carousel. Sand horses, send bills, paint horses, pay bills. Sand, send. Paint, pay. Round and round.

Round and round, change partners, Will, Barry, Tom-Dick-and-Harry . . . .

I fell into a dream where I was walking the floor of a carousel, walking against its turning. The horses whirled past me, as if they were running on their own, running across the desert. Dapple, bay, roan, piebald, buckskin. All of them needed work, but they spun by me too fast to touch. I couldn't make out the faces of the riders. I was looking for Joy and Alex to ask them why they took the doll. Most of all, I was looking for the palomino horse with Zuzene.

Aita said Taba must have kicked her. Mama, don't ride into the desert tonight.

28

MORNING SUN HIT THE PRISMS hanging in Charlene's kitchen window and shattered into a million pieces. They made me feel dizzy, so I sat down at the kitchen table with my back to them.

"How's your head?" asked Charlene.

"It's been better." I started to roll my eyes, but they seemed to have been sanded in the night. Possibly varnished as well. All seven coats.

"I made extra coffee. Help yourself."

"Do you think it works?"

"You mean, does it do anything for a hangover? I doubt it."

"I do, too." I poured myself a cup anyway. It probably wouldn't do any damage. Probably nothing short of one of Estebe's A-bombs could do any more damage.

We sat in silence for five or ten minutes. Or maybe it only *seemed* like five or ten.

"I had some weird dreams last night," I said.

"Not too surprising. I do, too, when I drink too much wine."

"I was trying to find my father." I didn't tell her the part about Mama.

"Where were you looking?"

"On a carousel. I was walking opposite to how it turned."

"Sounds like you were the ticket-taker. Did you see anyone who might have been your father?"

The coffee was not doing good things in my stomach, so I set the cup down and pushed it away to escape the smell. "I don't know," I said. "I don't know what he'd look like. But I didn't see *anyone* clearly."

"That's too bad. You can probably find him if you try, and it would be interesting to know if you saw him first in your dream."

"How could I find him? The university?"

"That, or check a library for things he may have written. Publish or perish, you know."

"He may have perished," I said.

"In that case, we *don't* want to find him. Not in person, anyway."

The idea gave me chills. "I meant academically," I said quickly.

"The university might forward a letter. Or maybe he's still there."

I thought it over. Did I really want to find my father? He certainly hadn't tried to find me. That was painfully obvious from the ease with which Jakinda's daughter-in-law had found Joy after all these years. If Alex had given a damn about me, he could have had my phone number in thirty seconds.

I'd heard of adoptees who'd made it a crusade to find their natural parents. They were often disappointed—sometimes by failing, sometimes by succeeding.

The things I already knew about Alex made me think I wouldn't like him. On the other hand, all I knew was Joy's version. And I no longer trusted anything Joy said.

"What are you thinking?" Charlene asked.

"Pluses and minuses of looking for him. Or of finding him, for that matter. He doesn't sound too nice."

Charlene leaned back in her chair. "You really have to feel sorry for the guy," she said.

"I do?" I hadn't been anywhere near *that* thought.

"Well, here he is—smart guy, black at just the right time to be black . . . ."

"Is that a tiny bit cynical?" I asked.

"Yeah, well, let me finish my tiny cynicism here. So, he's a guy on the way up, married. . . . Maybe has a couple of kids. . . . "

"Oh, Jesus—siblings." That idea brought me to a momentary halt.

"Half-siblings, to be pedantic." Charlene said. "Anyway, he's in the right place, right time, and then he meets a nutty, fascinating artist. Has an affair. Well, okay, guys do."

"You think they *all* do?"

"No, but it's pretty hard to tell which ones wouldn't."

I wondered how Charlene knew. She'd said once that I'd be surprised how many guys had a thing for big women. I decided not to ask.

"So, Alex has an affair. So?"

Charlene sipped her coffee and leaned toward me. "Don't you see? Alex is in great shape. . . . Nice setup—career, wife, mistress. Then the mistress gets pregnant."

"So?" I repeated.

"And then . . . . Well, I think the mistress usually has an abortion at that point in the drama. No offense intended. But this mistress doesn't."

"Catholic," I put in. The story was interesting, as a story. I could see how the pieces fit together, a complete puzzle like a mystery novel.

Charlene frowned. "Well, she *was* committing adultery— what's the diff? Or is it adultery only for the married one?"

"I have no idea. But I think a Catholic woman who got involved with a married man might still draw the line at abortion."

"Okay, so now he'll have to hide a child as well as a mistress. So, he and her sister persuade her to go on a long trip and come back with an adoption story."

"Using Basque Grandpa as an excuse." I was absorbed in the plot, my headache gone. I felt light-headed, nearly manic.

Charlene closed her eyes as if visualizing another world. "Five years go by with everything at gridlock. The child is growing up, asking questions, nearly ready to start school. The school will be asking questions, too. And the other kids will ask, 'Where's your daddy?'"

"Maybe he's afraid nutty mistress will get fed up with all the lying—she hates it. Even if she could deceive her father, she might not be able to tell a barefaced lie to a kid."

"Maybe Alex has tried to get other teaching positions, move somewhere else, but he hasn't succeeded," said Charlene.

"And nutty mistress has been hinting at marriage. It looks like the nice setup is coming apart."

"So, he gets nutty mistress to ride out into the desert one night, and he hits her over the head." Charlene finished the story with a flourish.

The hot air rushed out of my balloon. I was back to reality, staring at Charlene. All the grief I'd ever felt about my family hit me in the pit of the stomach. I drew in a ragged breath and started sobbing.

Charlene's face went red. "Oh, my God," she said, nearly whispering. "I can't believe I said that, any of it. Oh, shit, Mirai, I'm so sorry. I got carried away—I didn't mean it. It seemed like a story we were making up. I forgot it was real."

I nodded, hoping I looked less devastated than I felt. I could not say a single word. Because, regardless of whether we should have said what we had, I had a sick feeling that we'd come up with the truth, or something pretty close to it.

29

I BLEW OFF TRYING to go to the studio at all that day. Too wiped out to even feel guilty, I had a long, hot soak with Charlene's lavender bubble bath and took a nap. Charlene came in after a couple of hours and gave me a great back rub. I didn't ask if she'd ever been a masseuse—she probably had.

My mind felt completely erased, washed like a blackboard on the last day of school.

"I'm supposed to have dinner with Barry tonight," I said. "I think I'll call him and cancel."

"Why? If you stay home, you'll just get depressed." Charlene jumped up and jerked my closet door open. Hangers clinked as she paged quickly through my clothes. "Oh, my, what have we here?"

I glanced up from my bed and saw she'd found my daishiki, or whatever it was. Chartreuse and chrome yellow stripes, with a scarlet thread woven in here and there. A cross between folk-wear and couturier.

"Christmas present from Joy last year," I said. "I've never worn it."

"Why not?"

"It makes me feel like the queen of some new African nation, on a state visit to the White House." *Also it makes me think of Joy.*

"Hah. The queen wishes. *Joy* picked this out?"

"Actually, I think one of her volunteers did."

"Wow. I can't wait to see you in it."

"You really think I should wear this for dinner with Barry?"

"Yep. Make him sit up and look. He's seen you with paint all over your face and hands. Show him your glamour side."

"I'll think about it," I said, and drifted back toward sleep.

When I woke, it was late afternoon—too late to call Barry and cancel. The daishiki was laid out across my chair, and I didn't have the energy to put another outfit together. So, I slipped it over my head and found a pair of sandals that looked okay with it.

I went down to the kitchen, where Charlene was starting another pot of coffee. This time, coffee seemed like a good idea. "Me, too," I said, taking a mug off the shelf.

"Not till you put on a robe," said Charlene. "You look great. Too good to mess up with a coffee spill."

"That's another thing—Joy said that Mama was autistic, and that she always worried about me, because clumsiness is one of the symptoms."

"Yeah, well, it's one of the symptoms of rushing and not watching what your hands are doing, too. You clumsy with your tools at work?"

"No."

"Then don't sweat it. I wondered why Joy gets that funny look when you fumble something."

The electric coffeemaker was making the snorting noises that heralded the end of its cycle. I went to my room and pulled a robe over my outfit so Charlene would give me some coffee.

When I got back to the kitchen, she had two mugs poured. She handed me one, and I took a cautious sip. Better. Maybe it would actually do me some good.

We took our coffee to the living room. Charlene sat in an armchair in the sunny bay window and read the newspaper. I kicked off my sandals and folded up on the couch, knees to chest. I took a few sips of the coffee, then set the cup aside and forgot it.

We sat in a silence that was companionable, if not exactly happy. I didn't want to talk about my family anymore, and Charlene didn't push it. She didn't even comment on what was in the paper, supposing that any of it was worth mentioning.

When she left the room, I hardly looked up. The patches of sunlight slid away, and I barely noticed them, either. A few minutes before eight, I got up and turned on a few lights. The mirror over the mantel showed me I was still wearing my robe. I took it off and hung it behind the kitchen door to hide it. I didn't have enough energy to take it upstairs.

Now the mirror reflected the gorgeous daishiki, with my sullen face pasted above it. *I'm not wearing this thing, it's wearing me. Well, I don't look like an African queen. What I look like is a kid dressed up in her mother's clothes.*

Thinking "mother" zapped me like a cattle prod just as the doorbell rang. I pushed my mood aside, ran my fingers through my hair to fluff it up, and let Barry in.

"Wow," he said, looking me over. He smiled like a flashbulb going off in my face. I figured he was smiling at my dress, so I let it be the one to smile back at him.

"You ready?" he asked.

"Uh-huh." I tried to sound pleasant, at least. None of my problems were his fault.

He glanced down at my feet. "Uh . . . maybe some shoes?"

"Oops." I pulled myself together and retrieved my sandals. I tried to make light of my forgetfulness: "Ta-dah! *Now* I'm ready."

We walked to his car, parked half a block up the street. I expected it to be cluttered with junk of all kinds, but it looked as clean as if Charlene had been there.

I opened the door and settled into my seat. Barry pulled away from the curb and started describing a wonderful restaurant he'd chosen, a seafood place somewhere in the City, maybe out on the Avenues. I wasn't paying much attention. In fact, lulled by the motion of the car and the deepening twilight, I fell asleep.

When I woke, the car was parked. I looked around in confusion—we were still in Oakland. I could see the witch's hat of the *Oakland Tribune* Tower, and farther away, the Bay Bridge and the Golden Gate. A passing car silhouetted Barry still beside me, waiting quietly in the driver's seat.

"Oh, God, I'm sorry," I said. I felt like an imbecile.

"Don't sweat it," said Barry. "Are you okay? I mean, are you too tired to go out for dinner?"

"No, I'm fine." Right. I looked fine. I looked great, falling asleep in the middle of his discourse on Bay Area restaurants.

"Would you rather get dinner closer to home? I mean, that place is great, but we can always go there another night." He sounded easy and contented.

"Maybe that would be best," I said. "Why waste great food on someone who can't even stay awake?"

"Oh, there are good restaurants on this side of the bay. We'll do the seafood place next time."

I was sure he wouldn't ask me out again, but I smiled and nodded as if we were a real couple making real plans.

30

THE RESTAURANT BARRY PICKED in Oakland was a hole-in-the-wall sort of place. "Are we in Chinatown?" I asked, taking in the dime-store–Oriental ambience.

"On the edge of it," he said. "The food's great—don't let the décor throw you."

"You order, then," I said. "Just get whatever's good. I love Chinese food."

He nodded and went through a complicated conversation with the waiter. An older man came from the back and greeted Barry. Then the three of them discussed what we'd eat. Half the talk seemed to be in Chinese.

The waiter brought tea and chopsticks, and I spread a napkin in my lap. Sipping tea, I tried to salvage what was left of the evening.

"How do you know all these good places to eat?" I asked.

"I've written a few restaurant reviews."

"Is that what you do?" I'd always wondered who got to do those books—travel and dining guides, tour books, and movie reviews. It sounded like a fun job.

"Not a lot of it," he said. "I'm a freelance writer. Mostly I do corporate stuff, or government publications—education manuals, that sort of thing. Grant proposals. I stay away from advertising, because I don't like it. But almost anything else."

"My roommate's a fund-raiser," I said. "I think she does some grant stuff too."

"What's her name? I know a few of the local fund-raisers."

"Charlene Arthur."

He shook his head. "No, I don't know her. I may have heard the name, though. Does she work for a firm?"

"No. Freelance. Were you speaking Chinese when you ordered?"

"I know the names of some dishes, that's all. I'm sure I mispronounce everything. I probably really say, 'I need twenty light bulbs and a fried bulldozer,' or, 'Please let me sweep the carpet with my tie.' They know what I'm trying to say, but that doesn't mean they don't fall on the kitchen floor laughing, once the door's closed."

"So, you order food and spread happiness at the same time," I said. "Not bad at all."

The waiter brought a plate with mixed appetizers—barbecued spare ribs and fried wontons. The wontons had a hot scent of sesame oil. Ordinarily I would have found them appetizing, but I decided to pass.

I took one of the spare ribs and nibbled delicately. The sauce was intense: hot, tangy, and sweet. I laid the rib on the edge of my plate. The meat along the edge of the bone was gnawed-looking, like alley garbage chewed by rats. Or cats—around here, people called stray cats "alley rabbits." Supposedly some of the restaurants . . . . *Stop it, Mirai.*

I looked away, then back at the bone. It occurred to me that what was on my plate was a piece of an actual dead animal. Not much different from road kill. *Stop it.*

A gurgling belch came up my throat. Hoping Barry hadn't noticed, I patted my lips with my napkin.

"Did you grow up in Oakland?" I asked, hoping to distract him.

"No, in Rio Vista."

"Where's that?"

"Up in the delta. Halfway between Fairfield and Lodi. My dad owns a supermarket. What about you?"

"I've lived in Oakland since I was five," I said, not wanting to discuss Nevada and the Basques. I couldn't think of anything to ask about Rio Vista or the grocery business.

"Did you grow up living in the Catholic Worker house?"

Before we could get into that, the waiter came with bowls of soup. Hot and sour soup—the very thing for a hangover, I thought. The bustle of replacing the appetizer plates with soup bowls provided a break in the conversation. I hoped I could get the subject off Joy.

My stomach emitted a soprano whine. If Barry didn't hear it, he was deaf. His expression didn't change.

If I couldn't keep him talking about his background, maybe his work would get him going. "When did you do the restaurant reviews book?" I asked.

"It wasn't a book, just a series of articles for the paper. It was several years ago. I had a lot of fun with it."

"In that case, you should stay current in case they ask for another series. It wouldn't do to let your knowledge get out of date."

"That's what I thought, too." He grinned, showing a dimple I hadn't noticed before.

I tried to smile, but the soup was beginning to feel odd in my stomach. Maybe hot and sour soup wasn't the best thing for a hangover after all. I put my spoon down.

"Did you review this place when you were doing your articles?" I asked.

"Oh, yeah. I had a great meal here. Of course, the menu is more ethnic than a lot of Americans like. Lots of the tourists want sweet-and-sour pork or chow mein. But people who live in the Bay Area are pretty open about food."

"How is it different?" I asked. If I could keep the conversation on his interests, I might be able to handle the evening. Maybe the gross noises coming from my insides weren't as loud as I thought.

"Most Chinese-American cuisine is Mandarin. It's not bad, but it's the blandest of the regional cuisines of China, and restaurants here often tone it down even more. This restaurant is Hunan, much spicier—often a bit greasy for American tastes."

Plebeian American that I was, I was miserably aware of the fattiness of the food I'd eaten so far. I tried to steer the subject away from food.

"Where in China is it?" Geography would be a nice, safe subject.

"Hunan Province is in southeastern China—along the Yangtze River. There's agricultural land, of course, but there's also lakes, rivers, and mountains. The food is as much game as tame, if you follow me. A lot of seafood too, and a few delicacies like frog legs and turtle."

As he finished the sentence, a waiter passed our table with a cart loaded with steaming platters. Rich scents of sesame and scallops filled the air. I imagined frogs and turtles. My mouth filled with sour saliva, and I knew I had to get out of there.

"Excuse me a minute," I said. I jumped to my feet and scrambled toward the door marked Restrooms.

I made it with about two seconds to spare.

Part 5

31

WHEN I OPENED MY EYES the next morning, my bedroom was filled with sunlight, but a bad taste was in my mouth—in every sense of that expression. The beautiful daishiki lay wadded and stinking on my desk chair. I figured it was probably ruined. No more African queen for me.

I felt achy and listless. I knew I should get up and go to Mass. But the idea of even one more sip of wine made me feel sick again. Puking at the communion rail might be the only asinine thing I hadn't done yet. I decided to forget Mass and went back to sleep.

Charlene woke me, tapping at the door. She opened it and stuck in her head.

"Barry's on the phone," she said, as if that were good.

"Tell him I'm sick."

Her eyebrows went up, but she didn't argue. She closed the door softly, leaving me to kick myself in solitude.

I DRAGGED INTO THE STUDIO on Monday a few minutes before noon. Barbara and Louie were in the office bending over the desk. I stepped around and looked over their shoulders.

It was the first of Barbara's color designs. She'd drawn one of the giraffes and painted it with her color choices for my approval. As I looked, she slid a few more out of a portfolio and spread them out for me to see. She'd worked out designs for a horse, an ostrich, and the tiger.

It was damn good. Nineteenth-century carousels had been painted in intense colors, as the buildings of that era had been. By the 1920s, soft colors, even pastels, were fashionable. What Barbara had designed for this 1906 machine was in softened, but not pastel, colors for most of the large areas of the trappings, shaded with more saturated colors and trimmed with an intense palette. It was perfect.

The only problem was, it wasn't consistent with my own designs for the machine. I'd have to redo mine or tell Barbara to come up with another idea.

Barbara was waiting for me to say yes or no, her expression slipping slowly from delight in her designs to a neutral, self-protective look. I'd gone that route myself more than once, when a teacher didn't understand what I was trying to do.

"Hang on a sec," I said. "They're good. I'm trying to work it into the whole picture."

I looked over the designs again. There was no way I could combine them with the designs I'd already done. Too distinctive. At the same time, the ones I'd done were good. And I'd told Barbara I'd only consider her work if it blended.

But this was better. It was accurate but fresh, different from what anyone else was doing. I'd be a fool to lose this for my studio. That was the thought that finally cut through the mixed load of bull that was clogging my mind. *Someone else came up with a better idea. Live with it, Mirai. Worse things have happened, and the world's still turning.*

"It doesn't work with what I've done so far," I began. Barbara's expression closed with disappointment. I put up a hand. "Hold on. I'm thinking how I could revise mine, because this is great."

Her smile came out from behind the cloud for a few seconds, then disappeared again.

"What's the matter?" I asked.

"What about the ones you've already painted?"

"The differences aren't in the coat colors, they're in the trappings. None of that's been started. Let's take a look later this afternoon and decide how to make this work."

I had a twinge of giving up control, envious that her designs were better than my own. *This time,* I reminded myself. *This time they're better, and next time it'll be me with the brainstorm. And that's what partnership is.*

Partnership. There it was again, as scary an idea as ever. No way to dodge it now, because there was no arguing with the truth staring up at me from those drawings. Barbara was done being an apprentice.

WHEN I GOT HOME, I FOUND a bouquet waiting on the hall table, complete with a "Get Well" card, both from Barry.

"Looks like you have an admirer," Charlene commented, passing through the hallway as I opened the card.

"I doubt it, after the way I screwed up our date."

She stopped at the foot of the stairs. "Why? What did you do? Lose your temper?"

"No, my dinner."

"You mean you *barfed?* You *were* looking slightly green before you left."

"Yeah, well, the good news is I made it to the ladies' room." I read the card—a simple "Hope you're feeling better soon."

"I'd say the good news is your date being nice enough to send you flowers," Charlene said.

"Well, yeah. That too. But Barry's not exactly a date."

"Oh, why not?"

I tried to find an explanation.

"Nothing. I don't know. Maybe I'm not ready."

"What does it take to get you to look at someone? You're not into the 'dangerous guy' trap, are you?"

If Joy had ever asked such a thing, I would have pretended ignorance. Getting it from Charlene, I thought it over. Maybe I *did* get attracted to guys who seemed risky.

"I don't know," I finally said. "Men need to have some kind of glamour—or something like it, anyway."

Charlene snorted. "Like Will? Moth to the flame, and all that crap? Did you like the way *he* treated you?"

"No." I sniffed one of the flowers—nothing. I always checked when I got a bouquet, but florists' flowers were never fragrant.

"Would you make friends with women who acted like Will?" Charlene persisted.

"No."

"Then why the *fuck* are you wasting your time grieving over someone you don't even like?"

I didn't have an answer. I never did have an answer for really good questions.

"There's vases on the bottom shelf in the pantry," said Charlene. "If you cut a half inch or so off the ends of the stems, the flowers will last longer. Maybe even until you figure out that Barry's worth a second look."

She went upstairs to her office and shut the door. I wasn't sure if she was pissed at me or not. From the bouquet, a green scent of ferns and leaves was rising, faint but insistent.

32

I PULLED ON MY EXERCISE CLOTHES the next morning and headed toward Lake Merritt, wishing I were meeting Joy instead of walking alone. I was later than the sunrise joggers, earlier than the stroller-mommies, so the sidewalk wasn't mobbed. Even with a clear path, I dawdled and dragged. Every step set off a separate ache somewhere in my chest. "Heartache" was the usual word, but it wasn't really my heart. More like lungs, or shoulders, or even esophagus. *How romantic: I have an esophagus ache.* I did a few shoulder rolls, shifting the pain around but not reducing it.

The freshness had burned off the day. Looking toward San Francisco Bay, I saw that smog had built a brown wall across the horizon. I walked past shop windows, barely noticing the familiar tenants: a Christian Science Reading Room, a health food store, a small gallery I'd always enjoyed.

I stopped short. The gallery was gone, empty except for a broom in one corner. *The last witch missed her ride,* I thought. But it wasn't funny. The gallery had been a bright spot on the street, a place to buy beautiful gifts, and I'd miss it.

I stopped myself from turning toward St. Martha's when I got to the corner and walked downhill instead. Standing on the joggers' path, I looked around. The lake's surface lay flat and gray as a two-way mirror. The air was too still for rustling leaves or lapping water, but the low rumble of traffic would have drowned out small sounds anyway. I jogged a short distance along the path and then slowed to a walk, wiping sweat from my face.

"Unseasonably warm" was the official weather forecast. *How can it be unseasonably warm in a place with no seasons? Wonder what it's like now in Peregrine Falls.*

A sort of Grandma Moses pastiche scrolled through my imagination: harvesting, baking, and canning. It got good and sentimental for a while: sleds at Christmas, snowmen, carols . . . . I skipped forward to apple blossoms in the spring, plowed fields, slickers, and daffodils. With a faint snort, I consigned the imaginary calendar art to the trash. I didn't know if people in other places really had most of the things I imagined, or even if they noticed when they *did* have them. Maybe it was like all the San Francisco hype, stuff that didn't mean a damn to the residents.

I hope it rains this year. Not another drought—one more year when I can't even tell what month it is. Every day the same, nothing to look forward to.

I imagined celebrating Christmas for the first time without Joy. And birthdays, and Thanksgiving, and all the other holidays. Solitary walks on other streets, avoiding St. Martha's.

What if I *did* go there? Joy wouldn't refuse to talk to me, ever. She'd be her old self—she didn't hold grudges. I could talk to Joy, yes—but what happened when it was her turn to talk? What could she say that I'd believe? She'd lied to me about everything important. If she said it was a nice day, would I look out the window to check? If she said the soup needed more salt, would I taste it before I believed her?

If she said she loved me, would the words hang in the air between us, unclaimed?

I turned and trudged home to change for work. *I hope it rains this year.*

WHEN I GOT TO THE STUDIO, Barbara was already there with more designs. She must have worked half the night on them. She was so excited, she looked high. I still felt sad, and the carousel seemed trivial. But I did remember what it was like to feel what Barbara was feeling now, the creative delight and eagerness of a first big project. I didn't want to dull it for her, so I looked over all the designs carefully. I made a few small suggestions, but as a whole, I approved them.

"Get Louie to do the base coats for the saddles and ornaments," I said. I smiled at her. "Nice work, Barb," I made myself say.

"You sure?"

"Sure as sure."

She danced off to talk to Louie.

The designs *were* good. They were perfect. What I didn't say was that I was damn glad *one* of us could bring some enthusiasm to the project. All mine had vanished, at least for now.

Maybe I could get it back. I *had* to—Barbara couldn't manage the whole thing. Even if she could, it wouldn't be fair to ask her to. Not to mention, hadn't I already told her to keep her hands off the lion? Unless I changed my mind and assigned it to her, designs for the lead animal were my territory.

The lion had to be strong enough to dominate the carousel. If I planned to do it, I'd have to shake off my case of the blahs and come up with a spectacular design. Nothing less would "lead" the animals Barbara was drawing now.

Or I could admit defeat and turn the whole thing over to her. She'd do a wonderful job on the lion, and I could stand in the background and applaud.

I *could*. But I wasn't going to.

33

WHEN MATT, MY FRIEND at Portland Carousel Works, finally called, he hemmed and hawed before he finally came out with it: They couldn't give me a break on the price for the extra work.

"Why don't you get the owner to make up the extras?" he asked. "I'm sure it's in your standard contract, unless you changed it. Didn't we go through the same thing for that monster in Austin?"

"Yeah, we did, but that was an owner who had the money. This one doesn't."

"I wish we could do it. Maybe if I talked to Ben and Susan again . . . ."

"It wouldn't do any good," I said. "Thanks for asking them, but let's leave it at that." I didn't want to put Matt at odds with his partners. I wasn't even sure he'd really ask them—he sounded like he'd changed a lot since we were in school. "Don't worry about it," I added.

"Well, I'm sorry. Let me know if you think of anything I *can* do."

"Sure, Matt," I said. "Will do. Let me know when you're down here next, and we'll go out for a beer." Sure, he would.

We got off the phone, and I stewed for a while. I wished I'd never brought up the subject. I was worse off than when I'd started.

Barbara and Louie were in the paint room, putting base coats on the animals' trappings. Might as well lend a hand, I thought. At least for right now, I was striking out everywhere else.

Once I started working, my mood changed. Handling wood and paint, letting my sense of touch guide my judgment—as always, it was a homing to myself. I had no room for worry or hurt, nothing but the work under my hands and my satisfaction in it. Cleaning brushes at the end of the day, I felt a lot better than I had any reason to.

I GOT HOME AS CHARLENE was leaving. We hovered on the porch for a minute of friendly chat.

"Hail and farewell," I said. "Where're you headed?"

"St. Martha's"

"St. *Martha's*! What for?"

"I told you I was volunteering over there."

Yes, Charlene had told me. For some reason, I'd thought that was going to be off when Joy and I quarreled. I also realized now it was none of my business.

"Ah. Well, have fun."

I went into the house and paused in the front hallway, confused. I reminded myself that Charlene's interest in the Catholic Worker house started long before my falling-out with Joy. I had no reason to think she was up to anything.

Or did I? Charlene and Joy were two of a kind in a lot of ways. Idealistic world-fixers, both of them, not above a few shortcuts in a good cause. I didn't have a problem with that, but I didn't want to be the good cause.

I went to the kitchen, undecided what to do about dinner. I hadn't gone to the market lately, so there wasn't much to choose from. Unwilling to go to a restaurant, I scraped the last of the peanut butter over some nearly stale bread.

I'd only taken a couple of bites when the phone rang. I tried to swallow fast, but the peanut butter stuck to the roof of my mouth. My cheery hello came out as a muffled snort.

"Mirai?" It was Barry.

I made some more pre-language noises intended to convey I was going to the kitchen to get some water and would be back in a second. He was still on the phone when I returned.

"Hi," I said.

"Mirai, are you okay?"

I cleared my throat. "Peanut butter," I explained.

"Oh. Is Charlene out?"

"Yes—did you want to talk to her?"

"No, but I couldn't imagine you answering the phone with a mouthful of peanut butter if someone else was there to get it."

"True. Anyway, I was meaning to call to thank you for the flowers. I mean, after I finished the peanut butter."

"Is that dinner?"

"Uh-huh. I just got home from the studio."

"Would you like to go out? Peanut butter doesn't sound like much of a dinner."

"You ready to chance that again?"

"Oh, sure. Live dangerously—that's my motto."

"Must be. But I decided I was too tired to go out. That's why I was eating peanut butter."

"I could bring a pizza over. Unless you're too tired for company."

I hesitated. It wasn't that I was too tired for company, but I felt confused about Barry. I didn't know how interested he really was in me—maybe he was only being nice. It seemed sort of vain to assume he was smitten with me.

On the other hand, I didn't want to act like a tease. And I wasn't sure I was interested in *him*.

He was waiting for an answer.

"No, I'm not too tired," I said. "But be warned: The place is a wreck and so am I." That seemed a polite way of telling him I wasn't trying to impress him.

He laughed. "I'll mess up my hair so I'll fit in. See you in a bit."

I thought I'd been fair, letting him know I wasn't regarding this as a date. On the other hand, there was no reason to insult the man by looking absolutely awful. I took a quick shower and tore through the closet, unable to decide what to wear. I couldn't look dressed up, or he'd think I was interested in him, so I picked out a pair of jeans—not the skintight ones I'd worn to Will's, but better-looking than the ones I wore to work.

Choosing a top was harder. A peasant blouse—too sexy. He'd never believe I'd worn that to work. Checked shirt—too boyish. A knit shirt with Mickey Mouse—much too warm, with its long sleeves and high neck. A tank top with an Ankh symbol—cute, but I wasn't sure what an Ankh symbol meant. Better not wear a billboard unless I was sure what it said.

I paged furiously through the closet, pulling out clothes. Oh, good, a glitz number with sequins—what had I ever bought *that* for? T-shirt—too shapeless. A crepe blouse seemed a good choice, but when I checked the mirror, I decided the shoulder pads looked like falsies that had slipped upwards. I threw it on the floor as I turned to the ransacked closet. The Sally Army was going to do well out of this.

I'd rejected at least a dozen tops, and the room looked like an ill-kept dressing room in a department store. The doorbell rang.

I pulled on a Hawaiian shirt, knotting the tails at my waist. It was cool, at least, and the bright colors looked good on me. Without a backward glance at the room, I ran downstairs to let Barry in.

34

"Pizza man!"

Barry stood on the porch, balancing the pizza box on the fingertips of one hand. As I watched, he lifted it from shoulder level to above his head. He gave me a goofy smile as part of the parody, and I couldn't help noticing his dimple again.

"Come on in," I said, backing out of the doorway. I led him to the kitchen.

He put the box down, but he didn't open it. "Could I wash my hands?" he asked.

"Sure," I said. "The sink's right there."

"I guess I meant, could I use your bathroom."

"Oh. Upstairs, third door on the left."

After he was gone, I started wondering whether I'd closed my bedroom door. If he noticed the chaos in my room, my pretense of being cool about seeing him was gone. Unless he concluded I was a slob.

Of course, he didn't know which room was mine. Not that an observant person could mistake my clothes for Charlene's. But maybe he wasn't observant.

Damn the old building for not having a downstairs bathroom.

When Barry came back, he didn't comment about anything upstairs. Could I drop some kind of remark about going through my clothes to get a bag together for the Sally Army? Better not bring it up—he might not have noticed.

"Where do you want to eat?" I asked.

"What are the choices?"

"Dining room, or the coffee table in the living room. Or—it won't be dark for another hour or so. Want to eat at the picnic table down in the yard?"

"You have a yard?"

"Yes, and when I say down, I do mean *down*. The hill falls away from the house, so the yard is way down—like two stories. A trip best suited to mountain goats. But it might be cooler."

"Cooler sounds better. Let's be mountain goats, then."

"Do mountain goats eat pizza?" I asked.

"Guess they do. If they didn't before now, we'll start a fad. All the mountain goats will be ordering pizza to be delivered to the peak of Everest. Domino's will have to cope." He picked up the pizza box with a flourish, then stepped back. "After you, Madame—especially since I don't know how to get there."

I fished a couple of canned sodas out of the refrigerator and took the roll of paper towels from the holder above the sink. I knew I was sure to drop it all down the stairs, so I forestalled fate by collecting everything in a plastic grocery bag. Thus equipped for elegant dining, we picked our way down the stairs and through the yard.

I unrolled a few of the paper towels and brushed dust and leaves off the table. Barry put the pizza box down, and we edged onto facing benches. I put a couple more paper towels down for plates, popped the tops off the sodas, and passed one to him. He held it up in a toast.

"To lovely afternoons," he said. "May the face of every good news and the back of every bad news be toward you."

I raised my soda and clunked it against his. "That sounds like one of those Irish things. . . . You know. May the road rise, or fall, or something . . . and may you die in Ireland. Kind of an odd way to bless someone."

He laughed. "Hope the road stays put," he said. "Lots of those Irish toasts sound odd to us. 'May you be in heaven an hour before the Devil knows you're dead.' Or, 'May you live a hundred years with one more to repent.' It's a franker acceptance of mortality than we're used to."

He opened the pizza box and held it out to me. I took a slice and bit into it.

He took one for himself, then set it down. "It hadn't occurred to me before," he said, "but what a culture regards as a blessing must have a lot to do with whatever troubles they've suffered. That 'May you die in Ireland' bit probably has to do with so many Irish having to emigrate."

I tried to look thoughtful and intelligent—not easy with a mouthful of pizza. Swallowing, I said, "I suppose it does. Maybe the Basques in my family had similar sayings."

"Oh, your family's Basque?"

"Half of them," I said. "The other half, obviously, African-American—but I don't have the pleasure of their acquaintance."

Barry snorted. "I have a few relatives whose acquaintance I could dispense with."

"That's what Charlene said," I answered. "But I'm starting to think I might introduce myself."

"Why not?" Barry's tone was easy, unintrusive. "Who has a better right?"

I hadn't looked at it that way before—that I simply had a right to say hello to my father. I had a right to expect him to say hello to me.

"Is your family Irish?" I asked. Dumb question—between his name and his face, what else could he be?

He rolled his eyes. "They're Irish-American. Irish enough to go all-out on St. Paddy's Day. That isn't always a lot—anyone with two drops of Irish blood is Irish on the seventeenth of March. Bet it wasn't that way a hundred years ago."

"No Irish need apply?" I asked.

"Except for railroad work." He laughed and raised the soda can again. "May the roof above us never fall in, and may we friends who are gathered below it never fall out."

"And may you die in Ireland." I raised my own soda and took another slice of pizza. "Besides, there's no roof above us."

Barry squinted toward the house, looming over the yard. "If that's not *above*, I don't know what is."

Dusk drew in as we finished eating. Neither of us was in a hurry to get up when the food was gone. I brushed pizza crumbs from the table, wondering if sparrows would get them. Or ants, trudging along with outsize loads. Maybe a shiny beetle would grab crumbs in its pincers and take them to a nest of baby beetles. Nothing would be wasted.

I pictured the intertwined worlds of the yard, fenceless worlds where "ownership" extended only as far as today's pizza crumb. Family meant nothing to the birds and beetles—they didn't need aunts or fathers. The yard was theirs, not mine—not even Charlene's. If they noticed me at all, they saw me as an intruder.

A hummingbird hovered near the vines on the fence. We watched, nearly motionless, as if trying to hold off the moment it would fly away. And then it did.

"Hummingbirds are funny," I said impulsively. "They don't sing—they really don't do anything. People love them for being hummingbirds."

"That's the only way to be loved," he said. "For being whatever you couldn't help being, even if you tried."

As he glanced at me, his eyes shaded from dark blue to violet in the fading light. Even though it was still warm, I shivered.

"Let's go in," I said.

In the kitchen, Barry was quiet, and I was sure he was waiting for a cue from me. I could say, "Come up to my room," and he would. We'd open the door—supposing I'd shut it—and confront the shambles, the clothes covering every surface. I'd say, "I wanted so badly to look good for you," and we'd laugh together and clear the bed by pushing everything willy-nilly onto the floor.

"Thanks for dinner," I said. "I was getting pretty hungry."

35

I WORKED ON DESIGNS for the lion in the evenings. Even if I'd been able to spare the time during work hours, I couldn't do them at the studio where Barbara could watch. I was sweating bullets, trying to make the design work with hers. What I really wanted was for the lion to upstage her animals, to be the king of the carousel. I rationalized that it was supposed to—it was the lead animal.

Night after night, my color sketches went into a file, probably destined for the trash can. My best sketch was one with nineteenth-century colors, dark and intense. But when I visualized it with Barbara's designs, it faded into a shadow.

I tried a medium shade for the coat color, approximately the same approach that Barbara had used on the other animals. It didn't work. Or rather, it was all right—and that was worse than if it had looked bad. A medium lion wouldn't do. I pictured my lion on the turning carousel, with the other animals somehow passing him, like hotshot drivers on the freeway.

One evening, I sat at my drawing board and did nothing. As far as coming up with a design was concerned, I might as well have gone to a movie. I scratched on my paper with a soft pencil, doodling carousels.

What did it mean, I wondered, for an animal to be the lead animal? Was it only a convenient way to number the rows? I didn't think so. It was no accident that a lion or tiger would always be the lead animal on a menagerie. Even on machines that were all horses, the lead animal was special. Some of the carvers had even signed them.

Well, *my* lion designs weren't lead animals. I didn't feel much like a lead animal myself, for that matter, regardless whose name was on the studio door. Barbara was doing the designs. I couldn't get my friends in Portland to give me a break. I might not make my deadline. I paged once more through my file of sketches. Passing from discouragement to fury, I considered tearing them up, but why bother? Not worth the trouble—they were already dead.

I remembered how I'd asked Charles Looff to help when I'd first seen the carousel. Asked his ghost, anyway, or whatever part of his memory was still hanging around the machine. *If you're going to give me a hand, you'd better slide on out of the hereafter and do it.* I turned off the light and went to bed.

Lying in the dark, I imagined Looff in his studio, his sharpened chisel removing curling ribbons of pale poplar from the half-carved lion. The wood curlicues turned slower and slower, falling silent as snow. Watching them, I became dizzy, falling slowly through the wood spirals. Falling or flying, I couldn't tell.

The animals glide free now, glide through a forest, three abreast like on a carousel, with the lion in the lead. The canopies of trees arch high overhead so the light reaching the ground is greenish. No undergrowth—only ferns for a sort of lawn. In the dim glades, the lion stands out from the others—he is white as fresh poplar wood.

In the morning, the image wouldn't go away, and it seemed to be nudging a memory. Where had I heard of a white lion?

A trip to the public library in Berkeley reminded me: A few white lions had been found in South Africa. There were several books—one told of the discovery, another of the capture of the lions, supposedly to preserve them from predators and hunters. A third book said that the white lions had always been known to indigenous people, and that they were considered sacred. According to this book, they were "children of the sun," sent to earth to enlighten us.

The photographs in the books were breathtaking. The females and cubs were pure white, while the males had a tawny cast, the color of new basswood. All the males had golden manes. I went home and painted a sketch of my lead animal, modeled on the white lions of Timbavati, with trappings of royal purple and gold.

I fairly pranced into the studio with my watercolor pad. Barbara was talking on the office phone when I arrived—if she'd been a cat, her ears would have been back, her fur bristling.

"I have to go," she said into the phone. "See you tonight. Bye."

More trouble with Will, probably. I didn't want to hear about it. Louie came into the office and glanced at Barbara, then quickly away. Probably *he* didn't want to know why she was fuming, either. He turned to me, maybe to ask a question. But I couldn't wait to show them my design.

"Hey, guys, look," I said. I laid my artwork out on the desk.

Louie stopped short. "Wow!"

Barbara was more cautious. "Aren't we going to stick with natural colors?" she asked. "This is beautiful, but there's no such thing as a white lion, is there?"

"Yes, there is," said Louie. "I saw a movie about them."

"Albinos?" Barbara's tone was skeptical.

"No, they're just white," I said. "Or white-*ish,* anyway. They come from Timbavati, in South Africa. One writer says they're sacred."

She looked at the drawings again. "I can see why people might think so."

"I think we should eliminate gold on the trappings, except for his," I said.

"But I've got lots of gold in my designs!" Barbara protested.

"Can we use copper? Or maybe we could make the others a sort of greeny gold, with red gold on the lion."

Barbara considered this. "That should work. But he's a lot lighter than any of my designs. Isn't that going to make him not fit?"

"He's supposed to stand out, since he's the lead animal. That's why I want to make his trappings different. Let's save purple for him, too."

"Why would he stand out, if he's white?" Louie asked. "Wouldn't the ones with more color be the ones to stand out?"

"White always attracts the eye," Barbara told him. "That's why people on television don't wear it. You really see it—it's stronger than anything else."

She fished through the files and pulled out her color studies. I arranged them across the table and set my lion next to them. We all stepped back and looked them over. The lion was perfect. We had our design.

36

FUELED BY OUR VISION, we worked harder that day than we'd ever worked before. When evening came, I was exhausted, but still excited.

I wished I could tell Joy.

On the way home, I drove automatically, making the turns from habit. Between me and the traffic, a carousel danced, tiny improvements in our design flickering like soap bubbles. I pulled up in front of the house and hurried to the door, eager to go over every detail with Charlene.

But the house was locked. I let myself in, still hoping that Charlene was home, even though I knew she couldn't be. With all the windows shut, the tick of the mantel clock filled the front hallway. The rug was perfectly aligned, like a rug in a decorating magazine, and the squatty black telephone sat in the exact center of its shiny stand.

The phone number of St. Martha's popped into my head as if I'd asked Directory Assistance for it. I *could* call Joy—she wouldn't act any different than if we'd talked yesterday. I could talk to her whenever I was ready. And when would I do it, if I didn't do it now? Would I ever? Or maybe I could go on like this forever, and someone would come someday and tell me she'd died.

I touched the phone, then took the receiver off the hook. The dial tone reminded me of a conch shell Joy had once held to my ear. The shell had echoed the sea, unable to speak any language but its mother's.

I called Barry.

As soon as he answered, I started babbling about the design, the white and purple, and that I was the one who had designed the lead animal.

"Whoa," said Barry. "I take it this is Mirai?"

"Well, yes. Sorry to be so incoherent."

"That's okay. I'll know who to call next time the guys win a game."

"Does it happen that seldom?"

"No, fairly often. But I always get excited. So, you're ready to wrap up the painting on the carousel?"

"Not quite. Before we varnish, I have to get the client's approval of what we've done."

"What do you do, send them artwork? Or slides, or what?"

"I'll have to *go* there," I said. "Otherwise, they'll take forever and probably try to improve the design, and it'll be a disaster. It's already October, and we can't afford that kind of delay. I've arranged to meet with the committee on the seventeenth."

"You flying?"

"That's the idea," I said, "though I'm not looking forward to all the flight connections."

"Where in Idaho is Peregrine Falls?"

"South-central, more or less. Why?"

"I need to go up there for an article I'm doing about the forest fire."

"What forest fire?"

Barry laughed. "Guess you've been skipping the newspaper."

"Uh-huh. Among other things."

"There was a bad fire in the Boise National Forest over the summer. I'm doing a series of articles on rebuilding after disasters—actually I'm working on a book. So, I've been meaning to get up there. Why don't we leave on Sunday and drive up together, share expenses?"

I considered what else Barry probably wanted to share.

"Okay," I said.

WHEN I GOT OFF THE PHONE, I felt restless and unfocused. I decided to make dinner for Charlene, not sure if she'd even be home to eat it. Since I hadn't gone to the market in a while, I checked the kitchen to see if there was anything to cook.

As I might have expected, Charlene had the fridge and cupboards fully stocked. I started a chicken roasting and took out a head of romaine for salad. I put it on the cutting board and reached for a knife. But I jerked my hand back, remembering Will had insisted that any kind of lettuce be torn, not cut.

As I started to tear a leaf, I thought how Joy had laughed at the idea that cutting it would make any difference. Again, I stopped.

Cut or tear? Joy wasn't a gourmet cook—she did things the easiest way because she was in the kitchen so much. Will didn't cook at all, just read articles and gave orders to whoever was cooking for him. So, which was likelier to be right—tear or cut?

Why the hell did I care what *either* of them thought?

A wave of anger rushed over me. I was alone, but others were still orchestrating my every move. Was that what Joy had meant when she said that I'd go to extreme lengths to please people? If I couldn't make a salad in my own kitchen without everyone—including Joy—pulling my strings, she was right.

I didn't want to tear the romaine because that would be giving in to Will. And I didn't want to cut it because that would be giving in to Joy. However, unless we were going to gnaw it off its stem, I had to do one or the other.

Or forget the salad. Feeling like a kid having a tantrum, I threw the romaine in the refrigerator and took out a box of frozen peas. I didn't much like peas, but at least no one had ever told me how to cook them.

The breadbox revealed a beautiful round loaf, perfect to toast with garlic butter. I set it on the cutting board and automatically made the sign of the cross over it with the knife. And I pictured the kitchen at St. Martha's, Joy's hands or mine blessing the bread.

Tears rushed to my eyes, and I sat hard on the kitchen stool. Once I started crying, there seemed to be no end in sight, and I didn't care.

Light filled the room with a snap of the switch, and Charlene came in. I hadn't heard the front door over my own noise.

"Mirai, what happened? Did you cut yourself?"

I shook my head. The peas boiled over with a hiss, and Charlene stepped away from me to turn off the stove. I grabbed a paper towel and wiped my nose.

"What's wrong?" she asked again.

"Oh, God, I don't know. Everything."

"Will? Joy?"

"Both of them. Neither. Nothing new—everything sort of caught up with me."

Charlene sized me up. "Tell you what. I'll finish dinner, you go take a hot bath. Better relax in the tub—I'm not giving you any wine this time." She looked into the refrigerator. "Oh, good—a head of romaine. I'll make a salad."

37

Weekend or no weekend, Saturday was a work day. When I agreed to drive to Peregrine Falls with Barry, it had seemed like a great, romantic idea. I hadn't thought how much longer a drive would take—time away from the studio, away from finishing the carousel by Memorial Day next year. Now I realized I was going to have to put in a lot of extra work to make up for it.

I pushed that thought away. I hadn't had a week off for months. And if Barbara was so hot to be an equal—a partner— it was her turn to try managing the place. I wasn't going to let her be equal as a designer and leave all the boring responsibilities to me.

The morning was stifling—without being very hot, it was so still that the air seemed used, almost unbreathable. As I drove to the studio, I could see a quilt of smog covering San Francisco—a sight far from rare but one unlikely to be featured on a postcard.

I snorted at a quick vision of postcard racks filled with reality—pollution, and homeless people, and oil spills. But I had to remind myself not to get too cynical. Without our need to escape, why on earth would anyone pay money to climb onto wooden animals and go round and round?

Besides being a weekend, it was Barbara's birthday. Louie had volunteered to get a cake and a bottle of sparkling apple juice for a lunchtime treat. I hoped he wouldn't forget. He and Barbara had been getting along a lot better, and all I'd need would be for him to blow it on the day before I left town.

At noon, I looked for him to help set up, but he'd disappeared. Feeling put-upon, I lugged the office fan into the old snack bar section of the skating rink. I was so sweaty, my shirt stuck to my back, and I got even more damp as I crawled around on the ragged carpet, arranging the extension cord. The fan was too low to cool anything but my ankles, so I fetched a drafting stool to raise it. Then I set out some paper plates and napkins, with plastic forks and glasses.

Louie came in, clutching a huge potted cactus and a canvas bag. He put the cactus on the table as a centerpiece.

"Louie," I said, "I don't think that should go there."

"Why not? It's got a flower." He pulled a cake box from the canvas bag, carefully as if it might break, and set it beside the flower pot.

"Chocolate," he said, opening the box. "My favorite."

I waited, feeling irritated, as he studiously checked the frosting for damage, delicately lifted out the cake, and replaced the box in his bag.

Barbara appeared from the rest room, improved with fresh makeup and a clean shirt. She slipped into the booth, tossing her head so her hair fanned around her shoulders. Louie's mind seemed a million miles away from everything but that whirl of hair.

"Earth to Louie," I said, "This plant is too big. And someone might get a spine in their hand."

"Why would they do that? Everyone knows you're not supposed to touch a cactus."

"Maybe an accident? Get the other drafting stool for it, would you?"

"Oh. Okay."

He went to the office and returned with the other stool, pulling it behind him with a scrape like chalk on a blackboard. In place of the plant, he set a package wrapped in kids' birthday party paper with purple dinosaurs and red lettering. He'd used nearly a yard of tape and finished the job with a squashed green stick-on bow that was probably left over from Christmas.

I set my shop-wrapped present on top of his, hiding most of the dinosaurs. My gift for Barbara was a book—a copy of one of mine she'd admired. It was a technical work on identifying woods, including a foldout page with samples of dozens of species.

I poured the juice into the plastic wineglasses and cut three slices of cake. After the first line of "Happy Birthday to You," Louie joined me, sounding hoarse and croaky.

Barbara opened my package, laying the ribbon and paper aside as if she might be planning to reuse them. Taking care not to dislodge any of the wood samples, she showed Louie the foldout.

"What's that for?" he asked.

"Examples of different veneers," she said. "You use them to compare to unknown woods. Helps in identifying what you've got. Sometimes they used scraps of who-knows-what."

Louie glanced at the wood samples. "All the animals we have are the same."

"Yeah, we were lucky on this job," Barbara said. "But you can't count on it. Also, you can get an animal that's not original to a carousel. Sometimes the tip-off is that the wood's different." She turned to me. "Thanks, Mirai! I've wanted a copy ever since I saw yours."

She peeled the paper from Louie's gift, revealing the back of a book. When she turned it over, she stared blankly at it: a thick volume about carousel organs.

I was surprised—the book looked expensive, way more than Louie could afford on his pay. And I was puzzled that he'd buy it for Barbara. As far as I knew, she wasn't particularly interested in music machines. Louie hovered while she paged through it, frowning slightly.

"Thanks, Louie," she said. "Now I'll know what Will is saying when he gets started on his shop talk."

Louie's face froze into the kind of smile you get when someone's taking your picture and you wish they wouldn't. Barbara closed the book and tried a bite of cake.

"Pretty good, for chocolate," she said. "Who brought it?"

Louie cleared his throat. "I did."

"Did your mom make it?"

He blinked. "No."

That seemed to take care of the cake. I couldn't think of anything to say, and apparently neither of them could, either. The silence lasted so long, I had to remind myself not to bow my head and think of some worthy cause. Then Louie stood up, backing away from the table.

"What did the carousel horse say to the carousel lion?"

"I give up," I said.

"When you're not the lead animal, the view's always the same."

"I don't get it," Barbara said.

"It's a joke about sled dogs," he said. "When you're not the lead *dog*, the view's always the same."

"But a carousel's a circle," she objected. "The view would always be the same anyway."

"At least the lead animal is right behind the chariot," I said. "It wouldn't be looking at another animal's ass."

She shrugged. "It's still the same."

Louie hovered between the table and his stand-up comedian spot. "So, a carousel zebra meets a giraffe from another carousel in a bar. 'How's it going?' the zebra asks."

He was interrupted by a ringing sound. I got up to answer the doorbell, but the noise was coming from Barbara's purse. She opened it and grabbed a cellular phone, fumbling with its buttons.

"Hello!" She yelled like a kid with a walkie-talkie made from an orange juice can and waxed string. "No, we're at lunch! Mirai and Louie fixed a party!"

She smiled apologetically around the phone, and we waited, silent, like we were waiting to hear news of someone's surgery.

"I don't know! I'll ask!" She put her hand over the mouthpiece and turned to me. "Will wants to take me out for my birthday. Mind if I take the afternoon off?"

"Go ahead," I told her.

"I'll be there in fifteen minutes!" She stuffed the phone into her purse and pulled out a compact.

"Where'd you get the phone?" I asked.

"Present from Will," she said. She checked her face in her mirror and rubbed a smudged place on her lipstick. "Gotta go!"

"Don't forget your books!" Louie called as she hurried out. He picked them up, but dropped the band organ one with a bang. As Barbara turned, Louie barged into the stool where I'd perched the fan. He grabbed for it, but connected instead with the cactus.

"Goddamn son of a bitch!" Louie yelled. He bent over, his undamaged hand clutching the wrist of the other one.

Barbara wavered for a moment, her hand stretched toward the doorknob.

"I'll take care of it," I said. The door closed behind her. I pried Louie's hand open and led him into the office, where we kept the first aid kit.

He was near tears as I tweezed the first spines from his hand. Maybe he was in pain, but I suspected it was mostly humiliation. He didn't say, and I didn't ask.

"So, what did the giraffe say?" I asked as I finished the tweezers work.

"Giraffe?"

"When the zebra asked him how things were going."

"He said, 'Up and down, buddy. Up and down.'"

38

WE FINISHED THE DAY with a minimum of conversation. I figured Louie would probably prefer to be quiet for a while. He had a few things to get over, his injured hand being the least of them.

I'd intended to quit early, but we had to work late to make up for Barbara's short day. Not long before seven, we dragged ourselves out onto the sidewalk. It was dusk, with a quarter moon hanging in the sky.

"You need a ride home?" I asked.

"No."

He walked away into the twilight. I didn't think he was seriously upset, so I didn't call after him. I drove home, glad I wasn't part of the Saturday night traffic on the Nimitz Freeway.

I parked in front of Charlene's house and sat in the van for a while, too tired to go inside and face my chore list. My presentation for the committee was ready, but I still had to do laundry and pack for the trip—business suits for my meetings, and Victoria's Secret skivvies for my nights with Barry. The combination sounded like the perfect getup for a kinky film.

Trying to picture Barry as a porn star made me laugh like a fool, until a dark figure at the window made me jump.

"You okay, miss?"

A bicycle cop. Jesus.

"Yes," I said. "A comedian on the radio cracked me up. I'm okay. I live here, so I'll go inside now."

Apparently satisfied that I wasn't drunk, high, or nuts, he stood back as I got out and locked the van.

"Bit safer to have your fun indoors," he said. "Take care."

"Thanks."

I went into the house and closed the front door softly. The fussy tones of television news filtered into the foyer.

"Mirai?" Charlene called.

"No, it's the Marquis de Sade."

"Great," she said. "I *love* older men. *Do* come in."

I did. "What're you watching?"

"News." She moved to one side of the couch, and I sat down, struggling to make sense of the commentator's sentence.

"—Greek ship carrying meat believed to be contaminated by radiation from Chernobyl was refused entry to the port of Lagos, Nigeria. This follows controversy over the export to various African countries of grain believed to be contaminated with radiation, and refusal by Pakistan of a Dutch shipment of powdered milk, for similar reasons."

"My God—they're selling *radioactive food?*" The end of the sentence came out in a sort of squawk.

Keeping her eyes on the screen, Charlene held up her hand and rubbed her fingers together in the classic gesture for venality.

"Who would *want* food that glows in the dark?" I asked.

Charlene snorted. "It's the latest thing—helps you find your breakfast on a winter morning. Besides, 'snap, crackle, and pop' is so passé."

A thought struck me. "What do you suppose happened to food that was contaminated by the Nevada tests?"

"I think it got sold to Pakistan and Nigeria, maybe to you and me. What do you think?"

"I'm not going to."

"Joy says plutonium contamination was found in Nevada groundwater only a couple of years ago," Charlene said.

I popped up like a jack-in-the-box. "I'd better do laundry," I said.

Once I'd started a load, I couldn't make up my mind what to do next. Packing had to wait until at least one load was finished and dried. I didn't want to go to the living room and listen to CBS pick over the troubles of the world. I wasn't hungry, but I decided to go out for dinner anyway. Maybe after a walk, I'd be ready to eat.

I plodded along, thinking about radioactive food, nuclear weapons. The way I had it figured, there was far too much variation in human beings. It took a genius to discover radioactivity, but any damn fool could set off a bomb. Unfortunately, we had both.

Estebe had left Nevada to get away from the bomb tests—or had he? The dates didn't line up. He'd been worried about the tests before I was born, but he hadn't left until about the time Joy and I moved to Oakland. Why had he waited so long? Nuclear fallout wasn't a problem *I'd* shilly-shally about.

Far more depressed than hungry, I studied the menu in the front window of a coffee shop. I didn't want anything on it, but I went in anyway. If I was going to have dinner, I'd better get it over with and get home to finish my laundry and packing.

When the waitress came with a menu, I ordered a glass of iced tea and a tuna sandwich. She brought the tea right away, and I took a few sips, then pressed the glass against the side of my face. Somehow, its cool comfort made me feel worse about everything, from Louie to Chernobyl. A knot rose into my throat, and I knew there was no way I could eat a thing.

I grubbed in my pocket, found a ten-dollar bill—far more than the cost of my dinner—and dropped it onto the table. Without checking to see whether the waitress even noticed, I left.

It must have been habit that led me up the hill to St. Martha's. I stood for a few minutes on the dark sidewalk, just looking. They'd be at the table now, the guests, the volunteers, and Joy—or to use her real name, Nekane. Nekane, Dolores, Grief.

From the time I was a child, I had walked up the front path thousands of times. I'd crossed the patio and turned the doorknob. Now, staring at the hunk of brass on the door, I couldn't recall its feel against my palm. I couldn't believe I'd ever touched it—it was the knob of a stranger's door.

And my hand—it was a scientific fact that every cell in it, even in the bones, was different from when I was a child. It was not the same hand that had opened that door every day after school, not the hand that had held so tight to Joy's, Christmas shopping that day in San Francisco.

I drew a ragged breath and screwed my face up tight to keep back the tears. Not wanting my buddy the bicycle cop to catch me acting strange twice in one evening, I turned and went home.

Part 6

39

It was close to midnight when I finished packing. Since there was nothing to do but go to bed, I turned out the light. I lay still in the darkness, mentally replaying my troubles over and over like a tape loop.

I didn't want to go over all my grudges against Joy, but there were plenty more to choose from. I was mad at so many people, it was hard to keep track. Matt, Ben, and Susan at Portland Carousel Works, for not giving me a break on the price of restoring the extra animals. Barbara, for a dozen things in the past six months—the birthday party was only the latest.

What *was* it about Barbara, anyway? Why did men fall all over her? And Louie—what made *him* get a crush on her? He had to be ten years younger than Barbara. And unless she'd changed her mind, she didn't even *like* Louie. But that was guys, always wanting what they couldn't have.

I didn't get to sleep for hours, and I woke up later than I'd planned. Barry was due in a few minutes. Standing at the refrigerator, I bolted breakfast—a stale bagel and an apple. Then I raced upstairs to dress. Several days ago, I'd picked out clothes to wear this morning—in fact, I'd bought some of them for the occasion. He'd better be impressed—though not right away, since I felt pretty tired from my bad night.

He came right on time to pick me up, cheerful as always. It was the "as always" part that bugged me, and even though I knew I was in a bad mood, I felt a jolt that told me I was onto something real and fair. Barry was always kind, always smiling. But he must have a dark side—everyone did.

I thought it over as he helped me put my luggage in the trunk. I got in the car, and he drove along the nearly deserted streets of my neighborhood's Sunday. The sun wasn't quite up, and the city matched my mood—it was as gray as if a thin layer of paint had been poured over it during the night.

But if that had happened, it must have been while Barry was somewhere else. He was anything but gray-looking. He whistled as he merged onto the freeway, and smiled when he caught my eye. At that moment, he seemed the nicest man in the world. But the last thing I needed was to get close to someone like Joy, someone who pretended to be all good—and then surprised me.

"You're looking happy." I kept my voice as neutral as I could.

"Sure, now," he said, laying on a corny brogue, "an' why wouldn't I be happy, with yourself beside me?"

"Quit joking, could you? I really want to know why you always seem to be up."

His face went serious. "You haven't known me that long. And you really attract me, so I'm probably on my best behavior."

"That's it—what I want to know is, what's your *worst* behavior?"

"You think someone who's attracted to you would tell the truth about that?"

Actually, I did. One of the things I'd learned was that most people described their faults, or showed them plainly, very early in a relationship. The trick was to pay attention. But I didn't want to say that in so many words.

"Give it a shot," I said. "That way, I can't complain I haven't been warned."

"Well, I'm not the most patient person in the world. I can be self-righteous when I get on one of my crusades. I have a temper." He looked like he was trying to think of more, but he'd apparently run out. "So, what are *your* besetting sins? Fair's fair, you know."

"Anger," I said. "And holding grudges. I guess I'm down because I walked by St. Martha's last night."

"What's wrong over there?"

"Nothing I know of—but you know I haven't spoken to Joy for weeks."

I couldn't keep the bitter tone out of my voice. Barry's head turned quickly toward me, then back to watch the road.

"No, I didn't know. How did *that* happen?" he asked. "Last I heard, you were getting along fine."

"Joy really dropped a bomb on me. She told me she's my real aunt—I always thought I was adopted."

Barry looked puzzled. "So, she's your real aunt—what's so awful about that?"

"She lied to me all my life. That's the part I can't get over. I can't believe I didn't tell you this."

He braked as a pickup cut in front of him. I'd probably have been cussing, but Barry didn't show any signs of the temper or impatience he'd claimed as faults.

"Well, you *didn't* tell me. But I'm sure you'll work it out. Wait till you meet *my* family—classic case of can't live with 'em, can't live without 'em. I bet they're a lot stranger than Joy."

"Oh, I have tons of other weird stuff. I know my grandfather didn't want me because I'm black, and Charlene has a theory that my father killed my mother."

"That really would be weird. But it's Charlene's theory—do you know anything to make you think she could be right?"

"All I know is that his name is Alex Bowman. And that he was a professor at UNR. Of course, that was over twenty-five years ago. He's probably moved on by now."

Barry drove silently for a few miles. When he finally spoke, he kept his eyes on the road ahead.

"We'll be getting to Reno this afternoon," he said. "If he's still there, you might call and ask him to tell you his side of the story."

40

"Mirai."

The voice at the other end of the phone sounded pretty faint to be coming from anywhere close. I felt a surprise stab of disappointment—up till then, I'd been telling myself I didn't care if I saw him or not.

"Where are you?" I asked.

"I was going to ask you the same thing."

"I'm at a gas-station pay phone somewhere off I-80. Where are you? You sound kind of far away."

Alex cleared his throat. "I'm at home. Well, you know that. You called me."

"But I have no idea where that is."

"You *don't*?"

"No, I didn't even know if the listing in the phone book was the right Alex Bowman." I was getting more confused by the second.

"Why would you need to get my number from the phone book?"

"It's where I generally get numbers I don't know."

He took a deep breath. "This doesn't make sense. Joy has my number and my address. I told her I'd never move without giving her the new information."

"I didn't know that," I said. "Look, I don't know anything about what you might have told Joy. The first time I heard of you was about two months ago."

There was dead silence on the other end. "Hello?"

"I'm sorry, Mirai, I'm having a little trouble processing this. . . . If you hadn't heard of me, who did you think your father was?"

"I didn't have a clue. I thought Mama adopted me."

"Oh, shit," he said, sounding distant again. Tired. "The old lie, huh? Thought that was just for her father's benefit. That's what she's been telling you all along. Shit."

I remembered what the kids in school used to say—"Not here, it draws flies." It didn't seem like a good moment to repeat it.

"I was sort of hoping we could get together," I said. "I know it's short notice, but are you available?"

"Yes," he said. "I'm available." I didn't miss the irony in his tone.

"Would you like to meet somewhere?" I asked. "I mean, I don't want to barge in on your family or anything."

"No reason not to come to the house. There's only my wife and I, and she's out."

I grabbed a scrap of paper out of my purse and scrawled his directions.

"He says it's a couple of miles from here," I told Barry. "You can come with me if you want to, or you can do something else for a while."

"I think I'll tag along, if it's okay with you," he said.

I didn't remind him that Alex might have killed my mother, and he didn't remind me.

When we pulled into the driveway, Alex was standing in the front doorway. He might have been eager to see me, or maybe he was barring the way to his home. He was a tall, thin black man with short gray hair. I didn't remember him at all.

He smiled as we came up the walk.

"Alex—Dad—this is Barry Donovan," I said.

"You didn't come to announce an engagement, did you?" he asked, extending a hand for Barry to shake.

I was about to say no, but Barry broke in. "Actually, we did."

I blinked. I had no choice but to play along. I guessed Barry was establishing some sort of right to be in on a family conference, but it made me uneasy as hell. Alex looked like he'd won the lottery—what was I going to say when I had to tell him it wasn't going to happen? Or worse, if he found out we'd lied?

"Come in, come in," Alex said, shooing us through the entry hall.

We sat in the living room, making small talk for a while. I told him Joy was fine, although I had no idea how she was doing. That I'd never visited Paradise Meadow, never even been to Reno before. That the weather had been awfully dry lately, and global warming was probably to blame.

While I was saying these—and other—inanities, I looked around. The house was big, and the living room was well furnished. But it was strangely sterile-looking—not only super clean like Charlene's place, but also impersonal. It looked like no one lived there, no one cared.

"So, tell me your plans," Alex said. "Have you set a wedding date?"

"June 2," Barry told him, straight-faced. "We came to invite you. Of course, it'll be in California."

"I'll get there. Would you guys like a cup of coffee? If I'd known you were coming, I'd have bought champagne, but I guess we'll have other chances."

"Coffee's fine," I said. In fact, coffee would be great. I was feeling drained. When Alex left the room, I glared at Barry. In return, he blew me a kiss, like a good fiancé. I could have throttled him.

I waited impatiently while the coffeemaker gurgled noisily in the kitchen. It occurred to me that Alex might be scurrying around back there, throwing together a batch of cookies, and I had to stifle a fit of the giggles. When he finally brought the coffee tray, there was a small white box alongside the cups.

"I wondered if the two of you would want this," he said, offering it to me. When I opened it, I found the most beautiful ring I'd ever seen, a thin gold band with a high-set round diamond that threw a carousel of rainbows around the room.

"I bought it for your mother," Alex said, a catch in his voice. "It was going to be *our* engagement ring. I never got to give it to her."

"Joy told me Mama was talking about getting married," I said. "But I'm confused. Weren't you married already?"

"In a way. Fay was divorcing me. She dropped the action after your mother died."

"And you're still married to her?" I asked.

"She had a breakdown around the time she dropped the divorce. She needed me, and Zuzene didn't anymore." He hesitated. "It sounds shabby—I know it does. But I never had an affair before I met your mother, and I never did again. Fay was my high school sweetheart—we married when we were in our teens. But what I felt for Zuzene is the love you only get once. I'd really like you to have her ring."

I stood, still holding the ring in its box, and gave him an awkward hug. I didn't especially want to hug him, but it beat looking for something to say. After a moment, he held me at arm's length, studying my face.

"Mirai," he said, "I've probably thought about you every day since you and Joy moved to California, wondered who you were turning into, what you were doing. I promised Joy I'd leave the two of you alone, and I did, but it was hard. She wouldn't even take money from me, and I know she sometimes needed it.

"I guess I could have looked you up once you were grown, but by then I was afraid you didn't want to see me. It never occurred to me that you didn't know I existed. Now that you've found me, I hope I'll see more of you."

"What about your wife?" I asked.

"I don't know," he said. "I guess I'll find out."

41

"I DON'T THINK HE killed her," Barry said, merging onto the freeway.

"I am going to kill *you,*" I answered. "I'm sure I can think of a really painful way to do it, if I put my mind to it. What in hell possessed you to tell him we were engaged?"

"He suggested it. I would never have thought of anything so brilliant."

"If that's brilliant, you're a . . . giant green frog."

"*Ribbit.* Kiss me quick, and I'll turn into a prince."

I drew a deep breath and held it—the only alternative to screaming. After a few seconds, I let it out. "Can we at least be serious?"

"Look, Mirai, neither of us knew your father, and if someone killed your mother, it might have been him. I couldn't let you walk into that alone. On the other hand, he wasn't likely to tell you what you wanted to know in front of some looky lou. He solved the problem himself by assuming I had a right to be there. I went along with his solution."

"So, the Devil made you do it."

"No, I took a good opportunity in a crappy situation."

"Sorry to involve you in my crappy reunion with my father."

"It *was* your idea that he might have killed your mother."

That notion now seemed embarrassingly melodramatic. "All I said was that he could have. There wasn't any reason for you to get involved."

"Probably not." Barry's voice was infuriatingly patient, even pleasant. "At the time, it looked like there was. And you didn't have any objection."

"I didn't know you were going to pull that fiancé act. You're as bad as Charlene."

"Did she pretend to be engaged to you?"

"No, she talked me into . . . . Oh, never mind." He'd probably think the way I'd set up Will was sexy. Better not go into it.

Barry was quiet for several minutes, attention on his driving as if he were in the middle of a city. But the freeway was nearly empty, and the scenery stretched out on both sides as monotonous as our quarrel.

Finally, he glanced my way. "I can't say I'm sorry, because I'd do it again. I *am* sorry it bothered you, if that's any help," he said.

I figured I'd better shut up altogether. Just the same, I was pissed. Speaking of faults, Barry seemed to have some unsuspected talents in the direction of barefaced lying. On the other hand, if his charade for Alex was lying, what about the stunt I'd pulled on Will? *Takes one to know one, Mirai.*

I leaned against the door and pretended to nap. *One more lie,* I thought—and then fell asleep.

When I returned to the land of the living, it was to find we had stopped at a light. I looked blankly at a freeway village of hotels and chain restaurants.

"Where are we?" I asked.

"A couple hours away from Peregrine Falls. We can get dinner here, maybe stay over. What do you think?"

It wasn't evening yet, but the afternoon light was tired and flat, like overexposed film. The day wouldn't last much longer.

"Fine with me," I said.

We picked the least awful-looking of the hotel coffee shops, and did the best we could with the menu. It still wasn't a meal I'd want to repeat.

After dinner, I looked myself over in the restaurant's ladies' room. It was a great place for self-criticism—mirrors lined all the walls except in the toilet compartments. Maybe Barry was directly opposite me now, gazing into the mirror in the men's room and wondering what in hell *he* was doing and why. Maybe the mirror would disappear, and the wall. And we'd be looking into each other's real eyes.

Real eyes . . . realize. Shit, I was getting dippy. Maybe that glass of wine hadn't been a good idea. I leaned over the sink and splashed cold water on my face. But I knew it wouldn't help. The problem wasn't one glass of wine. What was hanging me up was that I didn't know what to do about Barry. Everything had been going fine, and then I'd watched him scam Alex, and I didn't feel especially good about him.

But I knew damn well he was expecting me to make love to him. We'd check into the hotel—I'd insist on separate rooms—and pretty soon, he'd phone and ask if he could visit me. There he'd be, tippy-tapping on my door, showered, shaved, and ready for action.

Years ago, I knew, sex had been a no-no. Now it seemed to be mandatory, and I wondered if there'd been any in-between time when sleeping with your date was optional. It must not have lasted long, or I'd have heard about it. Maybe it was only ten minutes or so, and no one noticed.

My reflections in the facing mirrors repeated with mathematical precision, presumably to some vanishing point. I leaned closer, trying to see how in hell I could possibly attract Barry so much. I got no clues. Short, skinny, tired-looking. I didn't look like a model. I didn't look like anyone special at all.

I backed up and shrugged at my image, watching it shrug in agreement. "All the children are above average," I told it.

A woman exiting a toilet compartment gave me a funny look. *She* looked like a model, tanned and trim, with straight blonde hair down to her heinie. I considered introducing her to Barry but couldn't figure out a way to suggest it to her.

With another quick glance my way, she left without washing her hands.

UPSTAIRS, IN MY SEPARATE ROOM, I showered and dressed in my sexiest skivvies, thinking how much I'd like to spend the evening alone. But when the phone rang, I answered it.

"Mirai?" Barry, of course.

"Uh-huh?"

"Can I come see you?"

I wasn't in the mood to make love to him, but telling him no felt like more trouble than it was worth.

"Uh-huh." I made it sound inviting—not that I thought it was necessary. We hung up. I imagined him pushing the elevator button over and over, trying to make it get there faster.

See me. Right. My annoyance rose to a new height. Maybe I could work out a striptease routine and let him look, and that's all.

Except I knew I wouldn't. As Joy had said, I went too far to please people. And this was about as far as it got.

I had a flash of fury—and then a strange idea occurred to me: If Barry was so set on having sex, he had damn well better make it worth my while. It was up to *him* to please *me,* not the other way around.

That was a new idea. I waited in the dark, smiling in anticipation.

42

"I DON'T THINK WE OUGHT to go that way," said Angelo. Or Tom. One of the restoration committee men, anyway.

I shifted in my chair—I was still sore from the night before. "What's the problem?" I asked.

He leaned forward, gesturing toward my carousel renderings taped to the conference room walls.

"They're all different," he continued. "In a way, it's the same as when they were painted rainbow colors—they don't look like a set. They look like any old herd of animals.

"When my wife and I went to Disneyland, we took the grandkids to the carousel. And every one of the horses was painted white. Like the guys in the white hats, or the prince on the white horse. White for the good guys, get it?"

Regina gave him a horrified look. "Well, Tom, I really don't think . . . ." She cast me a nervous glance. The faces of the other committee members were registering variations of shock and embarrassment. I guess they expected me to jump up and sing "We Shall Overcome," or "Carry it On."

Keeping a straight face was a real challenge.

"I think we agreed," I said, "to keep the treatment historical. Your suggestion would definitely come under the heading of redesign. Supposing that I were willing to undertake the assignment at all, it would involve extra charges and extra time."

"I don't see why," said Tom. "Wouldn't it be easier to paint them all white?"

"Not really," I said. "I'd have to redesign the trappings and redo some of the primer coats. And I might not want to put my name on a Disney-copy carousel at all."

"Why not?" said Tom. "Disneyland is a big, big tourist attraction. I'd think it would be a real plus to have a carousel like theirs."

One of the women spoke up. "Tom, painting the carousel white is hardly going to turn Peregrine Falls into Anaheim. I think it would look terrible."

"Well, I think it would look great," said Tom.

The woman shook her head. "It's not the same—"

Tom interrupted. "If it's good enough for Walt Disney, it's good enough—"

More voices joined the argument. To get their attention, I stood. It worked—the babble subsided.

"Actually," I said, "When Disney bought his carousel, it was natural colors, and he kept it that way. The horses were painted white ten years ago, long after his death."

Tom raised his hand like a grammar school kid, itching to get the floor. Ignoring him, I continued.

"I do need to tell you that I probably couldn't go on with the work if you decide to paint all the animals white. Of course, our contract contains provisions for cancellation—what you're required to pay, and what I'm required to do, and so on." I paused to let that sink in. "Maybe the committee would like to debate the issue privately and let me know your decision?"

They stole glances at each other, looking for cues. Finally, Regina said, "That sounds like a good idea, Mirai. I'll call you later."

I shook hands with each of them and left the room.

Back at the Clown Motel, I called Barbara.

"Oh, for God's sake!" she said, when I'd explained about the committee. "What now?"

"Keep going. We're responsible for meeting the deadline unless and until they cancel the contract. How's it going, anyway?"

"Tight. I don't know if we're going to make it or not. Louie's hand is infected where he had the cactus spines in it. He's slowed way down. And . . . Will's making problems again."

"Is he having trouble finishing the band organ?"

"No, he's done, or almost. But he's on a tear. He got pissed off about that book Louie gave me for my birthday."

"Why?"

"I guess it's an expensive book. I didn't know that, but of course he did, since it's about band organs. Now he thinks I must be getting it on with Louie, and he's picking me up every afternoon after work like some kind of warden."

"Louie probably doesn't even notice him."

"Will makes sure he does. He comes in and waits."

"So, go out and wait for him."

"I did. He went in anyway and got Louie to come out and admire his damn car. His "1964½ Mustang.""

"Sounds like a couple of dogs pissing on a fire hydrant. But now he's shown off his car, maybe you can wait outside. He won't go in to get Louie again, probably."

"Maybe. He decided Louie must have given me the wood identification book too, and he pulled all the chips out of their pockets and threw them on the floor."

"Jesus, Barbara. Is he nuts? My copy's in the office. Go ahead and use it as a guide for putting yours back together."

"He's also calling me every two minutes. This damn cell phone has turned into a leash."

"Lose it," I said.

"Can't do that, he'd only buy another. And they cost a fortune."

"Can't you turn it off?"

"I suppose I could."

But . . . but . . . but . . . . Barbara hadn't said that part, and she didn't need to. I'd heard it all before, from most of the women I knew. Hell, I'd *said* it all before—first complaints, then excuses.

"I have no use for Will's games, okay? Make me the bad guy if you have to, but don't let him keep you from getting your work done. And don't let him make trouble with Louie. Wait for Will on the sidewalk, and leave the damn phone on the desk in the office. You'll be in the paint room—you probably won't even hear it. Leave it on the desk and forget it."

She sighed. I knew she was thinking of a dozen reasons why not.

"Tell him I made you do it. Tell him I said I'd call that phone and you'd better not answer. Make me the bad guy, but get that carousel done. I mean it, Barb." If she was going to be a partner, she'd better learn to act like a professional. I made a mental note to tell her that, if this sort of bullshit came up again.

I made her give me the phone number. I had no intention of calling it, but I wrote it down anyway.

"How's it going for you, apart from our client?" she asked. "How's Barry?"

"He's gone to check out a forest fire site for a story he's doing. Up in the mountains—toward Lowman, if that means anything to you. He's flying to California from there, and *I'm* taking his car on a side trip to Paradise Meadow."

"You guys have a fight?"

"No, that's what he came up here to do. I'll tell you later. Right now, I'm stuck in Peregrine Falls till the committee makes up its mind, so I'm counting on you to keep the work on track."

She didn't ask why I was going to Paradise Meadow if the schedule was so tight.

After we hung up, I took a shower and washed my hair. Packing my stuff took only a few minutes, and then there was nothing to do. I was hungry, but I didn't want to leave the room for long enough to get lunch, so I dashed out to the lobby and loaded up on junk food. Maybe a cell phone wasn't such an extravagance after all. If I wasn't tied to the phone, I could be sitting in a good restaurant, supposing one existed in Peregrine Falls.

I trotted back to my room, leaving the door open to let in some fresh air, and laid out my disgusting feast on the table with a flourish.

"The filet of Hershey Bar," I announced to myself, "topped with a soupçon of year-old salted peanuts a la Planter's. Fricassee of stale granola bar with potato chips à la carte. And from our cellars, Diet Pepsi 1989. Aged for weeks in sparkling stainless steel!

"And the dessert . . . . Ah, the dessert! Nothing less than the *spécialité de la maison*! Pink Sno Balls wrapped in the finest cellophane! *Magnifique!*"

As I whisked the chair away from the table, I noticed a woman staring at me from the walkway. "Don't mind me," I said, "I'm talking to my pet cobra."

She backed away hastily, and I closed the door. Nibbling a few peanuts, I looked up entreatingly at the absent woman. "But he's wearing his clown suit to match the decor. Sure you don't want to meet him? He adores new people."

WHEN REGINA CALLED ME, she was apologetic.

"I don't know what got into Tom," she said. "I mean, he's a lawyer, for heaven's sake. Or he was, before he retired. Why he got the idea he could redesign the carousel, I'll never know."

"I think I do," I said. "Design looks like fun, and he doesn't understand that it takes years of training to do it above coloring-book level. How'd you talk him out of it, anyway?"

"I didn't try. I reminded him what you said about the cost of starting over. He still thinks you should do it his way, but he *can* read a contract. The rest of us *love* your design, by the way. It's gorgeous. I can hardly wait to see it finished."

"Thanks. So, we're cleared to do the finish painting?"

"Yes. . . . By the way, I do hope Tom's comments didn't . . . . I mean, I don't think he intended . . . ."

I figured she'd flounder for another couple of minutes if I didn't interrupt.

"No," I said. "I didn't take it personally."

On your marks, get set, go! I was out of there. I pretended I was leaving for good.

43

I DROVE INTO PARADISE MEADOW a few minutes before sunset. Joy had never said exactly where Estebe's hotel had been or if it was still standing—and even if I found it, there wouldn't be anyone there for me to talk to. But she'd mentioned an old friend at the rectory of St. Ignatius Church. I decided to start there.

I swerved into a gas station and filled the tank. When I went inside to pay, I asked the cashier for directions.

"St. Ignatius?" he said. "They're a couple of blocks away. But they don't have services there hardly at all anymore. The Episcopal church might be open."

"I didn't want to go to a service," I said. "I'm doing research on my family."

"You want to talk to the Mormons in Reno for that." He counted my change into my hand. "My mom looked up all her family. She meant to go all the way to Salt Lake to see what they knew, but then she passed away."

"It's not exactly genealogy. I'm looking for a friend."

"The old priest? He retired, but they never got anyone else. I think he still lives there, right by the church. Brick house, off to the left."

When I found the place, an old woman answered my knock.

"Are you Garaze?" I asked. "I'm Joy San Julian's niece, Mirai."

She stood stock-still for a second, looking confused. Then she held the door wide. "Come in and have a seat. How's your aunt? It was so nice to see her again last month, even though it was a sad occasion."

"Joy's fine. She mentioned that she'd stayed with you while her friend was in the hospital."

I stepped into a clean, shabby living room—shades of tan, as if the wind had blown the desert in. Brown curtains drooped at the windows, and a few plastic plants in plastic pots sat on shiny, rickety looking tables—maybe those were plastic, too. Desert-colored upholstered furniture was arranged for socializing, but the room didn't feel like it had seen a guest for years. An archway led to a dining room that seemed full of junk, and beyond that was a narrower archway to an unlit hall.

I sat on the couch, and Garaze took a seat in a chair nearby. She smiled. "I remember you—of course I do. But you were a little girl, the last I saw you."

I didn't recall her, but I smiled and nodded. "Joy was so pleased to see you again," I said. "I had some business up this way, and I thought I'd come by and say hello."

"It's very nice to see you again, dear. What kind of business are you in?"

"I restore old carousels. I've been working on the one in Peregrine Falls, Idaho."

"Well, now, isn't that interesting! My brother and I used to visit relatives over in Farmington in the summers and ride the merry-go-round there. I wonder if they still have it."

"Yes," I said. "It's still there, still running. Are you from Farmington?"

"Oh, no," she said. "My family has lived *here* for generations. I've been with Father Heguy since I was a young girl."

"I was hoping I could talk to him," I said. "I've been wondering about my family—we moved to California so soon after Mama died. I don't know anything about them. Is he in?"

"He's always in," she said. "But he's not well. Maybe I can help? I knew your family well."

"Joy's father—"

"Garaze!" A voice called from another room.

She didn't get up, only turned toward the doorway and called back. "Yes, Father?"

"Did you see her?"

"No, Father." She turned back to me, shrugging. "He doesn't mean you. He asks me that a hundred times a day. His memory's gone."

"Who's he asking about?"

"He doesn't know. So, anyway, about Estebe?"

"They told him I was adopted, but I wasn't."

"He knew that. I heard him."

I was stunned. "When was that?"

"Right before he went to Spain."

"Garaze!" the priest called again.

"Just a minute," she said to me. She got up stiffly and left the room.

I wanted to scream. Instead, I walked to the window and looked out. Another tired evening in a small desert town, nothing to see. I sat on the couch again and waited.

"Sorry," Garaze said, as she came back. "He's always restless after sundown. Where were we?"

"Estebe came to see Father Heguy before he left for Spain?"

"That's right. He didn't have an appointment or anything, as far as I knew. He turned up at the door one night, saying he'd come to say good-bye. Which surprised me, since I hadn't known he was going anywhere."

"What did you do?"

"I got Father and went back to the kitchen. I could hear every word—well, you can see for yourself there's no door to shut." She fidgeted in the chair, adjusting her skirt over her knees. "It wasn't confession, you know," she said. "Father heard those in the church."

"No way you could keep from hearing if he was right here in your living room," I agreed. Most likely she knew every secret in town. I imagined her pressed against the wall with a drinking glass to her ear. Or maybe that hadn't been necessary. "So, what did he say?"

"I didn't get the first part," she said. "But in a few minutes, Father told him to go with God, which is what he said to all the ones who went to the old country. I didn't hear any more for a minute or two, and I thought the old man had left, but then I heard him sobbing, big dry-heave sort of sobs."

"If he was that upset about going, why didn't he stay?"

She shook her head and fiddled with her skirt again. Her eyes flicked to mine, then away, scanning her dull little room.

"I never did tell any of the things I heard here," she said. "But I guess your grandfather's long gone. He was an old man then, and it was years and years ago."

"He died the year after he went to Spain," I said.

"And your mother—she'd been dead for a few months when he left. And he"—she nodded toward the dark hallway—"he's past caring anymore."

I kept quiet, hoping her scruples would turn my way. Finally she looked up at me. I didn't actually hear her sigh, but her whole body seemed to do just that, to deflate a bit. She slumped in her chair, hands on her knees.

"I guess you have a right to know," she said. "I never said a word—but that didn't mean I forgot."

"So, he was crying about going back to Spain?" I prompted.

"It wasn't that. He'd been talking to her, to your mother, that night in the desert. And he'd pushed her. That's what he told Father. He said he ran away from her then, but he never thought he'd hurt her."

"But then he thought he had?"

"He'd heard a loud neigh as he ran to his truck. He was too upset to think much of it then, but afterwards he figured she'd fallen back against the horse. They'll strike out, you know, if you scare them."

I closed my eyes and covered them with my fingertips, as if I could keep the scene from happening, even now.

"The night he came here was a couple of months after that," she said. "He'd decided to go to Spain, and he wanted to set it up for Joy to take you away."

I had no idea what she was talking about. "For Joy to take *me* away?"

"Well, I'm sure you know your aunt was studying to be a teacher with the Ursulines. She hadn't taken her vows yet, though. She was still in Missoula."

I didn't let on that Joy's plans to become a nun surprised me. It figured, in a way, but it was one more damn secret about herself she hadn't told. Still and attentive, I waited for her to go on.

"Estebe made Father Heguy persuade your aunt to take you somewhere else. He and Joy weren't on speaking terms at that point, so he got Father to talk to her. He said his grandchild wasn't going to grow up so close to the radiation from the testing. He had kind of a bee in his bonnet about it."

"But how did he know I was his real grandchild?" I said, confused. "They'd told him I was adopted."

"Well, that was why he had the fight with your mother," she said. "She told him the adoption story had been a lie—that you were hers, and that your father was going to divorce his wife and marry her. That's when Estebe pushed her—he called her a name and pushed her away."

Pushed her into the horse. And drove off. Maybe she lay there, watching his taillights dwindle to red specks.

"Thank you for telling me," I said. Feeling completely empty, I stood up to leave, but Garaze stayed in her chair.

"Everyone was surprised when he left," she said. "He'd always laughed at the ones who went to Spain. Father knew why he was going, of course, and I knew, but both of us could keep a secret."

"Does Father Heguy still remember?"

"I doubt it. He's been retired for a couple of years, and all this was coming on for a while before that. He got forgetful, and he sometimes said things that didn't make sense. One Sunday, he put the Host on a man's tongue, and he said, clear as you please, 'Good doggie!'"

"Oh, no." I was shocked, but I wanted to laugh too. I forced my mind away from it—the last thing I wanted was to be offensive about her trouble. "What happened then?"

"Someone must have complained, and the Bishop came and they closed the church. It's a mission now. One Sunday a month, they come out from Winnemucca."

"I'm sorry," I said. "I didn't know."

She stood to show me out. I turned toward the door, but she stopped me with a light hand on my shoulder.

"It was a terrible accident," she said. "Estebe never meant to hurt your mother."

"Garaze!" Once again, the voice from the dark part of the house.

"Yes, Father?"

"Did you see her?"

Garaze took a deep breath. "Yes, I did, Father. She was beautiful. Thank you."

44

GARAZE WATCHED ME THROUGH the front window as I got into the car. I wanted to sit for a minute and mull over what she'd said, but I was afraid she'd come out to see what was wrong—so I drove away and parked in the next block.

I was sure she was telling the truth. Her story explained things I'd wondered about—for instance, how Joy had gotten a job in Oakland when she didn't know anyone there. I could see that Estebe wouldn't have wanted to take in an illegitimate grandchild—especially an illegitimate *black* grandchild. Besides, he was going to Spain, maybe afraid of the law. Or maybe, finally, through with America.

And yet, from his old country point of view, I was family. I couldn't be abandoned, and he wanted me to grow up safe from the radiation. So, Joy had to give up her own plans and take me, and we had to go somewhere else.

One of Estebe's letters had mentioned the priest was from California. That's how Joy ended up there, I guessed. He must have known someone who'd helped her set up St. Martha's. Probably no one *but* a priest could have talked Joy into changing her plans.

A Catholic Worker house. What a perfect career for a frustrated nun who was stuck with her dead sister's child.

But why was Estebe's meeting with Mama so secret? Why didn't Joy know where Mama had gone? That still didn't make sense.

I started the car again and headed for the freeway. The familiar green signs directed me to Winnemucca, Reno, and—much more distant—Sacramento. I decided to drive till I got too tired, then find a freeway hotel or pull off at a rest stop. Right now, I felt like I'd never sleep again.

I turned on the radio to keep me company. Some classical music would sweeten the trip, I thought. But what I heard instead was a feverish babble of voices.

"—and we're asking people not to use the phones, either to call in or out. I repeat, do not telephone. Keep the lines open for emergency services."

Startled, I glanced at the radio as if an expression on some face would tell me more.

Another voice: "That goes double because the whole country saw it start. The baseball game at Candlestick Park had just come on the air, and someone said 'We're having an—' and then they went off."

Oh, God. An earthquake in the Bay Area. Maybe it wasn't too big. Maybe it hadn't affected Oakland very much. The one in 1906 hadn't. I scanned the radio stations, trying to get information, but no one seemed to offer much besides rumors.

"—6.9, with an epicenter in the Santa Cruz mountains. We do *not* have verified reports—"

It was big. But still, it probably hadn't shaken Oakland much. Santa Cruz was fifty miles away. I pushed more buttons on the radio.

"—major damage in the Marina area. No word of BART operations at this—"

"—rush hour. We are verifying a report that the Bay Bridge has collapsed—"

"—Cypress overcrossing of the Nimitz Freeway. Casualties are estimated at two hundred or more—"

Different voices said the same news over and over. If even half of it was true, the earthquake had hit Oakland pretty hard. I couldn't stand any more, so I shut off the radio.

I wished I could talk to Joy. Then I remembered I could have talked to Joy any time in the past couple of months, and that I'd made it a point not to. *She's okay. Don't be silly. She couldn't possibly have been on the freeway—she doesn't even drive. No way. . . .*

There wasn't anything to do but keep going, and I did. The evening afterglow looked like the gleam of fires beyond the mountains. Even that went out soon, and the desert went dark except for the freeway lights. The car seemed stationary, the highway like a treadmill rolling beneath it. The mile markers crawled by, slow motion. I wondered if I'd ever get to Reno, let alone reach home. A glance at the speedometer told me I was going way over the speed limit. Startled, I lifted my foot from the accelerator. All I needed was to blunder into a speed trap.

When lights from the opposite side of the freeway began to rasp across my eyes, I swerved onto an exit ramp and found a place to pull over. I locked the doors and squirmed into the passenger seat, looking for a comfortable position. After a few minutes of wiggling around, I unfastened my bra, took off my shoes, and wadded up my jacket for a pillow. But it was like trying to sleep during root canal work. Finally I gave up and drove on.

What about the carousel? Oh, God, it's insured, but I'll be sick if it's gone. How many of the animals are safe in Portland?

I should have known that number, but I was in a panic. I couldn't remember, couldn't think. As I passed through Reno, it occurred to me that Alex must be somewhere nearby, sleeping next to his wife. It had meant so much to me to find him, but at that moment, I couldn't have cared less. I stopped in Reno only a few minutes to buy two cups of coffee to go, but I didn't even consider calling Alex. I stuffed the cups into both sides of the front seat cup holder and got on my way again. All I wanted was to get home.

The car labored up Donner Pass, accompanied only by a few semis. It had been a warm day, but now a cool night breeze cut through the freeway fumes with a scent of pine resin—or maybe I was imagining it.

On the long slope down into California, I turned on the radio again. The voices leaped out of the dark in a babble of ruin and death. Devastation in Santa Cruz, fires in the Marina District, collapsed sections of the Nimitz Freeway, landslides, gas explosions, tsunamis, mud volcanoes—it sounded like the Day of Judgment.

And I was headed straight for it.

Part 7

45

As Mirai drove away, Garaze closed the curtains and turned back to the living room, seeing it through a stranger's eyes for a moment. As she had done, too, when Nekane visited.

Nekane—what a surprise it was to see her. "Joy," she calls herself now. I like the change, but I still slipped up when I talked to her.

And now little Mirai. She didn't just happen to be in Paradise Meadow—it's miles out of her way, if she was going home to Oakland from Idaho. She must have wanted her family story pretty badly, to come all this way for it. Odd that Nekane didn't tell her long ago. Hope I haven't let any cats out of bags. Maybe Nekane didn't know, herself. She and Zuzene weren't that close. Zuzene. . . . Well, I don't think she was that close to anyone.

She locked the front door—not that there was likely any need, but most people had started doing it. Not like the old days.

I used to pity old people, because they were closer to death than I was. Now I pity the young, because the world they have to live in is so much harder than the one I knew.

As if to underline her opinion, a car roared down the street, moving much faster than the speed limit, reducing the required stop at the corner to a brief screech of brakes, then accelerating again. Garaze looked into the kitchen, checking the back door, even though she knew it was locked.

Mirai's grown up to be a pretty girl. Restoring carousels—she's an artist like her mother, I guess. Must be a fun job. I didn't tell her, but I used to cry after I'd ride that merry-go-round in Farmington.

It seemed like a magical journey in a storybook, but when it was over, everything was the same. I always wanted to ride it again the next summer, though. Kids are funny. Well, people are funny. No reason to think I'd be an exception.

Those visits to Farmington—how I looked forward to them every summer, driving so far with Mama and Papa. Getting to my aunt's and uncle's house in the evening, tired and sleepy, but excited too, because I was seeing my cousins for the first time in a year. Their house smelled different from ours. I'd just breathe it in—it was the smell of summer and welcome and even a sort of coming home, because I loved them.

It's strange: The people I missed when I was young, it was because they were in another place. I could always see them by going somewhere. But now, most of them are in a different time, and there's no cure for missing them.

Garaze moved quietly as she got ready for bed, careful not to wake Father Heguy. Even if he wasn't disturbed, he never slept long.

Then he'll be calling and calling me to ask if I've seen someone—I have no idea who. Maybe when he's asleep he sees Our Lady, or his own mother. For all I know, he sees them when he's awake.

Well, if he does, God bless him. If seeing his mother is a comfort to him now, let him see her. What a hold our families have on us!

For bad as well as good. Imagine Mirai not knowing she was Zuzene's child—what point was there to that lie, even in the beginning? To get Estebe's blessing? Children will go on and on, half-killing themselves trying to please a harsh parent. No half about it in Zuzene's case, either—that lie, and finally telling the truth, took her life.

Garaze walked through the house one more time, making sure everything was ready for the night. As always, the kitchen was spotless. But looking around the living room and the dining room beyond, Garaze sighed with defeat.

Look how my housekeeping has slipped—I used to keep the place immaculate. Not that it's dirty now, but it looks old, saggy, worn out. Huh. . . . Just like me.

Garaze turned off the lights and went to bed. But she lay awake, as she often did, thoughts tumbling. Still thinking of Mirai, playing the visit over and over. Still adding to what she'd said, changing it, as if Mirai were still there to hear, to finally understand. She couldn't stop the monologue of explanation—or, she wondered, was it self-justification?

Either way, the past had all come back.

46

WHEN I OPENED THE DOOR, Mirai, and saw you on the porch—there in the dusk, with the streetlamp behind you—I thought I was seeing Rosa's ghost. It was a chilly fall evening, same as when Rosa first came, and you were short and thin and held your head the same chin-up way. I just stood in the doorway, stunned and stupid.

"Are you Garaze?" you asked. I couldn't get a word out. "It's Mirai San Julian," you said. "Joy's niece."

And then I remembered, though I hadn't seen you since you were a little girl. I had no idea you might have grown up to look so like your grandmother.

"Mirai!" I opened the door wider and stepped back. "What brings you here?"

"I was hoping you could tell me a little about my family," you said. I didn't ask why you'd need to come all this way and ask me. I didn't think I wanted to know.

I answered your questions. No more, though—I'm wary of telling tales. There was always gossip in Paradise Meadow when I was young. The story about me was that I was in love with Father Laborde. That tittle-tattle started as soon as I went to work as the housekeeper for the rectory. Then, when Father Heguy took his place, they said now I was in love with him. I ignored it. What else could I do? There weren't any other jobs in town but waitress work, putting up with the dirty things men say to waitresses.

No, it wasn't the priests I loved, it was the job. Making a home clean and comfortable, knowing for sure I wouldn't be bothered with any of that man stuff. I loved cooking and washing, and doing linens with the iron hissing and the toasted smell of starch. Watching the birds at my feeder outside the kitchen window, I wouldn't have traded my job to live in a palace, much less to share a bed with a smelly sheepherder. I like things decent.

My girlfriends felt sorry for me as they married, one after another. Of course, they didn't say so, but I knew. They'd ask me to dinner and seat me next to some single man—their husband's younger brother, maybe, or a cousin from out of town. It was a relief when they finally gave up—I was glad to be the old maid of Paradise Meadow.

I think they came to envy me after a while. I know Carolina did, after Jesús took to drink and after all the things he did to her. She'd come here for arnica from me and advice from Father. None of it did any good. In the end, she outlived him, and then she was free. "Till death do us part," they said, and then some of them found out how long that could be.

Not Rosa. I felt proud of her for leaving Estebe. But I missed her. She was a young girl like me, and we were best friends. I met her the day she came to town. She didn't know anyone, so she came to the rectory for help. I'll always regret that Father sent her to the Basque hotel, even though there wasn't anywhere else for her to go.

But who would have thought she'd fall for Estebe San Julian? He was old enough to be her father. Maybe she thought she'd be secure, with him owning the hotel and all—but what a mistake!

I tried to warn her what he was like, but she wouldn't listen. She got mad at me and didn't invite me to the wedding. Some wedding that must have been. No friends there for her at all, because I was the only one she had. Maybe some people from the hotel came to sit in the pews, or else the church was empty—only the two of them and Father, with a couple of witnesses pulled in from the street.

There might have been flowers on the altar, left over from Christmas. I can picture her in some cheap white dress, her eyes shining brighter than the candles as she promised Estebe her future. She wouldn't have listened when the wind whistled around the corner of the church, the way it did on a winter day.

She should have, because that cold wind was her wedding song. She'd married a man who was worse than winter. He never had a kind word for anyone. He and Danel Arauco had been in the sheep business before he bought the hotel, and they were the roughest of a rough lot. There was even a rumor that, back in the range war days, they'd lured a cattleman out into the desert and left him to die.

On the other hand, maybe it wasn't true. Those that said it were the same magpies who thought I was lovesick over Father Laborde. So, I didn't know what to believe.

What I do know is she rued that marriage soon enough.

47

I MEANT TO SAY A PRAYER for you, Mirai, after my bedtime rosary, but I don't remember so good anymore—not what happened today and yesterday, anyhow. The long-ago past seems more real, the older I get. Maybe one day I'll walk into it and shut the door behind me.

My good intentions slipped my mind because I couldn't stop thinking about Rosa. In fact, I didn't finish my rosary at all. I fell into memories and then tears, kneeling by my bed with my beads hanging useless in my hands.

We patched up our quarrel soon after the wedding. I wasn't sorry for what I'd said, but I *told* her I was, and that was good enough. She had Zuzene about nine months and one day after they were married, and I brought a baby present while she was still in bed. Zuzene was a homely little thing, all red and wrinkled, but I crossed my fingers behind my back and said how cute she was. What else could I do? Besides, it worked out to be the truth—she grew up into a beautiful girl, whatever else was wrong with her.

But Rosa worried me—she looked so run-down and frail. She could hardly lift her head off the pillow. I asked her, "Do you have someone to take care of the hotel for you for a while?"

"Oh, no. There's no need," she said. "I'll be good as new in a few days."

I didn't believe it. That hotel was a job for a *crew* of people, and she was running it herself, more or less. But I kept my mouth shut. I didn't want to quarrel with her again.

But it bothered me enough that I asked Father Laborde if I could take her a pot of soup or something.

"You can give to those in need whenever you want, Garaze," he said. "But the San Julians aren't poor. They must have *gallons* of soup at that hotel."

"Only if she makes it, Father," I said. "And she's not well now." I was embarrassed to speak to a priest about childbirth. But of course, I didn't need to—he understood.

"Surely she has kitchen help there," he said.

"Just a woman who comes in on weekends. Other than that, she does it all."

"Well," he said, "whatever you think would do her some good."

That was all he said about it to me, but he went to the St. Jude's Guild women and told them to go over there and help her. Then there was an almighty ruckus when Estebe threw them out.

A year later, when Rosa had her second baby—your Aunt Nekane—everyone knew better than to interfere. Estebe San Julian was a proud man. What he had to be so proud of, I never knew.

48

YOU'RE FROM A CITY, Mirai, so you wouldn't know this, but having an enemy in a small town is a serious business. Even if you can't stand someone, you avoid an open feud any way you can. Estebe and I almost didn't manage it.

Before your Aunt Nekane was two years old, Rosa lost her next child. She was *really* sick that time, and Estebe had to get help in the hotel whether he liked it or not.

I came around to help her, too, and he showed me a face like the Devil's. He had no love for me, that one.

He left me at their bedroom door, and I stepped in, shocked at the change in her—how thin she was, and how old-looking. It was a hot day, and her hair clung in tendrils to her sweaty neck. Her skin was grayish, and wrinkles showed on her face. Wrinkles! I knew how old she was, twenty-three, because she was born a month or so after me.

"Rosa!" I exclaimed, "You look—"

She put her finger to her lips and cocked her head toward the doorway. I understood she believed he was still out there listening. At first I thought, *Let him hear,* but I realized after a second that it would go harder for her if he closed his door to her only friend.

"Let me do your hair," I said. That would take a while—he'd have to go away before long to take care of his hotel. And hairdressing would reassure him—it was the sort of thing he probably thought women should do.

I took her hairbrush from the dresser and began to tease the snarls out of her long hair. It had been so beautiful, but now it was dry and dull.

"We'll put some olive oil on it when you're better," I said.

She sighed. "Maybe I should cut it."

I brushed gently a while longer. Then I heard the floorboards creak softly as he left his listening post.

"Rosa," I said, when I was sure he'd gone, "you have to stop working so hard. You're killing yourself."

She shrugged. "The work has to be done. Running a hotel is a lot harder than taking care of one old priest."

"I know that," I said. "That's why you need some help here. At least a man to do the heavy chores. Maybe a cook. The place is full—you can afford it."

"He doesn't think so," she said.

"And I know you want a family, but your body isn't going to stand having them all at once like this," I said. "You need to give yourself a rest between little ones."

"They do come," she said.

"You're not the Virgin Mary," I told her, angry she was throwing her health away. "The babies don't just come. You have to do something to get them."

"No, I'm not the Virgin Mary," she answered. "She had a choice."

I understood then that he forced her, and hot as the day was, I felt cold down to my bones. I stared at her, disbelieving my own ears. I had no idea a husband might do that to a wife. She saw the astonishment on my face and reached out to touch my hand.

"He wants a son," she said.

49

You wouldn't understand this at your age, Mirai, but old people don't feel old. I never realized I was, till the day I looked in the mirror and said, "When did this happen?" Because my mother's face was looking back at me. And she'd been gone for twenty years or more.

There's not many in town left from the people I knew when I was young. Father Laborde retired years ago, and he passed away shortly after that, God rest him. And the people I told you about, they're almost all gone.

Zuzene, of course, she died when you were a tiny girl. And Estebe . . . . Well, I knew he couldn't still be alive, but it still made me sad when you told me he'd died in Spain. That last night when he came to see Father, I showed him out. I managed to say, "Go with God," without any special emphasis on the "go."

I suppose Rosa's gone, too. She was so frail—I doubt she would have lived to be old. Maybe, though, once she got away from him . . . .

I helped her do it, and I've never been sorry. A year after the miscarriage, she had a stillborn child. She ended up in the hospital in Reno, near dead. Estebe never visited her.

She looked terrible—I almost cried out when I saw her. But at least we could talk there without him listening in.

She saw my face and shrugged, unwilling to complain. It made me mad.

"You didn't die *this* time," I said. "Maybe you will, if you try again."

"It was a boy," she said. Tears trickled down her face, but she didn't make any crying sounds.

"*Adopt* a boy," I said. "There's plenty of children who need homes."

"He'd never agree to that. He wants a son of his own."

"A live son is a son," I said. "A dead one is nothing but a headstone."

"He doesn't see it that way," she said. "He's more determined than ever to have a boy. You know how Basques are about family."

That made me madder still. "I'm Basque myself, remember? I know very well how Basques are about family. *Senide* means *everyone,* not only fathers and sons. *Senide* means the mother too."

Her face was a mess, so I passed her a tissue from the bedside table. *Good God,* I thought, *she doesn't even have enough gumption to help herself to a tissue.* But I was wrong.

"I've been thinking what to do," she said. "Here I've had four children, and two of them are dead. That leaves two, but Zuzene isn't right—no one ever says so, but you know it as well as I do."

I nodded. It was one of those small-town things. Zuzene was nearly old enough for school, but of course she'd never be able to go. I'd never heard the child say a thing. She could play with crayons or paints all day, singing wordless songs like a little bird. But this was the first time I'd heard anyone, much less Rosa, admit she was retarded.

"But your body isn't going to stand much more," I said. "You're dying, one pregnancy at a time. And in between those, it's the way he makes you work that wears you down."

"I know," she said. "I *can't* take any more. And he'll never change. I have to leave, but I don't know how to do it."

"Don't go home," I said. "Leave from here—it's much easier to get out of Reno than Paradise. Go to your parents." That was a blind shot, because—good friends though we were—she'd never told me about her family.

"I can't leave Zuzene and Nekane," she protested. "And my parents are worse than Estebe."

"That can't be true," I said. "Estebe is killing you."

She shrugged again, and I was afraid she was going to sink into helplessness.

"Look, Rosa," I said. "I have some money saved, and I'll give it to you. Go wherever you want and start over. When you get on your feet, I'll get Father Laborde to talk to Estebe and persuade him to let you take Zuzene and Nekane. If he wants a son so bad, he won't care enough to hang onto a couple of daughters."

I hope she forgave me someday for being so wrong.

50

I TOLD YOU SO LITTLE of what I know about your family, Mirai. But so much damage is done by gossip—the old hens pecking, and the roosters too. Still, I feel bad, in a way—maybe that's why I keep on telling you all this in my mind, long after you've left for your home in California.

When Rosa left Estebe, the town buzzed for weeks. But no one had the nerve to say a word to him. No one but Father Laborde, and he came home shaking his head.

"He's a stubborn man," he said. "He says he wouldn't have her back if she begged on bended knees. Not that she's likely to do anything of the kind."

"What about the children, Father?" I asked. "Shouldn't they go to their mother?"

He shot me a sharp glance. "Do you know where she is?"

"Yes, Father." I waited for him to tell me it was a sin for a woman to leave her husband, and a sin to help her do it.

"Don't tell anyone," he said gently. "Let her go. But the children . . . . He'll never give them up. Don't speak to him about it, Garaze, do you understand?"

"Yes, Father," I said.

So, I broke my faith with her. But Father was right—Estebe wouldn't have let them go. I could see that.

All the same, he had no idea what to do with them. Zuzene couldn't go to school in her condition, and Nekane was still too young. After a few weeks of trying to take their mother's place, Estebe went back to his old ways. He didn't let them run wild—he was strict and demanding. But as to mothering, he didn't have it in him.

I did my best for them. Nekane was four, and she often spent the day with me at the rectory until she was old enough for school. Those were precious days to me, because I loved children, even though I'd never wanted to marry.

She was a quiet little thing, and she loved to wait in the empty church while I cleaned and dusted there. She'd sit peacefully at the feet of our Madonna statue, gazing at her face, maybe imagining Mary was her mother.

Sometimes Zuzene came, too, but more often she spent her days alone. She wandered around town, always drawing, often on scraps of newspaper or whatever she could find. She'd draw pictures even in the sand, if she had nothing else. She didn't sing anymore, and she rarely spoke. From time to time, I bought her notebooks and crayons.

That was all I could do. I wrote to Rosa, giving her news of the girls, but she never answered. Eventually a letter came back with a stranger's scrawl across the envelope: UNKNOWN AT THIS ADDRESS.

I've wondered ever since what became of her.

51

GARAZE PULLED HER SWEATER snug around her as she walked, a little stiffly, through the cemetery gate. She liked to spend an hour or so every Saturday tidying graves. Not only of her own family but of all the Catholic dead—especially the old ones whose children had moved away, who had no one left to do for them.

It wasn't really the priest's housekeeper's job, but she felt better praying for them on Sunday if she knew she'd done what she could. She felt like God's colleague then, someone who had a right to ask.

Sometimes she weeded in the Protestant section too, if a grave looked neglected. God couldn't possibly mind, and if someone else did, too bad. She even tended imaginary graves—for the ones who died in the old country, like Estebe, or in some war-wrecked place like Korea or Vietnam.

As always, Garaze went first to her family plot. When she was young, she'd said a rosary here, but she couldn't stand so long anymore. Now she had a sort of wordless prayer, picturing their faces, reminding God of them—in case He needed reminding.

Walking on, she noticed a few long blades of grass on Jakinda's grave. She knelt to pluck them, remembering Jakinda's wedding day, and the future that seemed so sweet and certain as she and her new husband left for Cedar City.

And in the hospital, Jakinda's eyes . . . . Those eyes had seen each of her children trapped on their last bed, her husband too, all the ones she loved most. And finally, Jakinda was the one looking up at people who didn't know what to say or do. *When you think about it, every death's a crucifixion—God forgive me if it's a sin to say so.*

She crossed herself and stood, carefully testing her balance. After a moment, she bent and touched Jakinda's name on the headstone, as gently as touching a face.

No one in her family's left to tend a grave. What a terrible thing the testing was, all over that part of Nevada and Utah. But it wasn't close to Paradise—I thought Estebe was going overboard when he insisted Nekane and Mirai go to California. Still, I had to give him credit for taking care of them. At least, according to his lights.

As she made her rounds, she noticed Father Laborde's flowers needed straightening, so she took care of that. She pulled a weed here and there, sparing the dandelions. *Let someone else dig them out, if that's what they want.*

Dandelions—wonder why people hate them so. They're flowers, aren't they? Sometimes they're all the flowers we have. Everyone tries to get rid of them, but they keep coming back. Like the Kingdom of Heaven.

So much to do in the cemetery—more every year, of course. The town I knew is here *now. Most of it, anyway.* Coming to the headstone Zuzene shared with her stillborn brother, she paused to remember Rosa, then walked on.

A scrap of paper blew across the path, and she bent to pick it up. It was weather-bleached, illegible. She dropped it into the trash can near the gate, hesitated a moment, and then sat heavily on a nearby bench. She was in no hurry to get home—to the television, with its earthquake news. Of course, she could turn it off, but somehow, she didn't. After trying over and over to call St. Martha's, she'd given up. The television seemed a thin connection.

It was such a blessing to see Nekane last summer, even with all our grief over Jakinda. Joy, not Nekane—wonder if I'll ever get used to that. I hope she's all right. I know she'll phone me when she can.

And little Mirai. What a pretty girl she's grown up to be. The more I looked into her face, the more I saw Rosa's eyes looking back at me.

God? Now that I'm thinking of it, there was something I wanted to ask. Why is it that our love lasts and our bodies don't?

She shivered in the autumn breeze and wrapped her sweater tighter. As her hands took shelter in the pockets, her fingers found a forgotten rosary and automatically began to tell the beads, each one calling up a name, living and dead together.

Mama, Papa, Nekane, Mirai, Father Heguy, Jakinda, Zuzene, Father Laborde, Estebe, Rosa. . . . Grant them peace.

Part 8

52

NEAR SACRAMENTO, I CHECKED into a motel. There was no way I could go any farther without sleep. From a display of snacks and sundries in the office, I picked out another junk food meal and a package of over-the-counter sleeping pills. The clerk, absorbed in the earthquake news on the lobby television, pushed my change blindly into my hands, and it scattered across the floor.

"Oh, sorry." She made no move to help pick it up.

I went to my room through a maze of dirty corridors, trying to breathe too shallowly to notice the smell much. I wouldn't have stayed two minutes in such a crummy motel if the situation hadn't been urgent. As it was, I fell on the bed without undressing. The last thing I needed was sleeping pills.

When I woke, a thin sliver of light was coming in at the edges of the window shades. I felt fine for a few seconds, then all my worries dropped on me like a spider off the ceiling.

I grabbed the phone and dialed the number for St. Martha's, but all I got was a message that there was no phone service into the area. I tried Barbara's cell phone number with the same results. I didn't see a clock anywhere, so I got up and peeked around the shade. My view was blocked for a second by someone walking along the balcony. So, people were up and about. Time to get going.

I took a quick shower and rummaged in my bag for toiletries and a clean T-shirt. Then I turned on the TV to catch up on the earthquake.

A coiffed, somber-voiced news guy announced that parts of the Bay Bridge had collapsed, and so had a long section of the freeway. He said it was the most costly natural disaster ever to hit the United States. All utilities were disrupted, no gasoline was available, stores would be closed indefinitely, and so would financial services like ATMs and credit reporting. Thousands of homes were destroyed, and thousands of people were injured. Estimated fatalities were two hundred or more.

I wanted to reach into the television and strangle him. Since that wasn't possible, I grabbed my bag and slammed out, leaving him gloating over aftershocks to an empty room.

My hands were shaking so much, I dropped my keys twice before I got the car door open. In the driver's seat, I sat staring blankly at the motel parking lot for several minutes. I realized I had to get hold of myself if I was going to drive. I took one deep breath, then another.

As I turned the ignition key, the governor's voice blared from the radio speakers—some genius pronouncement about having thought the bridges were safe. I turned the volume down, pulled out of the parking lot, and took the first freeway entrance.

By the time I got through Sacramento, I realized I might not make it to Oakland today—it was usually an easy drive, but I had no idea what to expect of freeways and local streets near the quake area. I might run into detours or dead ends. The radio was an endless irritant, but I kept listening—they might say which routes were closed.

Now that the news was getting old, the stories were more varied. I heard that bystanders had rescued dozens of people from the freeway collapse. That volunteers with flashlights had directed traffic when the power went out. That bucket brigades had helped fight fires where the water lines were broken. That tent cities were being put up to house thousands of people who were suddenly homeless.

A picture of what home would be like hit me full force. My heart started pounding and tears came to my eyes. I took the next exit and parked along the access road.

Looking around, I saw the familiar fall landscapes of California—rolling hills with the grass baked to hay by the summer's drought. I'd always said that our fall color happened on the ground rather than in the trees. Now, in mid-October, it was nearly time for winter rains to bring back the green—usually a beautiful turn of the seasons. But today the idea was sickening—too many people would have no roofs over their heads.

And maybe one of them would be me. Or Joy.

Jesus. I pushed another button, another station, another voice. I wanted to hear someone say, "Attention, Mirai San Julian! All the people you love are safe. St. Martha's is safe. Your studio is safe."

Don't dream, *Mirai. Do* something.

First chance I got, I stopped and spent a precious hour shopping for emergency supplies. The whole back of the car was packed, and so was the front—the only space left was barely large enough for me to squeeze in and drive. I'd *better* get to Oakland today. With all motels in the area sure to be full, I'd have a choice between sleeping in the driver's seat and bedding down somewhere outdoors.

I had food, water, a first aid kit, emergency blankets, even a camping stove. And I hoped my friends didn't need any of it.

53

My estimate of how long it would take to get into Oakland turned out to be pessimistic. Except for a few snarls, traffic was light. So, it was broad daylight when I pulled up in front of St. Martha's and surveyed the damage.

The house was still standing, but I wondered if it would be much longer. Between all the pairs of French doors around the patio were long cracks in the walls. Giant X's, as if someone had crossed off the building.

Without thinking of anything but Joy, I jumped out of the car and dashed across the yard. The patio glinted with broken glass, but I crunched right through it. The front door was jammed half-open, and I pushed into the living room.

"Absolutely perfect chaos," I muttered, echoing Charlene's long-ago description of her moving day. "Absolutely *perfect* chaos," I said again, stupidly. This time, it wasn't an overstatement. If there was anything that could still fall or break, I couldn't imagine what it might be.

"Joy!" I yelled. "Are you in here?" Kicking aside a landslide of books, I pushed into the dining room. No one there, either. When I looked into the kitchen, I had to back off and shut my eyes. It wasn't possible that *everything* from the cabinets had been dumped on the floor. When I opened them again, I saw, yes, it was possible.

I stood and listened for anything, any breath or movement, anything to tell me I wasn't all alone. But the silence was complete, like sudden deafness. It took me a moment to realize that the schoolhouse clock had stopped.

"Joy! Are you here?"

Nothing. I went to the bottom of the stairs and called again. The staircase seemed twisted, pulled an inch or so away from the wall. I could tell it was dangerous, but I went up anyway, calling over and over, even after I was sure no one was there. I looked for a note, anything to give an idea what had happened. Nothing.

An aftershock punched the building like a big fist, and I crouched in the hallway with my heart pounding and all my spit dried up. When it was over, I crept downstairs and got out.

The car felt safe and familiar, so I sat in it for a while, trying to figure things out. Maybe Joy and the guests had gone to another Catholic Worker house, or to one of the public shelters. I might not catch up with them soon—maybe not till the phones were working again. Or longer. I hoped Joy would call me, but I'd been such a shit, maybe she wouldn't. No, she would. Of *course* she would. A pit of sick dread opened in my stomach.

No use going on a wild goose chase. Maybe Charlene would know where they were. Home was a short trip, but long enough for me to imagine dozens of possibilities, each worse than the one before. I was sure I'd see the house lying in rubble in the yard.

But when I got there, the place looked like it always did. I unlocked the front door and stepped warily inside. I was ready for another scene of devastation, but everything I could see was eerily normal, as if Charlene hadn't let the earthquake happen here.

"Anyone home?" I called. No answer. As I passed through the rooms, I noticed some things were missing. Broken, I guessed. Charlene wasn't in her office upstairs—she wasn't home. *She* hadn't left a note, either.

The door to my room was open. My bed was stripped, and a couple of big cardboard boxes sat on the bare mattress. I stopped in the doorway, shocked. Charlene couldn't be moving me out, could she? I peered into one, and saw my bulletin board, the photos snarled in their ribbons and pins. The other had an assortment of items, most of which had probably been on the floor when I left.

I couldn't suppress a snort of laughter. Trust Charlene to have the place clean a few hours after the earthquake. Anyway, she must be all right—no one else would have done it. And—I allowed myself a flicker of hope—Charlene wouldn't have, either, if Joy was in trouble.

Better check on the studio next. If Barbara had made sure the animals were in their racks, everything should be okay—unless the whole building collapsed. But if she hadn't . . . . Carousel history was full of disaster stories. Quite a few machines had been lost in fires. The idea that the Looff animals could be destroyed because of our negligence made me feel sick again.

I had to take a roundabout way to the studio because of rubble-blocked streets. By the time I got there, I was prepared for the worst.

But the building didn't look any worse than usual. The door was unlocked, and I entered warily, afraid that someone might have broken in. I was ready for desperate strangers, ready for trouble.

Instead, I heard quiet voices. There was no light in the building except in the office, the only room with windows. I looked in cautiously.

The office was crowded. Near the windows by my desk, Louie and Charlene bent over a newspaper. The guests from St. Martha's sat on kitchen chairs in one corner, eating bread from a plastic bag. In the opposite corner, two figures slept on the floor in a tangle of sheets and cushions. One of them was Barbara—I recognized her hair, spread in a gold fan across the sheet.

Charlene looked up. "Mirai!" she yelped. "Good God, where did you come from?"

The other person in the corner sat up, rubbing her face with the heel of her hand.

"Joy!" I was across the room before I knew it. Joy looked up at me, and I knelt and hugged her. Like nothing had ever come between us. Of course, from her point of view, it hadn't.

"What are you doing here?" I asked.

Joy winced. "Did you see St. Martha's?"

"Were you hurt?"

"Sprained my ankle." She pulled the sheet away to show me her elastic-bandaged foot. "It'll be all right. Did you see St. Martha's?"

"Yes, I did. How did you sprain your ankle?"

"I fell down the stairs, getting everyone out." She didn't sound especially concerned about the ankle—typical Joy—but her face told me she was in pain. "We went to your place, but there's no water there. So, we ended up here."

"That's what we did!" said the woman from St. Martha's. What was her name, Winnie? No, Ginny. "We came here! I helped a lot, I carried pillows."

"That's fine," I said. "Thank you." I turned to Joy. "We have water?"

"Yes, but no power." Joy shrugged. "They're putting up tent cities. . . . We could have gone to one of those, I guess."

"No," I said quickly. "I'd never have found you." I glanced at Barbara, but she slept on. "Is she okay?"

"No," said Ginny. She sounded excited, gloating. "Poor thing, she—"

Louie stood up quickly. "Come on out here a second." He looked around the room. "'Scuse us."

He pulled me through the door and shut it behind us. We stood together on the sidewalk in the afternoon sun. The whole world smelled of dust and smoke.

Louie didn't say anything at first. He looked exhausted and dirty, ten years older than the last time I'd seen him.

"What's going on?" I asked. "Is Barbara hurt?"

"Not exactly," he said. "We were in the paint room when it hit—nearly ready to go home, but then everything started shaking."

"What about Barbara?" I was ready to scream. Why couldn't he answer my question?

Louie seemed to be searching for words. "We ran out. At first there wasn't anyone around, then people poured out of the buildings. Like an anthill when you . . . ." He broke off. "It was like a movie—someone said to come help, the freeway had collapsed. Right down the street."

"I heard about that," I said.

"Some guys were going under and trying to get people out. The whole thing could have fallen down any minute. Barbara got the shakes, and her teeth were chattering. I told her to go home, but she didn't want to. So, she waited while I went in to help. I'd only been working half an hour when I saw Will's car."

"Will's car!" I was so shocked I couldn't quite get my breath. "You mean, he was on the freeway? Are you sure?"

"Yeah. All I could see was the car's rear end. The rest was crushed. I knew it was his, on account of the plate—ORGAN4U. I went back to Barbara and told her we had to get out of there."

"Maybe he lent someone his car," I said, clinging to a last cobweb of hope.

"Did he ever lend that car?"

"No. Stupid idea." Will would never in a million years have lent his 1964½ poppy-red Mustang to anyone. He wouldn't have lent it to God.

Stupid idea, hope.

54

WE STOOD THERE a few seconds—I didn't know what to say, and he probably didn't, either. It was almost too much to think about. I felt myself go numb, though I knew I wouldn't stay that way.

A couple of the neighborhood bums drifted by, but they didn't ask for money. Probably the liquor store was closed, so they didn't need any.

I struggled to get my bearings. "So, you and Barbara left," I prompted Louie. "You didn't tell her?"

"Later I did. After we got here. I didn't want her to go see for herself or anything. There was nothing she could do." He frowned. "She was really upset for a while. Then she kind of sacked out."

"She taking tranqs?"

"Maybe. If she has any. I didn't ask."

"Jesus." We stood silently for a minute. "Were the animals damaged?" I asked. It sounded stupid, after everything else, but I had to know.

"One fell over. I think it's sort of trashed. The others were in their racks. I haven't had a chance to look."

"Let's do it now. Got a couple of flashlights?"

"Yeah. We're saving the batteries, though. We need them to go to the bathroom."

"I have more," I said impatiently. "Let's go see."

Louie stepped into the office and collected flashlights from the desk drawer. He handed me one, and we went out onto the dark floor of the studio. It was hot and still—stifling. The dark was like a blanket a few inches beyond my nose. I squelched a panicky feeling. No time for that kind of crap.

At first, we played our lights on the floor in front of us, to make walking easier. After less than a minute, I realized I had no idea where we were.

"Hang on, Louie," I said. "There's no north star in here."

"Huh?"

"Where are we? I thought the paint room was that way."

We stopped and shone our lights around until we found the paint room door.

"The paint should be okay," Louie said. "We put it away good." He sounded worried.

"What about the animal?"

"A stander. I think it fell."

We looked in, crisscrossing the paint room floor with the lights. He was right: The paint was safe, and the animal, the zebra that had already been repaired once in Portland, was lying on its side with a big crack. It would have to be sent again.

Louie's voice sounded tearful in the dark. "I'm sorry," he said. "The lights went out, and we ran. Then there was Will. . . . "

"Don't sweat it. You did the right thing. Let's take a look at the storeroom."

Everything was in place, secured in the racks. I moved the light around, and animal faces with glittering eyes blazed from the dark as the beam touched them, then were gone. A horse with flaring nostrils, the lion's snarl. Like a bizarre dream. As far as I could tell, they were all fine.

"You did great," I told him. "Don't worry about the zebra. We have insurance for this stuff."

"Thanks." I hoped the breath I heard was a sigh of relief. "Can we still make the schedule?" he asked.

"Act-of-God clause in the contract. We'll do our best, but if we don't make it, we're covered on that too."

"Oh. I see." He was quiet for a moment, his light trained steadily on an empty spot on the floor. "Are the St. Martha's people here to stay?" he asked.

"I guess so. We'll have to get the work done around them."

"I couldn't tell them no," he said, sounding a bit defensive. "They couldn't stay at St. Martha's, so we found places for them here."

I thought it over. I wished I didn't have to run a Catholic Worker house out of my studio, but what else could I do? Even when the water at Charlene's place got turned back on, I couldn't ask her to take them in. Maybe one of the bigger Catholic Worker places could, but I doubted it.

"Doesn't sound like you had a choice," I said slowly. I felt guilty that I didn't want them to stay, but that didn't make me feel better about the prospect of having them underfoot. I was royally stuck.

Louie shrugged. "We couldn't think of anything else. They don't have anywhere else to go."

"Okay," I said. "But we have to set the place up better. We can only camp in the office for a few days. Once the power comes on—or before that, if we have to—we'll have to make some kind of bedroom back here. I have stuff to get out of the car. Let's go ahead and do that."

We trailed through the studio, turning off the flashlights as we neared the front door. I glanced into the office as we passed, but nothing had changed.

"Why didn't you bring mattresses?" I asked. "You could have used the van."

"No keys," Louie said. "Didn't think you'd like for me to hot-wire it, you know?"

"Oh, shit." I hadn't left the spare keys. One more thing to feel guilty about. "Well, we can do it now, anyway."

"Fine with me," said Louie. "Sleeping in a chair isn't too good. And it looks like we'll be here for a while."

"Now that we have the van, we can get whatever we need," I said. "Make a list. We have to get a mattress for Joy for tonight."

"Yeah," said Louie. "Also, we need food and stuff. Barry's gone to get what he can, but the stores are closed, mostly."

"Barry!" I was so confused, I wondered if my mind had a short circuit. "Is *he* staying here?"

Louie shrugged. "For a night or two. We thought there might be looters. Also, he figured this is where you'd turn up."

"I do have his car," I said.

Louie grinned. "I doubt that's his main reason."

As we neared the curb, he did a double take. "What's all *that* in it?"

"Food and stuff. I guess we'd better unpack it."

"Wow," he said, sounding like a teenager again. "You brought food. Is there any chocolate?"

"Louie . . . . Oh, never mind." I stifled my annoyance. Let him be a kid for a few minutes, if that's what he wanted. It sounded like he'd had far too much responsibility for the past couple of days. "I don't remember what I bought. Why don't we get going and unload? Any chocolate you find is all yours."

55

THAT WAS THE BEGINNING of what we called "St. Martha's North." As if the guests were *my* guests, as if they were welcome.

They damn well weren't.

As much as I loved Joy, I'd never been able to understand this side of her. In my opinion, her "guests" were a bunch of irritating losers. And for all her talk about helping people rather than pleasing them, she let them run all over her.

As soon as the power came back on, I'd given her an alcove that once held rental skates, according to the sign still painted on the wall. Except to go to the bathroom, she never came out. She sat on the mattress in her room, or lay on it. The crutches the hospital had given her lay on the floor. She hadn't even bothered to learn to get around on them.

I carried her meals in on trays—if I hadn't, she'd probably have gone hungry. It was only slowly that I realized the main problem wasn't pain in her ankle.

For Pete and Frank, the St. Martha's guys, we'd set off a corner of the basketball court. Each of them had a mattress, and we'd hauled a couple of chairs back there, but they didn't like it much.

"Why can't I have my own room?" Frank groused. "I don't want to share with Pete. He snores."

"You snore, too," Pete said. "You snore worse than I do."

"*Ginny* doesn't have to share," Frank said. "This is like jail."

I bet you know *that, too,* I thought. "Ginny has a corner of the snack bar," I said. "That's hardly the Hyatt Regency. And if there were another woman, Ginny would have to share it with her."

Ginny joined in. "I want a room, too. My little boy might come and stay."

"Your little boy's not coming," Frank said. "He's grown up. He'd've been here a long time ago if he gave a damn about you."

Ginny made a squeaky sound, and tears ran down her crumpled face. I wanted to comfort her, but I couldn't think what to say. Brutal as Frank's remark had been, he had the facts straight, as far as I knew.

I handed her a box of tissues and she fled, presumably to her lair in the snack bar.

"Always makin' a fuss," said Frank. He conveniently ignored his own role in the fuss.

I ignored it, too. I had no intention of stepping into the housemother role. I had time for only two things: Joy and the carousel.

At least I knew how to fix the carousel.

We packed up the poor, hard-luck zebra to send back to Portland Carousel Works. I called Matt to explain what we needed.

"How you doin' down there?" he asked. "Hear you had some rock and roll." He sounded like it was a joke.

"I'm living in the studio," I said. "My apartment doesn't have water. My aunt's place was wrecked, and she's living here, too. We're sleeping on the floor. Barbara's husband got killed."

"Oh, Jesus," he said. His voice was real now, the Matt who used to be my friend. "I'm sorry. Your aunt's place—you mean the halfway house?"

"Catholic Worker house," I said, keeping my voice neutral.

"What happened to the people?"

"They're here, too. We don't know yet if St. Martha's can be fixed up."

"Shit. How's Barbara?"

"Not good."

He was silent for what seemed a long time.

"Look," I said, "I'm using Barbara's cell phone—there's no regular service yet, so this is costing an arm and a leg. I have to get going."

"Right," said Matt. "I need to think this over and get back to you. Don't worry about the zebra, though. We'll get him done ASAP."

Even if they did, I didn't think it would help much. The earthquake had given me a perfect, legal excuse to throw away the schedule. But I didn't want to. I wanted that carousel to open on Memorial Day.

Will had nearly finished the band organ. But I had to find someone to pick up where he'd left off and then install it. I would have liked to have left that to Barbara, but she was still more or less incommunicado, either asleep on a mattress in the storeroom or sitting in the office staring into space like a mad-woman in a Victorian novel. Or going off on long, unexplained errands I assumed had to do with things like identifying Will's body—things I'd rather not know. If she wanted to talk, I'd be a friend and listen. I sure didn't want the details enough to drag them out of her.

I had Louie, when he wasn't hanging around Barbara. But the two of us couldn't finish the carousel by Memorial Day, not even if the alternative was to get shot at sunrise the morning after. Even supposing the St. Martha's crowd stopped getting in the way, which I knew they wouldn't. Even assuming Joy wouldn't need major help from me, which I knew she would. Even if Barbara pulled herself together faster than I had any right to expect. Hell, a *year* from Memorial Day was more like it.

I was mulling over this well-rehearsed list of troubles when Barry came into the office. He'd been in and out to help with supplies, but this was the first time we'd been alone together since the trip.

He held out his arms and I went to him. Just having someone to be close to—God, it felt good.

"How are you doing?" he asked, still holding me.

I pulled away. "I don't see any way I can finish the carousel on schedule," I said.

He touched my face lightly. "I didn't mean that—I meant how do you feel?"

"Jesus—I don't know," I said. "I don't have time to think about it. I'm the only person around here who isn't falling apart."

"Well, don't put yourself on hold forever, or you'll be sorry. But if the practical stuff is what you want to do first, let's start on that."

He dropped into the guest chair hard enough that I was worried it might collapse. I sat at the desk again.

"I really can't think what you could do," I said.

"Let's just run through the problems, and we'll see."

"Okay," I said, and took a deep breath. "I don't know how to get the band organ finished, Barbara's down for the count, Joy is in some kind of shock, I've got both of them plus three crazies living in my studio . . . . That enough?"

Barry nodded. "That's enough. Let's start with the easy ones."

"There's an easy one?"

"Well, there is the physical problem of housing all these people. That one's pretty clear-cut. I doubt we can go out now and rent a house. Too many other people looking. Would Barbara rent her place to St. Martha's, now that it's just her there?"

"I don't feel like asking. I mean, it's her house and her memories."

"Sounds like even the easy ones aren't easy," he said. "If Barbara's place stays empty for long, it'll get looted."

I rolled my eyes. "You tell her that."

"I will. But first we'll have to come up with a better plan than sending her back to an empty house. What about Charlene? Would she take Barbara in?"

"Probably."

"Would she take the St. Martha's guests?"

"I doubt it."

"What about fixing St. Martha's? Have you taken a second look at the place?"

"No. I've been sort of overwhelmed here."

"I'll take care of that part. I have a club guy who's an engineer."

"A Boys and Girls Club guy? I thought the club was for kids."

"Well, he's an alumnus. He started out on the streets and ended up getting an engineering scholarship at Cal. I'm sure he's busy right now, but I bet he'll take a look if I ask him."

"Go ahead," I said. "We're going to have to face it sooner or later."

He stood up to leave, then held out his arms again. We hugged for a long moment before I spoke again.

"When I was in Paradise Meadow, I found out what happened to my mother. She and my grandfather had a quarrel, and he pushed her into her horse by accident, just as he was turning to go. He didn't even realize what had happened till later."

He held me closer for a second. "Well, now you know," he said. "It's not a good thing, but it's not as awful as you thought, is it?"

"I guess not. I haven't had that much time to worry about it."

"Yeah, you're probably more upset about all the stuff that happened here."

I nodded, keeping my face turned away. My eyes were filling with tears I didn't want to have to explain to Barry.

Not that I still loved Will—I damn well didn't. But the thought of the body I'd caressed being crushed under tons of concrete made me quickly turn my thoughts somewhere, any-where else. The trouble was, they kept coming back.

56

TWO DAYS LATER, BARRY and I stood outside St. Martha's with the engineer. The morning was gray and chilly, threatening rain. I thought again of the tent cities and shivered in spite of my sweater.

Vince, the engineer, was a big, friendly guy. He looked tired, and I guessed he'd been working hard the past week. Sort of like being a doctor in an epidemic.

Seeing the building made me feel completely hopeless. It looked even worse than it had the first time, if such a thing was possible. Yellow tape was hung all around like garlands. Danger and Do Not Enter were apparently the themes of the day. A red card on the door said, Unsafe to Enter. I wondered how anyone could be expected to fix the building without going in.

"Did the city put the tape there?" I asked. I didn't even *want* to go in, not after my scare with the aftershock. But it was upsetting to be told I couldn't. It was my house, where I'd grown up. My house, even though I'd left it.

Vince nodded. "I'd say so. They've been inspecting buildings since the morning after the quake. Let's walk around the outside."

He didn't comment on the nearly knee-high dandelions and foxtails as we made our way through the yard. He looked at the building intently, not spending more than a few seconds on anything but taking it all in: cracks, broken glass, everything. He busily made notes on a clipboard, and once he walked up to a crack in the wall, took a coin out of his pocket, and tapped the wall with it, up and down both sides of the crack. Seeing my puzzled look, he smiled.

"Checking to see if the stucco's peeling away," he said. "If it makes a hollow sound, there's some separation."

"Oh." I had no idea why that would matter.

"Let's take a look at the back now," he said.

He took the brick path to the gate, and Barry and I followed, brushing against Joy's rosemary. The scent of the bruised plants heightened my sadness, recalling past times in Joy's garden. I stopped for a moment, fighting tears.

If Vince noticed, he pretended he hadn't. When we got to the front of the house, he tucked the clipboard under his arm.

"I need to go inside and take a look," he said. "But since it's red-tagged, you guys shouldn't go in. Why don't you sit and wait for me awhile?" He gestured toward the bench where Joy often sat to rest and play her flute.

Barry and I sat, watching uneasily as he pushed aside the tape and disappeared through the front door.

"I hope he knows what he's doing," I said.

"I'm sure he does."

"He probably knows what's dangerous and what's not."

"Has to."

We sat quietly for a few minutes. I pulled my sweater closer around me. The day of the earthquake and the few days after it had been hot, but after that, the temperature had plummeted. Then, as if adding insult to injury, the skies had opened and the rainy season had begun right on time—or even early. The tent cities of homeless earthquake victims were now mires of misery.

The rain had also given new energy to the weeds at St. Martha's. Foxtails covered the front yard like a field of wheat. I leaned down and picked one, pulling a few of the seeds loose, feeling their sawtooth roughness, twisting them free of the ear. I could still smell rosemary on my hands as I again pulled my sweater tighter.

"Are you cold?" Barry asked. He put one arm around my shoulders and drew me close for warmth.

"No, not really."

"Want my jacket?"

"Uh-uh. You're plenty warm, just like this."

"Mirai," he said, caressing my shoulder, "remember how we told your father we planned to—"

"Well, look who's here!" blared a woman's voice from the sidewalk.

We turned awkwardly, still sitting. I almost blurted out, "Oh, shit," because it was Nancy—the woman who'd made the fuss about the doll, that day I'd brought Joy home from the airport.

She came up the walk quickly, as if this was a moment she'd been waiting for.

"I guess this neighborhood can forget your precious band of criminals," she said. "When are you tearing the building down?"

"We're not," I said. "We're going to restore it."

"We'll see," she said. "The city may not let you. My husband says it's a nuisance building, and he says there's a lot we can do about it now."

"Is there anything I can do for you?" I asked. "I mean, besides taking your abuse?"

Her face turned red. "Oh, you can do something for me. You can do something for the whole neighborhood. Get out!"

At that point, Vince emerged from the front door. He looked at Nancy quizzically, then turned to Barry and me. "It's repairable," he said. "You probably aren't required to do more than repair, but I'd advise some strengthening so it'll perform better next time."

Nancy laughed. "You won't need to worry about that. I doubt very much there'll *be* a next time."

Vince stared as she stomped off. "Who the hell is *that*?"

57

WE SPENT THE NEXT fifteen minutes standing in the yard, talking about depressing things like budget and schedule. When we'd finished and Vince left, I was feeling close to hopeless.

"Want to go to lunch?" Barry asked.

I shook my head. "I really need to get to the studio," I said. "Anyway, I have a headache."

"But we need to talk. What if I come over around three? Would that work?"

"All right." I didn't really want to, but when would I *ever* want to? We kissed quickly, and I started back to the studio, wishing I could get away from all the problems. I'd stretched the truth about the headache, but by the time I arrived, my karma had caught up with me—I had a real one, throbbing harder by the minute.

The sound of a television somewhere in the back didn't help. In the office, Charlene was reading the newspaper.

"What's going on?" I asked. "Where'd the TV come from?"

Charlene folded the paper neatly and laid it on the desk. "I got it from home," she said. "Louie asked me to do house-mother duty, because he had to take Barbara to something about Will. But the guests were squabbling more than I could stand."

I sat in the desk chair and rubbed my temples. It didn't help. "Where'd they go? Barbara and Louie, I mean." I could hear where the *guests* were.

"I didn't ask," she said. "But I'd suppose it's whatever you do when someone dies. . . . Arrangements. . . . I don't know." She didn't sound especially interested.

I glanced at her, startled. It wasn't like Charlene to be unsympathetic.

"Yeah," she said. "I'm having a hard time with this one, for some reason. I can't stand to think about it. It only makes it harder that I honestly thought the guy was a bastard."

Boy, did I understand *that*—well enough that I changed the subject. "Where's Joy?"

"In her room. I think she's on a real downer, Mirai." She improved the crease in the newspaper and lined it up perfectly with the edge of the desk.

"Well, finding out how much it's going to cost to fix St. Martha's isn't going to make her feel better," I said. "That's where Barry and I went—he dragged some poor engineer over there."

"A lot, huh?"

"Sounds like a lot to me. I don't know how much earthquake insurance she had, if any. The engineer says she can get money from FEMA, but I bet she won't."

"Why not?"

"Catholic Workers don't take government money. They have an idea that the government could interfere with them if they did."

"FEMA money isn't like that," Charlene said. "Program money like block grants—those can get tricky. But FEMA couldn't care less how people use the buildings." Charlene sounded sure of it, and I reminded myself she was a professional fund-raiser.

"Well, I wish you'd tell her that. I mean, if she *does* object to FEMA money. The engineer couldn't give me a definite figure, but he said it would probably cost around three hundred thousand dollars to fix the building—and that's if nothing else goes wrong."

Charlene's eyebrows went up. "Does Joy have any money?" she asked.

"I don't think so. I know she bought the house with what Estebe and my mother left. Their property, you know, and my mother's artwork. I doubt there was much left over."

"So, what's she been living on, all these years?"

"Mostly donations, I guess. Typical Catholic Worker house. She might have kept a stash for repairs, but it wouldn't be anywhere near enough. Also, it's going to be more than a year before they can move in. Supposing they can at all—that woman who was so nasty about the doll is taking action to try to keep them out."

"I see." Charlene sounded thoughtful. "Tell me, what did the guests usually do during the day?"

"Some of them have had jobs," I said. "Mostly, though, the ones who could work would pull themselves together and move on. I don't know, Charlene. Ginny hasn't been at St. Martha's long. Frank worked for a while, but he's been unemployed for months, and I doubt he's looking. Pete's been there forever. I don't think he's ever done much except watch TV and read."

"Is that good for *him*?"

"Probably not. Most of the Catholic Worker houses do a lot more rehab than Joy. But there's no official policy, and St. Martha's has turned into the house that'll take the hopeless cases."

"Maybe it's circular, though. They're living the life of Riley over there. Who wouldn't *want* to be a hopeless case?"

"I've said the same thing to Joy, and I think you're right. It's one of the reasons I couldn't live there. Let me ask you, though, since Barbara's not here—could she stay in my room? I mean, would you mind? Or could Joy?"

Charlene looked down at her folded newspaper and carefully pressed the creases with her thumbnail. They were perfect. "As far as I'm concerned, they could *both* stay at my place. There's plenty of room—no need to turn *you* out, either. You ever coming home, by the way?"

I shrugged. "How can I, as long as the guests are here? I can't leave them alone in the studio."

"Can you find someone else to take them?"

"I can try. But can you guess how many people in Oakland are looking for housing right now? And even if there was anything, I can't imagine who'd put up with them."

"What's going on with you and Barry?" she asked.

"We sort of got together during the trip, but I don't know what's going to happen now. All I've thought about since I got home is other people's problems."

She looked straight at me then, and her face was serious. "Maybe I'm talking out of turn here. But you'd be a damn fool to keep tending to other people's business and neglecting your own. If you throw away a great guy like Barry, don't be surprised if you never find another as good."

"But what can I do?"

"Take care of Joy as best you can, and your carousel, and Barbara. But take care of yourself too. Give the guests reasonable notice, and then get on with your own life. The party's over. They're going to have to go somewhere else."

If I hadn't been so uncomfortable, if I hadn't been evading Charlene's eyes, I wouldn't have seen the flicker of motion in the hallway. It only lasted a second or two, but I was sure that one of the guests had been standing there, that one of them had heard.

58

"WHAT'S THE MATTER?" asked Charlene.

"Someone was in the hallway."

She glanced that way, but of course the person was long gone. "One of the guests, you mean?"

"Had to be. The outside door's locked. One of them heard what you said."

"Good. It's what they need to hear." She folded her arms.

I stared at Charlene, speechless. My headache gave another drum roll. She put up her hand.

"Okay, okay," she said. "I know it sounds mean. But you remember when Joy told you she thought you tended to be a pleaser?"

"Yeah, but—"

She barged on through my protest. "Ever hear of the pot calling the kettle black?"

"Well, but—"

"Think it over." She stood and tossed the newspaper into the trash, wasting all that folding, all that arranging. "I gotta go. Let me know what Joy and Barbara want to do—I've got plenty of room."

I sat idly for a while after she left, applying generous doses of self-pity to my headache. It wasn't effective, so I decided to try something else.

I found a bottle of aspirin in the desk drawer and swallowed a couple dry. They tasted nasty, bitter, and sour. I went out to the snack bar for a drink of water.

That taken care of, I looked around. We'd tried to make the snack bar into a sort of common room, but the results weren't anything you'd be likely to see in the pages of a home magazine.

The room had a serving counter and two lines of booths. Ginny's cot was squeezed into the end of the aisle between the booths, with a hoard of objects taking up most of the nearby tables and seats.

How, I wondered, had Ginny managed to collect so much junk? They'd fled from St. Martha's with nothing more than the clothes they had on, as I understood Joy's story. And since then, the guests had rarely left the studio. They *could*—they weren't prisoners—but there was nowhere to go and nothing to do, in a rough neighborhood made rougher by desperation. But Ginny had somehow assembled a rat's nest around her bed. I sighed. I hoped none of it came from looting.

Even without Ginny, though, the room would have been less than inviting. All its flaws were dramatized by an overhead light that managed to be glaring and dim at the same time. And there were plenty of flaws to go around.

A shelf behind the counter must have held food and soda machines, but they were gone, all stolen or sold before I'd moved the studio in. All but a big hulk of a popcorn machine, probably too heavy for thieves to bother with. Since the wall had been painted a time or two while the machines were there, it was piebald with patches of green, beige, and black.

The empty spots on the shelf were piled high with the supplies I'd bought outside of Sacramento. When I first moved into the place, I'd brought in a small refrigerator, now stuffed with food and stacked with teetering columns of cans.

The seats of the booths had plastic upholstery, split in places with the stuffing poking out. Or mended with silver duct tape, a real decorator touch.

The picture was completed by the worn-out, grubby linoleum flooring, peeling in places, stuck down with more duct tape. If I'd been looking for a backdrop for depression, I couldn't have found a better one. And I knew the living spaces we'd thrown together were every bit as bad. Charlene had a point that Joy and Barbara might feel better if they'd spend most of their time somewhere else.

As I stood there thinking, I realized the building was quiet— no more TV noise. Worried, I checked to see if the guests had left. There was no one on the main floor, no one in the paint room or the storeroom. I finally found them talking quietly in the men's dorm section of the basketball court. Under the circumstances, that wasn't exactly reassuring. They looked up as I approached, but no one spoke. They looked united for once, hostile and resentful. I left them alone.

Since I was in the back of the building anyway, I went to the skate shop, Joy's new quarters. The door was closed, as always. I tapped on it and got no response—again, as always. I opened it quietly, in case she was sleeping, but she was sitting up on her mattress, legs straight out in front of her, staring at the wall. She didn't look up when I came in. She made me think of an abandoned plastic doll.

I didn't know what to say. I'd already given her sympathy, and she'd pushed it aside brusquely, almost—for Joy—rudely. I'd asked how I could help, tried to talk business—everything I could think of, always with the same result. Joy didn't want to talk.

"Hi," I said—an original opening. She looked up.

"Hi," she answered dully. Not much of a handle for conversation.

I sat cross-legged on the floor so I wouldn't have to bend over her like someone training a dog. At least we were on the same level.

"Joy," I said. "We need to figure out what to do next. We have to find another place for St. Martha's."

At least she looked up. Nothing more, but it was a start.

"I *have* to get on with the carousel, or I'll never finish it by Memorial Day," I said. "I'll probably have to do a huge amount of the work myself, or else find someone to hire in Barbara's place. She's off today to make some kind of arrangements about Will, and she's sure to be a basket case when she gets back. I feel sorry for her, I really do. But—I can't help it—life goes on."

"It would be better to go ahead and tell them you can't meet the deadline," Joy said. "I know you love your work, but I think taking care of people is more important right now." I waited, but she'd made her pronouncement and had retreated into her depression.

Frustrated, I blurted out the truth. "Barry and I met with an engineer at St. Martha's. It's going to cost over a quarter of a million dollars to fix it. Supposing you have insurance. Or that your principles will allow you to take a handout from FEMA."

"I have some insurance," Joy said. "The bank insisted on it when I bought the house. But it won't cover all of that. And I'm not taking money from the federal government."

"Then I hope you have an awful lot stashed in the bank."

She started to speak, but it was my sermon, not hers.

"Even if you have the money, someone has to house your guests for at least a year before the building's livable. And you've made it very hard for anyone to do that, Joy. I could be home if I didn't have to keep an eye on them—someone has to, every minute. They steal, they eavesdrop, they quarrel, they demand to be waited on like kings. Living with you has made them *more* helpless and unrealistic, not less."

"Mirai, dear," she said with exasperating patience, "Catholic Worker houses have always dealt with people with problems.

Dorothy Day said she knew many of her guests took advantage, but she didn't care. It's an act of Christian charity to care for them."

"She also believed in the dignity of work," I said. "I know you think your people are some kind of exception, but as I recall, you're the one who told me that pleasing is not the same as helping. And if Christian is what you're after, tell me this: What miracle of Christ made anyone end up *worse*—blinder, lamer, deafer, whatever. Show me even one, and I'll put up all three of your guests at the Hyatt Regency for as long as they want."

I stomped out, leaving the door open behind me. If she wanted to shut me out, she was damn well going to have to get up and do it herself.

59

BACK IN THE OFFICE, I fumed. The TV blared suddenly from the snack bar. That ruled out paperwork, unless I was willing to have a showdown with the guests—and at the moment, I wasn't.

I was too restless to sit still, so I wandered to the storeroom. All the animals were in there, partly because I hadn't had a chance to work, and partly for fear of aftershocks.

I turned on the light and started making a mental to-do list. The chariots were stripped, but they hadn't even been primed. At least the animals were fully painted. But we hadn't even started the varnishing, and it was a big job. How was I going to get it done, now that the studio had been turned into a crash pad?

Barry was due any minute. Hassling with St. Martha's was the last thing I wanted to do, but someone had to, or I'd never reclaim my studio. Especially if we ran into trouble with Nancy and the other neighbors. Maybe he'd have another idea or two. At least I could *talk* to him.

I heard the front door open and close.

"Anybody home?" Barry's voice.

"Back here," I called.

"Back where?" His voice had moved, but I couldn't tell if he was getting any closer.

"Storeroom! Come on back!" I yelled.

"*Back here* covers a fair amount of territory in this place," he mock-grumbled when he found me in the storeroom. "Looking at what's left to do?"

"Yeah. We're way behind." I felt exhausted thinking about it. And it didn't help that I'd been sleeping on a pad on the office floor ever since the earthquake.

"What if you don't make it?" Barry asked.

"Nothing, now. Act of God, et cetera. I still want to."

I wanted it so much, I could almost see the crowd, kids and grownups lined up to buy their tickets. Every animal would be perfect, down to the last jewel in the harness. I could hear the starting gong and the band organ. . . .

Barry broke into my wishful reverie. "What's left to do?" he asked.

"For the animals, just varnishing. But it's *seven coats* on every one of them. The chariots have to be painted *and* varnished. And all of it has to be sanded between coats."

"Six months sounds like long enough for that."

"It's not six months to finish the animals. It's six months till *everything* has to be done. Installed. Running. Open for business. In Peregrine Falls."

"The team may be able to help with the varnishing, if you can teach them how to do it right," Barry said. "They have school, and their parents may need their help, too, right now, but some of them can probably help. We can ask."

The front door opened and closed with a slam. We both looked up, startled. Barry put his head around the storeroom door and called to them.

Barbara came into the room, trailed by Louie. The depressed look was gone. Barbara was blazing.

"Guess what," she began.

"Tell me," I said. "I'm beyond guessing."

"Will wasn't alone in the car. They found a woman too."

"Oh," I said. My mind felt like a carousel lagging to a halt, the ride over, the horses gliding slower, slower. "Uh . . . maybe he was giving her a ride to the baseball game?" It came out sounding idiotic.

Barbara shook her head. "I don't think so. For one thing, they would have been way late for the game. Also, there was a suitcase in the trunk."

Ah, the trunk. From Louie's description, the only part of the car that hadn't been pancaked by the collapsing freeway deck. I shut my eyes for a second. Everything—the animals in their storage racks, the conversation, the change in Barbara—seemed out of kilter. I tried to imagine Will running away with some-one—leaving his studio behind. I couldn't.

"You mean, they were leaving town?" I asked.

"It didn't look like it," Barbara said. "There was nothing in the suitcase but a pair of ice skates."

"Ice skates!" I was starting to wonder if one of us had gone nuts. "Who told you all this?"

"The police. They wanted me to identify her. I refused. I said I had no idea who she could be."

"Ice skates!" I repeated stupidly. I flashed to the only pos-sible explanation. Will and whoever-she-was must have gone to a hotel for a screw, must have stuffed something heavy into a suitcase to take with them so they'd pass for respectable travel-ers. I imagined the bag falling open in the lobby, the ice skates tumbling out, embarrassment spoiling the party. I nearly, unfor-givably, snickered.

What stopped me was a detailed picture of how the party really had ended—broken concrete and tangled steel, broken bones and tangled limbs. The colors flashed at me, gray, red, gray, red. Freeway map, chart of the nervous system, then black snow, and then nothing at all.

60

"Lie down for a minute till you quit feeling dizzy," Barry said. "You damn near brained yourself on the concrete floor." Kneeling beside me, he eased me into a flat position.

"Not possible," I said. "No raw materials." Barry didn't seem to get it, and I didn't explain.

Louie and Barbara stood above me like mourners looking into an open grave. It would make an interesting group portrait. I could call it *From Supine*. Or maybe *The Lazarus View*.

I closed my eyes. Someone had once told me you couldn't feel dizzy if you were lying down. They were wrong.

"Shit," I said, and sat up. The room gave a quick spin. Barbara crouched on the floor beside Barry.

"Take it easy," she said. "Don't try to get up right away."

"I'm fine," I said. I wasn't fine, but I didn't feel bad enough to let them make me into a patient, either.

"Let me know when you can stand up," Barry said, "and I'll take you home. You've been sleeping on the floor here too long."

"I don't have a bed at home anymore," I said. "I believe Frank has my mattress."

"Well, he can un-have it." Barry looked up at Louie, who was hovering in an undecided half-crouch. "Louie, can you take the mattress to Charlene's?"

"Uh . . . sure."

"Haul those lazy bastards away from the TV to lend a hand." Gee, I thought, Barry *isn't* always polite. Louie headed for the snack bar.

"Tell Joy we're all leaving," Barry called after him. He looked down at me. "You ready?"

I heaved myself to my feet, supported by Barry's arm around me. Barbara scurried to my other side and held that arm. As we left the building, I thought I must have looked like a drunk being eighty-sixed out of a tavern. Nothing that would attract attention in that neighborhood, of course.

By the time we got to Charlene's, a cold drizzle was falling. Barbara settled me on the sofa while we waited for the guys to bring my mattress. Charlene came down from her office and sized up the situation.

"Welcome home," she said. If she sounded ironic, well, that was Charlene. "So, what's going on? You sick?"

"I'm okay, really," I said.

"Sure," Barbara said. "She passed out cold on the studio floor. Louie's coming in the van with her mattress."

Charlene opened an armoire and got a blanket, shaking out its perfect folds. She laid it over me, and I pulled it close. The sight of rain sliding down the front windows made me feel chilled.

"I can't say I'm all that surprised," Charlene said. "So, who's in charge of the nuthouse now?"

Barbara shrugged. "Joy, I guess."

Charlene's eyebrows shot up. "She feeling better?"

"I hope so," I said. "For all I know, she's feeling worse. I kind of sounded off about the guests after you left."

The conversation was cut short by the arrival of Frank, Pete, and Louie with the mattress. Charlene let them in and directed them up to my room. I could hear bumping and bumbling up the stairs, and a sharp exclamation from Charlene.

Barry and Barbara stayed in the living room with me. Barbara rolled her eyes at the mattress-moving ruckus, still audible as they crashed along the second-floor hallway.

"I hate to say it, but they drive me nuts," she said.

"Well," I told her, keeping my voice down, "if they were good roommates, they probably wouldn't have to live in a shelter."

She laughed, a quick snort that she tried to stifle. Barry looked from one of us to the other.

"It's not my business, but I think you need to have a meeting and decide what to do about Joy's guests," he said. "The city won't let you use an industrial building as a hotel for long, you know."

That idea hadn't crossed my mind. Since the earthquake, people were living anywhere they could. It hadn't occurred to me that the city would *make* me kick them out. It was a happy thought, but I was too tired to deal with it.

The moving crew came downstairs, escorted by Charlene. She showed them out and came into the living room. I stood up slowly, like an old lady.

"Barb," I said, "I'm sorry about Will. I'm really sorry about everything." That time, I meant it.

She nodded silently. Charlene turned to me.

"I've got your bed made. Can you walk upstairs?"

"Yeah. It was Will and everything. It got to me. . . . I couldn't stop imagining—"

"Well, stop now," she said. "Giving yourself the horrors won't make anything better." She took my blanket from the couch and began folding it. I dragged my way upstairs and fell into bed, feeling like a little kid.

At first, I was so exhausted and achy, I couldn't fall asleep. I lay in a sort of buzz of plans, ideas, and frustrations. I'd start to drift off, then wake myself up with a jump.

Suddenly, I was in a desert corral, looking at a big palomino mustang. I held an apple in my extended hand. I thought, *If he'll eat this, he'll talk to me. He can tell me what happened.* But he stayed against the far fence rails, wild and wary.

"If you won't tell me, I'll find out on my own," I said, and began to eat the fruit myself. As I bit into the dream apple, I woke, still feeling it in the clutch of my empty, cupped hand.

61

THE ROOM WAS DARK, the house silent. I got out of bed, waiting to see if I'd feel dizzy again. I didn't, so I stepped to the window, loving the feel of the cool wood floor under my bare feet. The rain had stopped, and I opened the sash, shivering in the night breeze. I had no idea how late it was, but the neighborhood was quiet.

If you won't tell me, I'll find out on my own. I had so many other problems, I couldn't imagine why I'd begun to think about Mama again.

I looked out at the street lights, the deep shadows between buildings. I'd learned, as women in the city did, to stay out of dark, lonely places.

In the desert, it wouldn't have been a lot different, except that the dangers weren't human. Rattlesnakes might be around on summer nights, and a rider was always in danger if the horse stepped wrong.

So, why would Mama go to meet her father there in secret? She could have met him any day on the main street of Paradise Meadow, and no one would have thought a thing of it.

Another thought struck me: Joy had said Mama and Estebe weren't even speaking. How had the meeting been set up? Joy hadn't said, and maybe she didn't know. But months ago she'd told me she had a box of old papers in the attic at St. Martha's. They'd still be there, in the empty building. But could they tell me anything I didn't know already?

I was still dressed—all I had to do was put on my shoes. I crept downstairs. At the archway to the living room, I heard a faint rustling. Startled, I went in. By the light coming in from the street, I could see that someone was sleeping on the couch. I moved closer, careful not to run into the coffee table, and bent over. It was Barbara, scrunched under the blanket I'd used earlier in the day. A light patch on the coffee table turned out to be her jacket.

I hadn't brought a jacket downstairs and didn't want to go back to my room to get one. Barbara wouldn't mind if I used hers for an hour or so, and it was probably chilly outside. I tried it on, still undecided about going out. It fit well enough, and when I put my hand into the pocket, I found her cell phone. That decided me—with a phone, it would be much less dangerous to go to St. Martha's and look for the papers in the attic. I slipped out the front door and began to walk. *If you won't tell me, I'll find out on my own.*

No one was on the street. Judging from the darkened houses, it must be very late. I walked softly, trying to see into every shadow, listening for anything behind me. Nothing. After a few blocks, I began to relax, to even enjoy the cold night air, the gibbous moon riding so high above it all. I'd been indoors so much lately, being outside and free was a delight.

But I hadn't walked halfway there before I started to have second thoughts. Maybe I should turn around and go home—of all the stupid things I'd ever done, this was the stupidest I could think of. Was I really going to take advantage of Joy's absence from St. Martha's to raid her personal papers?

What if the police came along and thought I was a looter? What if I fell through the ceiling? What if there was another aftershock?

If I was scared to look, I'd never know. I had to find those papers—what if something happened to them while the building was empty? Then I'd *never* find out—according to Joy, she hadn't read some of them herself.

I wasn't really doing anything wrong—Joy had told me about them, had promised to look through them with me. Didn't that amount to permission?

My rationalizations made me feel worse. And why did I think the information I wanted would even be there? Why would Estebe have written down the account of how he'd killed his daughter, if that's what he'd done?

By the time I reached the corner of Joy's street, I was a mess—I'd stirred up a full-blown compulsion to see the papers, while my conscience was screaming. I stopped in front of the house next door, suddenly struck by a thought: Even if I found the papers, I wouldn't be able to read them. They'd be in Basque—Joy had told me that the last letter was the only thing she had from Estebe that was in English.

I drifted slowly up the sidewalk, feeling stupid, disappointed, and relieved, in approximately equal parts. I was about to go home, when I saw a light behind St. Martha's.

No one should have been there in the middle of the night, and I knew the electricity was off. I grabbed the cell phone like a security blanket and headed through the gate to see who was there. Nobody was—but the kitchen was in flames. I took one astonished look, backed away, and dialed 911.

It must have taken only a few minutes for the fire trucks to get there, but those minutes went by in slow motion. Then came the relief of shrieking sirens and men shouting and running to save what they could.

While they were there, I sat on Joy's bench in the front patio and shook, pulling Barbara's coat tighter and tighter around me. I waited for news of what they'd been able to save, the way you wait for news when someone you love is in surgery. I should have called Joy, but it didn't occur to me—as if the little phone were a magic charm I could use once and then never again.

Part 9

62

THE NEXT DAY, I DROOPED around my room with a sort of event hangover. Barry came by late in the morning, on his way to meet Vince at St. Martha's again to look at the fire damage.

He had a surprise for me: a copy of the day's *Oakland Tribune* with a feature story on St. Martha's. Byline, Barry Donovan.

I read the article eagerly. It told the history of the building—which I hadn't known—as well as the mission of St. Martha's and its difficulties since the earthquake.

There were photos of the building, prominently featuring the Do Not Enter signs, and even a sidebar about the fire.

"The idea was to generate support and maybe even contributions," Barry said. "I wanted to more or less spike the guns of the neighborhood crazies."

"They may have spiked their own guns," I said. "It looks like the fire was set on purpose, and guess who's at the top of the suspect list?"

"Not you, I hope."

I stuck out my tongue at him.

He laughed. "Next time you decide to go on some cocka-mamie expedition, I want to go, too."

"As my bodyguard?" I asked, expecting a lecture on how dangerous it was.

"No, I want to be in on the fun," he said. "Gotta go, or I'll miss Vince."

He kissed me, holding me close. My body remembered our night in the hotel, and I wished he didn't have to go.

My next visitor was one I had to go downstairs for. Charlene came to my room and announced that a man from the fire department was waiting in the living room.

He stood as I came in, and held out his hand. After we'd introduced ourselves and sat, he told me, "I'm investigating the fire last night. I understand you called in the alarm"—he quickly checked a clipboard of notes he had on the coffee table—"at 3:10 in the morning."

"I didn't have a watch," I said. "But that sounds right."

"What brought you out at that hour?" he asked. His voice was friendly, courteous, but "What were you doing there?" was the gist of what he wanted to know. He had a right to ask, but I wasn't about to tell the whole story.

"I couldn't sleep," I said. "I'd been sick that afternoon, and I got up after everyone else had gone to bed. I felt uneasy, so I went for a walk. I guess it was habit that took me to St. Martha's. It's my aunt's place, you know, and I grew up there."

"Taking a walk in the middle of the night isn't a great idea in that neighborhood," he said. "You were lucky you weren't mugged."

"I suppose I *was* lucky," I agreed. "It's not something I'm in the habit of doing. Like I said, I'd been sick. I guess I wasn't thinking too clearly."

"How far along was the fire when you got there?"

"I don't know—I saw a light at the back and went to check. As soon as I saw the fire, I called the fire department from my cell phone."

"You happened to have a cell phone with you?" He sounded suspicious.

"Yes—actually, it's my business partner's phone. She was sleeping over at my place, and I borrowed her jacket. It was in the pocket."

"You realize we're treating this fire as suspicious." His eyes searched my face.

"If someone did it on purpose," I said slowly, "I suspect it was Nancy."

"Who's that?" His voice managed to convey distrust of me, of the information, and of Nancy, all at the same time.

"A neighbor. She's complained to the city a lot about St. Martha's—the yard, the residents, that kind of thing. Yesterday she found out we were planning to rebuild, and she freaked. I guess you could get her name from city files—it would be on the complaints."

"Can't get anything from the city now," he said, and I remembered that City Hall was closed, all its departments relocated. It wouldn't be easy to find a grass-mowing complaint amongst all that.

"She lives a few houses west of St. Martha's," I said. "I could show you, if you like."

"I expect we can find her," he said. "We'll probably need to talk to you again, though."

He stood, gathering his coat and clipboard. I showed him out, hoping he wouldn't need to come back.

IT WAS JUST AS WELL I hadn't counted on getting much rest that day. Along came another visitor: Joy.

Once again, we sat facing each other in Charlene's Victorian chairs, as we had when we'd begun our journey into the past. This time, though, Joy was slumped in the chair, her injured foot sticking out stiffly. She was empty-handed, and her fingers twisted and clasped one another, let go, and twisted again. She didn't seem aware of what they were doing.

"Charlene told me it was you who called the fire department," she said. "Thank you for saving the building."

She looked gray and distant. Old, uninterested, polite.

"I'm glad I happened to see it," I said. "It was a fluke I was there."

"Why *were* you there? It was the middle of the night."

That seemed to be the question of the day. But now, I'd have to tell the truth.

"I sort of got a thing about your father's papers," I said. "I kept wondering what might be in them. I still don't understand what happened, what made Mama ride out into the desert that night. I started thinking the papers might get destroyed in the empty building."

"Aita's papers!" She sat up straighter, and her hands stilled for a moment. "But I read them to you!"

"Not all of them. You told me there were more in a box in the attic, things you hadn't read yourself."

"Well, that's true. But he didn't keep a diary or anything personal—I told you that. I think all that's left is records from the hotel. I didn't read them because they didn't look interesting. They wouldn't have told you anything. Besides, they're in Basque."

"I remembered that just before I got there," I said ruefully. If ever there were a fool's errand, going out to get those papers was it.

"So, you went out alone, in the middle of the night. Didn't I teach you any better than that? What in the world possessed you, Mirai?"

"You don't understand how important it is to me to find out about my family," I said. "I looked up Alex while I was on my trip. I would have told you before, but you didn't want to talk. I even went to see Garaze."

Joy said nothing. I couldn't read her expression.

"You don't understand," I repeated, as if saying it twice might make anything change. "You didn't grow up with a big question mark in your mind about who you were and where you came from."

"Just about who my mother was and where she went," Joy countered. "I made myself set aside such questions, and I think you should, too."

"Some of us care about stuff like that." I knew I was needling her, but I wanted to make her come back to life. Anger had brought Barbara to her feet—maybe it would work for Joy.

"I care," Joy said, her voice rising. "But I don't care enough to risk my safety. As you did. You could have been mugged, or raped. Or killed, for that matter. You are so much like your mother, Mirai—you went out without thinking of the risks, the way she . . . ."

She stopped. Her hand went out in an awkward gesture.

"The way she *what*?" I said. "Why don't you tell me? It's all these hints and half-truths and evasions that make me frantic enough to take risks."

Joy glanced sharply at me, then her eyes wandered to the window, as if she were looking for somewhere else to go. "Zuzene was obsessed with Ama," she said. "She painted her picture over and over, as if she were trying to bring her back. And she went out that night thinking she was going to meet her."

I was stunned. "How do you know? You weren't there."

"She phoned me, of course. To her, it was the biggest news of her life. Someone had left a note at her house, supposedly from Ama. It asked Zuzene to go to Pyramid Lake that night.

I told her it was ridiculous, it made no sense, she shouldn't go. That it couldn't possibly be Ama. But Zuzene was determined.

"I thought it was a cruel practical joke, but I also thought it would teach her a lesson about obsessing over the past. What could I have done, anyway? I was in Missoula."

"So, she went out into the desert," I said. "Do you know who met her there?"

"No," she said. "I told Aita what she'd said, and he said he'd told the police. But they never talked to me."

"Who did you think it might be?" I asked.

"Alex's wife," she said, so quickly that I knew she'd thought about it over and over. Then she paused. "Anyway, that's what I thought at first. Then the coroner ruled Zuzene's death was an accident, probably a kick from the horse. So, the note had nothing to do with it. And Aita told me not to talk about it."

"Why not?"

"He said Zuzene must have made it up, that she'd been getting crazier and crazier. He said it was a family shame, not to be aired."

"What did *you* think?" I asked. Surely she could see what was right in front of her.

"I didn't know what to think," Joy said. "And I had her estate to settle and a distraught five-year-old child to take care of. And Aita had a kind of collapse, maybe because they'd never made up their quarrel over Alex. Shortly after that, he went to Spain, and I never saw him again."

She looked at me then. "So, I let it go. I had no evidence of anything—I hadn't seen the note. Either Zuzene was delusional like Aita said, or she'd been the victim of a cruel joke—what difference did it make? I didn't want to know."

I opened my mouth and then shut it. If she hadn't put it together in all these years, she really *didn't* want to know.

63

It DIDN'T TAKE MUCH persuasion to get Barbara to stay on at Charlene's. In fact, it apparently hadn't taken any. Charlene mentioned it in an offhand way over dinner, a beautiful cheese soufflé that she'd invited me to share. She'd also made a salad with a spicy dressing, and she'd bought croissants to go with them.

"I didn't see any need to check with you, since we'd already discussed it," she said. "Or at least we'd discussed putting her in your room while you stayed at the studio. Since there's a couple of spare bedrooms, though, I thought I'd put her in one of those. I assume you're not going back to sleeping on the studio floor."

"I hadn't planned on it," I said. "But someone has to keep those guys in order."

"Well, here I am talking out of turn again," said Charlene, as she set the soufflé dish on the table. "But if I were you, I'd lock up anything that's valuable or confidential. And tell Joy that she's responsible for their behavior, and if she can't keep order, she'll have to find them another place."

"What about daytime?" I asked. "I really do need to work."

"There's acres of room at your place," she said. "Tell her they have to stay out of the way while you're working."

It wasn't going to be easy to get that tough with Joy. I sighed. I had too many memories of Joy being on my side when it really mattered. *Please allow me to introduce my niece, Mirai—and what's your name?* Joy had always been behind me, even in my brat years, when I didn't deserve it.

I couldn't let St. Martha's fail if I could prevent it. But I had no idea what to do. I didn't want to fall into the same trap with Joy that she had with the guests. There was the riddle—how to do what was best for people without mixing that up with what they wanted at the moment.

Hell, I had enough trouble sorting that out for myself. Why would I think I was smart enough to say what was right for someone else? Anyway, wasn't she the one always giving *me* lectures on the difference between helping and pleasing?

Saturday morning, the basketball team hit the studio an hour after I got there. They milled around the workroom floor. Barry was with them, like a proud papa.

"How many players on the team?" I asked.

"Depends if it's casual or competition," Barry said. "Why?"

"There's more guys here than I expected."

"Well, we let anyone on the team who wants to play," he explained. "When we compete, they play five at a time. But you must know how many guys we have. You've seen them often enough."

"I guess I wasn't paying much attention." I'd seen them out of the corner of my eye, but I'd ignored them. Now I was face to face with over a dozen teenaged guys.

"Is there a girls' basketball team?" I asked, momentarily distracted.

"Sure, there is," Barry said. "Someone else coaches it, though. Why do you ask?"

"Just curious." So much male adolescence was overwhelming. They all seemed to be talking at once, and a couple of them were jumping around as if it were practice time. I hoped Barry could get them into some kind of order. I knew he expected they'd be a lot of help, but it seemed likelier they'd make things worse.

Barry got their attention with a quick, shrill whistle.

"Okay, guys, sit down for a few minutes, and Ms. San Julian will explain what she's doing and what you can do to help."

They all sat on the floor. Before I started to explain, I noticed that Pete was standing nearby.

"Did you need anything, Pete?" I asked. If he was going to make problems, I'd have to deal with that too. I wished for the millionth time that Joy's guests would go away. Anywhere, as long as it was away.

"No," he said. "I was wondering if I could listen in."

"Sure," I said, a bit ungraciously. Why was he looking to me for entertainment—was the TV broken?

I turned to the team and surveyed their faces. They looked to be anywhere from twelve years old to maybe eighteen—the bridge between boys and men. All so different. A children's rhyme popped into my head: *Rich man, poor man, beggar man, thief* . . . . Barry would be doing his best to give them better choices.

They were attentive now, waiting for me to start. A sideways glance told me Pete was, too. For the moment, anyway, he looked a lot like them, and I wondered what he'd been like when he was a teenager, if anyone had tried to help *him*.

After I'd told them the basics—about carousels in general, a bit about this one, and what I needed them to do—I divided them into groups of five, thinking that sticking to their usual team size might make it more natural for them to work together. That made three groups, and I assigned each group an animal to start with. I didn't want the boys to start milling around again, so I asked Barry if he could get the animals.

Pete cleared his throat. "I could help bring them out," he said. "Might be easier for the two of us, you know?"

"Sure," I said, trying to hide my surprise. "Thanks, Pete."

64

BARRY AND I SURVEYED the three groups of boys.

"Why don't you supervise one group, and I'll alternate between the others?" I suggested.

The guys were getting unruly again, and I wasn't sure this idea was going to work. But after ten minutes or so, I realized that the unsupervised group was quiet and busy. When I checked, I saw that Pete was there, demonstrating how to sand with the grain. He looked up with a sheepish expression when he noticed me watching.

"I used to be a carpenter foreman," he said. "Never did no painting, but I know a few things about wood." He held up a piece of sandpaper. "Like this paper here, how it's cracking? If you have some heavy tape, we could put some on the back—then it won't."

"Let me see," I said, and went to the office. I found a roll of fiber packing tape and took it to him.

"This'll do great," he said. I watched in surprise—I thought I knew every sanding trick in the book. When I saw how well the tape worked, I asked Pete to explain his idea to all the boys.

He looked happier than I'd ever seen him.

So, I wasn't surprised when Ginny and Frank joined us on Monday morning. I doubted they'd stay, since neither had any experience with woodworking or painting, but there was no reason not to give them a chance. Before long, I realized I could leave the three of them and Louie to sand, and that Barbara and I could get on with varnishing.

In the paint room, I took a sea monster, gorgeous in green, blue, and gold, and she selected a camel with red trappings. We closed the door to keep sawdust out and moved the animals to wheeled stands for varnishing. We eyed each other for a moment over their backs.

I noticed how tired Barbara looked. Even with her decent bed at Charlene's, she was as listless as when she'd been sleeping on the floor. My wooden monster seemed slightly more alive than she did.

I opened a can of varnish and poured some off into a paper pail for us to work from. Selecting a couple of brushes, I handed one to her.

She gestured toward the sanding room. "How did you manage that?" she asked.

"I didn't. They wanted to, and Pete had some experience . . . ."

"Surprise," she said. She sounded ironic, but I guessed she felt as ashamed as I did. We'd dismissed the guests as useless, when all they needed was something to do. We varnished in silence for a while.

Then she sighed. "Mirai, as far as I can see, Will had his repair work finished. The band organ pieces are almost all crated, ready to ship. Harvey can probably install it. I'm thinking it might be a good idea for me to go to Peregrine Falls pretty soon—Evangeline's renting a double-wide up there somewhere, and I can stay with her. If I'm there, I can see to it that the band organ works and call in someone if Harvey's not up to finishing the job. And you can start shipping animals as soon as they're painted."

"What about all the stuff we need to do here?" I asked.

"Let's wait and see. I think we'll be fine if the team and the St. Martha's guys keep helping. Oh, and Barry, of course." She gave me a mischievous smile, the first sparkle I'd seen from her in a while. "Somehow I think he's likely to stick around."

"How long would you want to stay up there?" I could imagine how much she might want to get away from Oakland right now, but I wasn't sure I could do without her.

"I don't know. . . . Maybe quite a while. I want the band organ to be perfect, as a sort of memorial to Will. He wasn't much of a husband, but . . . . I guess it's just that I don't want to leave his work unfinished."

I nodded, smoothing my varnish coat with the tip of the brush. I'd miss Barbara, and I'd probably have to work harder if she was gone. But it would be good to have someone on the scene, too.

"Also," she went on, "I've been talking to Joy, and I think I'm going to let her use my house till St. Martha's is repaired. I wouldn't want to go back there now."

"They say you're not supposed to make big decisions like that for a year," I said.

"I know, but a year should see Joy through, and then I can decide whether to rent it out or sell it or what."

We varnished in silence a few moments more. Then I asked, "What about Louie?"

Barbara glanced my way, then studied her camel as if she expected it to speak for her. Finally she said, "What about him? He's getting pretty good—I'm sure he'll help you a lot."

"No, I mean . . . . You know perfectly well he has a huge crush on you."

She studied her varnish job more carefully than was necessary. "He's kind of young for me."

"He's kind of nice too," I said. "Besides, he's grown up a lot lately, don't you think?"

She stood away from the finished camel, eyeing it for flaws. "I guess the earthquake did that too," she said. "I don't know, Mirai. Maybe that's another one of those things where you have to wait a year."

"What are you going to do with all your stuff when you let Joy have the house?" I asked.

"Some of it, they can have. It's mostly Will's things anyway, and I don't want them—not now. His studio—maybe I can find someone to run it. Or maybe you could add it to your shop. Especially if Louie's interested in the mechanical music side . . . ."

She trailed off. I could see she'd been thinking about the future and that it could well include Louie. And that she was a little embarrassed about it.

"Maybe I could," I said. "That's probably another one of those things we'll have a better line on in a year."

65

MOVING ST. MARTHA'S NORTH to Barbara's house was set for Thanksgiving weekend, when the basketball team could help. By Wednesday night, our borrowed truck was loaded with furniture and supplies, ready to go first thing Friday.

That meant Thanksgiving dinner had to be at Charlene's. Barbara was already staying with us, and we'd invited Joy, Louie, Barry, Ginny, Pete, and Frank. And when I came downstairs before they'd arrived, I found a surprise guest—Matt, my friend from Portland Carousel Works.

Or ex-friend. I wasn't sure how I felt about Matt, since they'd refused to cut me any slack on the repairs to the Peregrine Falls animals. He sized me up with his typical teddy-bear geniality.

"Hey, babe"—he called nearly everyone babe, so it wasn't an endearment—"we won't spoil the party by talking business. But I have a proposal for you that I got Ben and Susan to agree to, and I think you'll be happy with it. We can go over that tomorrow, while all these nice people are playing musical chairs with their apartments."

I started to thank him, but he held up a hand in a let-me-finish gesture. "*And* I have a surprise. You don't get to hear it yet, but that doesn't mean we can't start celebrating now!"

He rummaged in a tote bag and brought out a bottle of champagne. "Not rotgut," he said. "I promise!"

I laughed, because he and I had shared more than one bottle of terrible wine when we were students.

"Put it away for now," I said. "Maybe we can have some later with Charlene and Barbara, but Joy doesn't serve alcohol to her residents."

"More for us," he said, laughing.

I wondered what he might be up to. But not for long, because Barbara came downstairs and the guests started arriving.

First were Joy and the St. Martha's people. Over the years, I'd sat at many Thanksgiving tables with Joy's various guests, but this was the first year it hadn't felt like "Thanksgiving at the orphanage." Pete, Ginny, and Frank had been helping in the studio for several weeks, and I'd gotten to know them. They were co-workers now.

It made more difference than I'd expected—in them too. Among other things, they'd been far more respectful of the studio—kept their sleeping areas clean and kept the TV off till the workday was done. I had to laugh—they'd become easy to live with, just in time to move out.

Also, their work was helping a lot. It might turn out to be what made it possible to finish the carousel by Memorial Day. I was starting to wonder if some kind of training arrangement might be a way to get them on their feet again. Maybe for other guests too, as they came along. I'd need to find out more and talk to Joy. Looking at my three helpers, though, I was sure I was onto something.

Barry arrived, and the party lit up for me. He gave Joy a hug and a kiss, and winked at me over her shoulder—*I have a few of these for you too.*

I collected one of each right away.

"Let's go to the kitchen for a minute," he said. He patted a shopping bag he'd brought. "I have things to put in the fridge."

In the kitchen, he pulled a couple of bottles of sparkling apple cider from the bag, followed by a bottle of champagne. Everyone seemed to have the same idea, one that wasn't going to work at a party for the St. Martha's residents.

"We can't drink wine at dinner," I said. "Joy doesn't serve it in front of her people."

"We'll have some later," he said. "I brought the apple juice for dinner."

Barry snitched a couple of tiny tarts from a platter on the kitchen table and passed one to me. He ran a featherlight finger along the outline of my cheek.

"How's the carousel going?" he asked.

"The team's been a big help," I said. "I'm thinking of paying them for their work. Would that be okay?"

Barry shook his head. "I don't think that would fly with the Boys and Girls Club. You can make a contribution to the club, of course."

"I'll do that." I took a bite of my tart. It was good—well, everything Charlene cooked was good. The filling was messy but delicious.

Wiping my mouth with a napkin, I checked to make sure we were still alone in the kitchen. "I want to do something for the St. Martha's people too. But Joy's not going to like it if I do."

"Why not?"

I shrugged. "I think they should be growing, not just being sheltered. They've improved so much in the past few weeks— having jobs and responsibility. But I don't think Joy's willing to let go."

"Was she always like that?" he asked. "I mean, when you grew up and wanted to be on your own, did she cling to you?"

"No."

"So, what's the difference?"

"St. Martha's is her dream, so she won't let go of it. But she was more or less stuck with me."

"Why do you think that?"

"I always thought it was because I wasn't family. Not really."

"But actually, you *were* her family, and the guests weren't."

I thought that over, and shook my head.

"I didn't see it that way, and I still think I was right without knowing why. Garaze told me something when I was in Paradise Meadow. . . . Before Mama got killed, Joy was planning to be a nun. The priest in Paradise talked her into taking me instead, and probably helped her set up St. Martha's—he was from California, and she didn't have any connections here."

"So, St. Martha's was sort of a substitute for joining an order?"

"Because she had to take care of me, yes. It fits."

"Why?"

"She gave up what she really wanted to do," I said, my voice thick with sadness. "For my sake."

Barry gave me an analytical look, reminding me he was a journalist, used to interviewing people and sifting what they said.

"Did she ever tell you that?" he asked.

"No. Like I said, I found this out when I met Garaze. And then we had the earthquake, and everything's been a mess ever since."

"Why don't we ask her now? I'll go get her." He headed out to the living room.

I stood in the kitchen with my mouth open. I felt like a rat in a trap.

66

I DIDN'T HAVE MORE than a few seconds to collect myself before they came through the kitchen door.

"Barry said you had something you wanted to ask me," Joy said.

I thought fast—I wasn't ready to talk about her giving up the convent.

"I was thinking it might help the St. Martha's guests if I set up some kind of training in the shop," I said, spilling my whole idea, unconsidered as it was. "They're doing so well—it could be anything from woodworking to office work. Maybe I could set up savings accounts for when they're on their feet enough to leave. . . . I thought they might benefit . . . ." I trailed off.

Joy was beaming. "That's *exactly* what we need," she said happily. "I've noticed how well they're doing, but I had nothing like that to offer them. Oh, Mirai, that's wonderful! We'll work out the details when we're done with the move." She looked like an angel had descended and given her a present.

I figured I might as well get the rest of it over with. "Joy . . . when I went to Nevada . . . . Well, I told you I went to see Garaze."

"Which I already knew," said Joy, nodding. "I'd called her to let her know we were all right. She said you were a little like Zuzene." She smiled. "And a good bit like me."

"She told me you'd meant to be a nun."

"That's true, when I was young, I did."

"You gave that up because you had to take care of me." There, I'd said it.

Joy frowned. "You mean you got the idea I'd made some great renunciation of my vocation because Zuzene died?" She laughed. "Don't underestimate God, Mirai—if He'd wanted me to be a nun, I'd have been one, no matter what. The truth is, I didn't seem to have a call. I kept waiting, wondering if I'd already had one and hadn't understood. Then God opened up my path for me."

"Some path," I said, not taking in what she'd said, still feeling miserable and unwanted.

She hugged me for a long moment, then held me at arm's length and studied my face. "Yes, dear, it's been some path. I wouldn't have missed it for anything in the world."

She wiped her eyes and turned to Barry. "Now, Barry, I hope you'll excuse all this—here we are discussing family matters you can't possibly be interested in."

"It's all right," Barry said, smiling.

She patted him on the shoulder and left us.

"You San Julians are really something about family," Barry said. "Could an Irishman possibly join?"

Somehow, a ring had appeared in his hand, and he was studying my face quizzically. I gave him my left hand, and he slipped it on my fourth finger.

"You can wear that ring Alex gave you on your *other* hand," he said. "I'm giving you one that's just us."

We were still in a tight embrace when Charlene appeared at the kitchen door.

"Jeez, guys," she said. "How're we gonna get dinner on the table with your romance blossoming in the kitchen?" She winked as she checked the oven to see how the turkey was doing.

"Go on out and join the party," she added. "I think everyone's here now."

In the living room, I had to smile at the way the dinner guests had mixed. Matt was talking seriously with Ginny. Frank and Louie were laughing at something Barbara had said.

Pete circulated with a tray of appetizers and tiny napkins. When he got to Barry and me, he smiled broadly, showing a mouthful of bad teeth—but looking sweet anyway.

"Barb says you girls are near finished with the painting," he said.

"Only a few more to go." I wasn't nuts about "girls" but it wasn't a point I needed to make to Pete. "How's the varnishing?"

"I think we may make it in time."

"I'm beginning to think so, too." I held up crossed fingers for luck.

Pete nodded and held out the tray. Barry and I each took something, and Pete smiled again and moved on.

"Guess you'll be working out some kind of training scheme," Barry said. "In your spare time, of course. When you're not working on the carousel or helping plan our wedding. When did we tell your dad it would be?"

"I think you said June 2," I said. "That's more than six months away."

"Right," said Barry. "And four or five days after Memorial Day."

"Oh, my God."

Charlene appeared in the kitchen door, holding a damp-looking dish towel in one hand.

"Plizz to tebbell," she said, flourishing the towel as gracefully as a damp towel could be flourished.

"Which restaurant's waiters are you spoofing today?" I asked, laughing.

"All of them," she answered. "In fact—this is a secret, but"—her voice dropped to a piercing theatrical whisper—"there *is* only one waiter. In this whole city, maybe in the entire world—*There Is Only One Waiter!*"

We laughed and helped bring the food into the dining room. When we'd taken our seats, Matt lifted a wineglass filled with sparkling apple juice.

"To Charlene," he said, "who I met for the first time today— though I feel I know her already, from talking and talking on the phone."

I looked up in surprise.

"While I was helping out at the studio," Charlene explained.

"And we have an announcement!" Matt said. "Charlene has set up a benefit project with Portland Carousel Works. We've asked our clients all over the country to participate, and the responses have been almost all positive. So far, it's over fifty carousels that will donate their earnings on Memorial Day to rebuilding St. Martha's."

We were so astonished, no one could find anything to say but Pete. "How much would that come to?"

"Memorial Day is a big day for all the carousels," Charlene said. "It should amount to about eighty thousand dollars."

"So, a toast to Charlene, who made it happen!" Matt said. We toasted Charlene, and Matt as well.

"I'd like to thank you both," said Joy. "And Barry too, whose newspaper article brought in another twenty thousand in pledges. With all this plus the insurance money, I believe we'll have enough to repair St. Martha's—especially since Barbara is letting us use her house rent-free."

Then she raised her glass to me. "And I have a toast to offer, too. To my niece, Mirai, who has decided to help St. Martha's with a paid training program for the residents."

Glasses were raised again, accompanied by cheers from Pete, Ginny, and Frank.

Barry stood then. "I don't have a toast, but I do have an announcement. Mirai and I are engaged." He smiled sheepishly at the tumult this brought on.

Barbara jumped up and hugged me. Joy did, too, and then Matt.

"Why isn't anyone hugging Barry?" I asked.

"We're leaving that to you," Barbara said. "When's the wedding?"

"After the carousel's finished," I said.

"Where?" she asked. "In Peregrine Falls? Get that carousel off to a good start by having the reception there?"

I started to say that Oakland was good enough for me. But our church had been nearly destroyed by the earthquake. It wouldn't be ready for a wedding in six months. And I thought of Garaze, who probably couldn't come to Oakland. And Alex, who might be kept away by complications with his wife.

"In Paradise Meadow," I said.

Matt raised his glass. "To Mirai and Barry!" he offered. Everyone joined in the toast, and we started our Thanksgiving dinner.

Joy made the sign of the cross over the bread, as she had so many times at St. Martha's. "For these and all our many blessings, God's holy name be praised."

It was a blessing she used often—but this time, I heard her voice tremble.

67

On Memorial Day, I woke in Barry's arms, and for a moment I felt a wonderful sense of peace. Then the clown pictures on the wall reminded me where I was, and everything that had to be done. I slid quietly out of bed, leaving Barry asleep, and made a pot of coffee—I'd learned my lesson about the coffee at the Clearwater Cafe.

When it was done, I took my cup to the window. It was early but getting light fast. I thought of the morning creeping west, waking carousels all across the continent, and how they'd start to twinkle and spin. All the carousels of Charlene's and Matt's benefit project, singing their songs, saving St. Martha's.

I took a deep, ragged breath that sounded like tears and felt like joy.

Barry stirred and sat up. "You okay?" he asked.

I sat on the edge of the bed, next to him, basking in his warmth. "Never better," I said.

He sipped some of my coffee. "Any more of that?" he asked.

"Uh-huh," I said. I brought him a steaming cup.

He took a few sips and ran his fingers through his hair. "Worried about Saturday?" he asked.

I thought it over. I'd decided not to let the wedding turn into a big production. Once I'd arranged for a priest to come from Winnemucca to Paradise Meadow and also made sure Alex could come, I'd let everything else take care of itself.

"No," I said. "If I can get through today, Saturday should be a picnic."

He laughed. "So, what's on for today?"

"Well, speaking of picnics, there's one for the whole town. That's after the carousel dedication. And speeches by the mayor, the head of the committee, and me."

"Really? What are you going to say?"

"Not much. And I think they're also having a moment of silence for Will."

"Hmmm," Barry said. "Very proper. Besides, it's likely to be the only moment of silence all day."

"Most likely it will. But a carousel spinning in silence would be spooky."

"Like my mother's idea of the ideal jukebox," Barry said. "We used to go to a café that was great, except my mom didn't like the noise of the jukebox. She used to say she wished they had a selection for three-and-a-half minutes of silence."

"Barry, about your parents . . . . They're okay . . . I mean . . . about us?"

"Sure."

I hoped he was right. I knew they were good Catholics, and that meant that they wouldn't be likely to come out with any overt prejudice. But they *were* from a small city in the Sacramento River Delta. . . . I stopped my thought, realizing I was getting into some prejudices of my own.

"About the ethnic thing, though . . . ," he said.

I waited.

"My mom is likely to hit you up for Basque recipes." His grin told me he'd more or less read my mind.

"Basque recipes!" I said. "I can't cook!"

"Better sic her on Joy, then." He ran his hand over my cheek. "If we stay in this bed, we're going to be late, because I'm going to have to make love to you again."

"*That's* not a bad idea. We can run out at the last minute and do the dedication ceremony in the nude. No one will even notice, probably."

But I got up and dressed. By the time I was ready, Barry was, too, so we went over to the Clearwater for breakfast.

"Let's get a booth," I said. No way was I going to sit at the big table where I'd seen Will's wedding ring for the first time.

"Won't the others be coming?" he asked. "Others" included our whole entourage: Joy, Charlene, Louie, the St. Martha's bunch, as well as people we were meeting here—Barbara, Matt, our crew . . . . I didn't even want to consider breakfast with that many people.

"A booth, okay? If they come in, we'll wave hello in a really friendly way."

He laughed, and we took a tiny booth in the corner, barely enough room for the two of us.

When we were nearly finished breakfast, Joy and Charlene came in. While I was hugging them, Pete, Ginny, and Frank joined us, followed closely by Matt. I knew Barbara, Louie, and the restoration team couldn't be far behind. Happy as I was to have them all there, I wanted to get away from the chatter.

"Let's go look at the carousel," I said to Barry, and we left for Northern Lights Park.

We found city workers setting up chairs for the party all around the carousel building. More workers were on a platform that had been built for the occasion, fiddling with a sound system. No one paid any attention to us as we approached the open doors of the carousel.

Inside, the lights were on, and the animals, rounding boards, and mirrors glistened in like-new perfection. In the corner, the band organ waited. For just a brief moment, I could see Charles Looff beside it, and thought I saw him nod and smile before he disappeared. Maybe he and his men *had* helped us finish, as I'd asked them a year ago.

"What are you looking at?" Barry asked.

I started to say, "Nothing," but changed my mind. "Charles Looff," I said. "He's gone now."

I turned to Barry and hugged him hard, remembering how near I'd come, when he first called, to telling him he couldn't use the studio. He would have vanished from my world as irretrievably as Charles Looff.

We walked among the animals, gazing at one delight after the other. The designs—my work and Barbara's together—reminded me how she and I had recovered our friendship, and that made my happiness complete. This was the best moment, the moment when the carousel was still mine, knowing I was about to give it back, ready for the town to treasure again.

A female voice from the doorway said, "Can I help you?" And then, "Oh, hi, Mirai! Didn't realize it was you."

Regina, the committee chairperson, came into view from behind a camel.

"Hi, Regina," I said. "I'd like you to meet my fiancé, Barry Donovan."

"I'm delighted to meet you," she said. She gestured to the carousel. "Well, Mirai? What do you think?"

"I'm very pleased," I said, and with that, the carousel was no longer mine. I'd given it away—but I *was* very pleased. And that was mine forever.

ONLY THE FORMALITY of the party remained.

At the dedication, the mayor made a long speech that seemed aimed more at the next election than anything else.

Regina made a short one that celebrated the carousel's history and the town's help in the restoration. She told about St. Martha's and the benefit, which the committee had decided to join. She also led the solemn moment of silence for Will, and I thought of all he'd done, good and bad. Once again, I silently cussed at him, even while I grieved. This was his last carousel.

My speech was last. After Regina introduced me, I looked around the crowd wordlessly for what felt like a long time.

Finally I said, "What are we *waiting* for? There's a *carousel* over there!"

The surprised silence lasted several seconds. Then the gongs clanged, and the band organ started up with "In the Good Old Summertime."

I scampered down from the platform and reached for Barry's hand. Eagerly, we ran to begin our ride.

Anne L. Watson, a retired historic preservation architecture consultant, is the author of numerous novels, plus books on such diverse subjects as soapmaking and baking with cookie molds. Anne currently lives in Friday Harbor, Washington, in the San Juan Islands, with her husband and fellow author, Aaron Shepard. Please visit her at **www.annelwatson.com**.